I0629468

BOOK 1 *OF THE* JUSTICE CYCLE

DEATH

J.W. KIEFER

JWKIEFER.COM

Front cover image by Joshua Recene.

Edited by Lauren Moore
Laurenmoorebooks.com

For information contact :
Website-www.jwkiefer.com
Email-Authorjwkiefer@gmail.com

Fourth edition: February 2024.
13, 12, 11, 10, 9, 8, 7, 6, 5, 4

This book is dedicated to the people who have had the most impact on its creation, My Armor Bearers. Steve Caponey (Flatline), Jon-Mark Menta (Hollow Point), Sean Nemi (Sgt. Edge), Jeremy Wagner (Flash), Josh Strunk (Fortress) and David Devigili (Sidewinder). The time we spent running around upstate NY creating worlds, characters and stories will always be some of my fondest memories.

Foreword

Like most things worth doing in life, this book took me a long time to write. Even though it is my first, it rises off of the backs of many failed manuscripts that have since been lost to crashing computers, the beguiling of new ideas or simply to the ever-moving sands of time and neglect.

J R R Tolkien once replied when asked why it took him so long to write the Lord of the Rings, "Life happens." I have found this to be the case. Like all humans my time is extremely limited, and the pressures of work, family, church, and much needed personal time seem to always be vying for its attention. This is still the case for me, but I decided once my kids grew up and started their own adult lives, that it was time for me to seriously pursue the one thing I had always wanted to do since childhood, become a writer.

This novel is the result of that decision. My life is still filled with many distractions, and I would like to say that I have mastered the discipline of writing every day, but that would be a lie. I have, however, found that continual small steps forward produce bigger results in the end than great leaps on occasions. For those of you who read this book I hope you are inspired to keep moving forward in your journey no matter how small the steps may be; and you will find, as I have, that in time, you too will accomplish your dreams.

Jay

Chapter One

Binghamton New York
*October 19*th

It was an unusually chilly October evening, even for upstate New York. A cold front from northern Canada had blown through, bringing with it rain, a bitter wind, and temperatures that dropped into the forties. According to the radio meteorologist, this night would be the worst of it. Dismal and forbidding, the stormy evening fit the mood of the lone figure making his way down the empty streets.

The man was hunched and weather-beaten, his long black trench coat flapping wildly in the wind. He made no attempt to draw the coat around himself, but let the wind have its way. Drenched as he was, any normal man would've been shivering, but he was no ordinary man. Ever since he had been chosen, his body had become impervious to the elements of the mortal world.

He was short and lithe of build, with jet-black hair pulled tight into a long ponytail. He appeared to be of Asian descent, and most people would not have given him a second glance, except for his haunting eyes. He'd once had beautiful dark brown eyes that had charmed many a young lady with a glance. Now those eyes were gone, replaced by shadowy black holes of darkness that seemed to writhe and twist with a life of their own.

He missed his old eyes, that used to see the joys of life and love. Eyes that looked on the world with such innocence. Nothing escaped his gaze now, nothing at all. It saw everything, even the hearts of men. No action escaped his notice. He saw every sin, no matter how big or small. He saw the hidden and the veiled, those things which men thought they had concealed and would never be held accountable for.

It was a dreadful power that his heart had grown weary of. He understood what that meant, and he welcomed it. The end was near; he could sense it. He would soon be free of his burden. It would pass to another.

The man turned down a narrow alleyway, leaving behind the brightly lit streets for the shelter of the shadows. He shied away from the light, preferring to travel in the darkness away from prying eyes. He missed the sun and its warmth. This nocturnal existence was poetic, he supposed, as most evil deeds did take place in the dark of night. But it grew old.

He passed a few scattered silhouettes lying on the cold, wet ground and felt a twinge of pity. It had been years since he'd felt anything at all, so the feeling came as a shock. It was nothing more than a small stirring in his heart, but to someone who had felt nothing for so long, it struck like a bolt of lightning.

A single tear tracked down his cheek. He reached up and touched it, wondering at the wetness on his fingers. He'd been incapable of crying for so long that he'd forgotten what it felt like.

The homeless man closest to him stirred and mumbled something in his sleep. He was filthy, dressed in tattered rags, his white hair gnarled and a tangled beard long. He shivered and tossed, trying in vain to shake off the chill.

The dark figure stooped and fixed his shadowy gaze upon the sleeping person. In a moment, the person's life flashed before his eyes like a sped-up movie, and he saw everything.

Alcohol and drug abuse had brought this man to this place. Addiction had taken everything from him including his wife and children, but addiction had only been a symptom of a greater pain.

His gaze saw all. Saw the homeless man as a child watching as his father, who was unable to deal with his own failures at life, brutally beat his mother until she eventually fled. That was when his father turned his wrath upon him.

The boy eventually escaped his seemingly unending torment when his father had finally succumbed to liver failure. He watched as the boy, now a young man, dumped a full bottle of whiskey on his father's grave before getting wasted. He watched as the young man tried to move forward from the demons that haunted him. Watched as he fell in love and built a family of his own, vowing not to follow the same path his father had. But the American dream comes at a cost. Two layoffs and no work eventually took their toll, and he heard the call of the same demons his father had. Demons that eventually changed a loving man into a monster who, in a fit of alcohol-induced rage, murdered his ten-year-old son.

The man removed his trench coat and settled it over the sleeping man. His shivering subsided.

"Sleep tight, David," he said, in a hollow voice. He watched the man a moment before continuing on into the shadows.

He moved quickly and stealthily, more shadow than man. Without his coat, the man appeared out of place here. "Out of time" might be a better description. A sheathed katana hung from his hip, and a black Japanese kimono dangled loosely on his wiry frame. Even though he did not wear the trademark armor of a samurai, he carried himself as a warrior.

Before the man reached the end of the alleyway, he crouched and sprung upward, then scaled the brick wall of the building on his right. When he reached the crest of the wall, he stood on the rooftop like a bat, peering down into the darkness below him. His black eyes pierced the thick gloom, searching for anything out of the ordinary. Not a minute went by before a slight movement caught his attention. A shadow darker than the night moved silently below him.

The figure in the alleyway snapped his head upward toward the movement just in time to catch a blur of black before the man was gone. The person chuckled to himself and stepped out of the shadows and into the center of the alley. Dressed in what looked like a black French musketeer uniform, the man wore a rapier at his side and a large brimmed black hat on his head. But where the musketeers of old wore a cross, this man wore a skull.

His long, slender mustache twitched with a smile. "Shogun, why must we continue to play this cat-and-mouse game? It is becoming very tiresome. Still, protocol requires it, so I will not begrudge you your whims. Ready or not, here I come." He leapt up onto the rooftop in a single bound.

The Musketeer's blade slid out with a ring as he flipped through the air and landed on the roof. He scanned the empty rooftop, then lowered his sword.

The Musketeer had the same nightmare black eyes as the Shogun and his gaze was just as keen. He saw every raindrop as it fell to the earth. Nothing escaped his penetrating eyes.

"I know you are here, mon ami. I can sense your presence. Why make this difficult? The outcome is inevitable."

"Why must you always talk so much?" came the whispered reply from everywhere and yet nowhere at all.

"I suppose it is my nature," the Musketeer said. "Much like your nature is to be depressed and gloomy."

"It was not always so," said the voice again, reverberating like an echo.

"Ah, do you find yourself longing for the past?" The Musketeer continued to search for anything that would give away his opponent's position.

"What do you care?" came the reply. This time it seemed to be coming from directly behind him as if someone was whispering in his ear.

The Musketeer chuckled. "You hurt my feelings, Shogun! I have enjoyed our little game more than you could ever know. We are brothers, you and I!"

With lightning speed, the Musketeer dropped into a crouch and pivoted, slashing backward with his rapier at shin level. The blade sliced harmlessly through the night air, hitting nothing more than raindrops.

"It will not be so easy."

The Musketeer's grin faded, and his eyes glinted. "Your tricks will only prolong the inevitable. You can sense the end is near for you. Why resist it?"

"What you say may be true, and it may not. You have been known to lie."

The Musketeer let loose a laugh. "So, you still have a sense of humor left in you after all these years? It is a pity that it only revealed itself now."

He held his sword in front of his face with both hands. As he did, the blade glowed with an eerie violet-black light, illuminating his angular face. "I must admit this banter is quite entertaining, but like all good things, it must come to an end."

He slashed downward and a flash of dark energy surged forward, arching right then left, as if searching for something. It finally struck an object about twenty feet off in a torrent of violet sparks.

The air around the impact shifted until the illusion the Shogun had created dissipated entirely. He stood there with his blade held up in a defensive position, his katana arcing with similar mystical energy.

The Musketeer launched forward and was upon the disoriented Shogun in a single bound. He struck with ferocity, forcing the Shogun into a corner. Again and again the Musketeer attacked, not allowing the Shogun to gain any advantage.

But the Shogun parried every deadly strike. He deflected a cut to his head and then whipped his blade back and forth, fending off two quick jabs to his midsection. Two more swift thrusts to his head forced his blade upward, and he had to shift his footing in order to keep his balance. He had to do something fast, and he knew it.

"Soon I will have you, Shogun," said the Musketeer between strikes, his free hand edging toward his belt.

Noticing the movement, the Shogun lunged forward and struck the Musketeer with his shoulder. The maneuver caught him off guard and sent him stumbling backward. Never losing his momentum, the Shogun followed through with a quick uppercut, slamming his fist into the Musketeer's chin. The blow sent the man flying, and he flipped twice in midair before slamming into the roof with a thud. His hand slipped out of his shirt, a dirk in his fist.

Kicking himself up, the Musketeer landed on his feet like a cat, his weapons at the ready. This time, however, it was the Shogun's turn to go on the offensive, and he attacked his opponent with savage ferocity. The dance began again, and the night was alive with the deadly song of the clashing blades.

The Shogun parried a hasty jab to his midsection and slashed down at his opponent's head. The Musketeer blocked the strike with both weapons, and the two fighters slid their swords down, their blades locked and arms straining with exertion.

"So, mon ami, where do we go from here?" the Musketeer panted.

"We finish it," replied the Shogun, and pivoted to the side. The Musketeer stumbled forward at the sudden release of pressure, leaving him wide open. The Shogun slashed upward, cutting deeply into his stomach, doubling him over.

The rain halted in place and the clamor of the universe ceased as time itself came to a standstill. The Musketeer hung limply from the Shogun's katana. He chuckled and his dirk dropped to the ground with a clang. Strangely, no blood flowed from the gaping wound.

"Get on with it already!" he growled through gritted teeth.

The Shogun nodded and slid his blade forward and yanked up, finishing his cut. The Musketeer fell to his knees, his hands dangling at his sides.

"Goodbye," whispered the Shogun.

"Go to hell!" the Musketeer spat.

"Never." The Shogun swung his blade to decapitate the injured man.

Before the blade could hit its mark, the Musketeer threw himself forward and the katana missed his head by inches. With a renewed and supernatural vigor, the Musketeer rolled to the side, away from the crouching Shogun. Holding his insides in with one arm and using his sword as a crutch, he managed to get to his feet, stumble toward the roof's edge, and throw himself over.

The Shogun charged after the fleeing Musketeer but was not quick enough. He peered over the edge, hoping to find a broken corpse lying shattered on the street below, but his heart knew better. There was no sign of the injured Musketeer.

The universe snapped back into motion and he was buffeted by the sudden clamor of the storm. A ghostly chuckle echoed on the wind but was lost in the downpour.

Chapter Two

Not far from the supernatural conflict, a young woman jogged down the relatively quiet streets of Binghamton, New York. The storm had driven most of the city's nocturnal inhabitants indoors for the night, so the streets were empty.

Amanda Pratt was a twenty-seven-year-old fit and attractive blonde. She had debated with herself on whether or not the exercise was worth getting wet over, but the heaping bowl of ice cream she had eaten after dinner made the decision a no-brainer. In today's society, the cardinal sin was not murder but being fat. It didn't matter what you did, as long as you looked good doing it.

She turned onto the street that led to Otsenango Park and picked up her pace as she crossed the bridge. Amanda was mildly afraid of heights, and her heartbeat quickened as she sprinted across the hated bridge. She slowed when she reached the other side and quickly checked her Fitbit. The rain was steadily increasing, and the wind was blowing hard, making the run uncomfortable and difficult.

Should she turn back? She sucked in deep gasps of air and shook off the rain that drenched her from head to toe.

What was I thinking coming out here this late at night and in a horrible storm no less? she thought. *It's not like anybody's gonna notice, anyway.*

Somebody had noticed her, though, and had followed her since she'd left her house. The fact was, he had come out here in this miserable weather just for her. She had been on his mind for quite some time.

Amanda noticed the man slowly approaching her as she turned to start the long run back home. He was a tall handsome man, whose long wet black hair clung to his face. The man was dressed all in black and wore a leather coat that came to his waist.

Her hand slipped up to her hair—she knew it was a matted mess after jogging—and she blushed as the handsome man approached. But as the man drew closer, a feeling of dread washed over her. The feeling was so overwhelming that it took all her willpower to keep herself from bolting in the opposite direction. She took a step back, her heartbeat quickening as she looked for a possible way of escape.

A few paces away, the man stopped to pull out a cigarette. He lit it with a Zippo lighter and took a long drag. "Hello, Amanda," he said, blowing smoke out his nostrils as he spoke.

Blue eyes. Ice-blue eyes.

"Do I know you?" she replied. The fact that this man knew her name made her feel even more uncomfortable.

The man smirked. "I'm a bit hurt that you don't remember me, Amanda."

Shivering in the rain, Amanda tried to back away. She was definitely terrified now and began to think it would be best if she left at once.

"Where are you going?" the man asked casually. "Don't you have time for an old friend?"

"I don't know you, mister, and I don't think I want to," she replied as she turned and bolted toward the front gate to the park.

"Now, don't go and make this hard on me," he called out as she fled down the street. "Amanda, please come back. I just want to talk and catch up on old times."

She was nearly hyperventilating by the time she reached the old creaky wrought iron gate to the park and found that it was locked with a chain. The smell of wet leaves filled her nostrils and the sound a something metal clinked somewhere in the darkness. A gust of wind rattled the large wooden sign that hung from the gate. The man called to her again and she frantically pulled on the gate, her muscles straining as she desperately tried to force it open. Her eyes darted up toward the intersection. If only she could make it to the brightly lit street.

"Amanda," called the man, taking another drag of his cigarette. "You don't really think you're going to be able to break that chain, do you?"

With a determination that Amanda never knew she possessed, she squeezed her way painfully through the small opening in the middle of the gate. Her coat caught on something sharp as she pushed through, preventing her from fleeing farther into the park. She screamed and pulled on the coat as the man strolled closer.

Seeing her stuck on the park gate, the man picked up his pace. Just as he was about to reach her, the coat tore free, and she fled as fast as she could into the park.

The man took one last long drag from his cigarette and flipped it away. He exhaled and pulled the torn remains of her coat off the gate and put it into his pocket.

"Well, I guess this saves me the trouble of dragging her into a dark alley kicking and screaming," he said to no one in particular.

With fearsome strength the man tore the chain from the gate, snapping the bars completely. He threw it into the bushes and shoved open the gate with a bang.

"Oh well, more fun for me," he said with a shrug and walked into the park, whistling as he went.

****

The Shogun leaped from rooftop to rooftop, running as fast as his legs could carry him. He'd come to this small city for a reason, and his little skirmish with the Musketeer had cost him precious time. It was strange that he should encounter his old enemy here. What possible purpose could he have for being this far upstate?

The Shogun reached the end of the row of buildings and leaped into the open air. He flipped once, then fell five stories to land lightly on his feet. The sword in his hand glowed, and he touched it lightly to his forehead.

He must hurry, the sword told him, or it would be too late for yet another innocent person. Sheathing his sword, the Shogun set off in a dead run, speeding down through the city streets like a blur, his feet barely touching the ground as he ran.

He reached the Otsenango Park gates and stopped to examine the split bars. Damage like this could only have been done by someone with immense strength. The Shogun had dealt with all manner of beings in his long years. Many possessed such power, some beings supernatural and others not. He was certain, however, that it was a human he was pursuing, but no average human possessed such strength.

The sword glowed again, and he saw what had transpired here only minutes earlier. He saw Amanda Pratt as she jogged, unaware of the evil that watched her from a distance. Likewise, he saw her flee, escaping into the deserted park. It was when he finally saw the wild eyes of the man pursuing her that he knew it that he had to move fast if he was going to stop him from killing Amanda.

Perhaps it would already be too late to stop him, but the Shogun would bring justice to the brute, regardless. He had slain many serial killers throughout the centuries, and, strong or not, this one would die just like all the others.

****

Amanda ran blindly down the dark footpaths of the park in a frantic attempt at losing her stalker. She struck her foot on a jutting tree root and painfully snagged her skin as she stumbled into a briar patch. Exhausted and out of breath, she stopped and leaned up against a small tree. She was cut and bruised from running headlong through thickets and sharp branches, and every muscle in her body ached with fatigue.

She had come here every day since she was a kid and knew that the clearing ahead led down to the river. If she continued in that direction, she would be trapped on the river's edge with no place to run or hide.

Before she could decide on which direction she should go, she heard a faint whistle coming from behind her. Her eyes went wide with such a sudden fear that overcame her rational mind, and she took off again.

Amanda ran and ran as self-preservation overcame the burning in her muscles. But no matter how fast she ran, the whistling always seemed to be just behind her. Tears streamed down her cheeks, and she screamed for help. No one was within earshot, and she knew it. She cried out anyway, in the faint hope that someone might hear.

Her chest burned, and just when she was about to give up, she stumbled into the clearing that led to the river. She fell to her knees and gasped for air, coughing violently from exertion. When she finally managed to stop her fit of coughing, she heard the whistling again, and her heart sank.

Chapter Three

O Tsenango Park was a beautiful recreational area surrounded by lush forests and small ponds. Many people spent their summer days there picnicking or competing on its many sports fields. Others came simply to walk the paved roads and enjoy the beautiful scenery of upstate New York.

The Shogun, however, was here for a different reason. He sprinted down the paved pathways past picnic tables, grills, softball fields, and playgrounds. Like watching a holographic overlay of the events that had just transpired, the Shogun saw every turn the woman made in her attempt to flee her pursuer.

He watched as Amanda ran off the paved path and into the dense woodlands that surrounded the park. He also watched as her stalker calmly mirrored her every step. The sword informed him that she was heading toward the river and that soon it would be too late. That's when Amanda's cries for help pierced the night air.

He gritted his teeth and a fury like he had not experienced in years welled up within him. The inferno burned like wildfire, the heat coursing through his being. He gave into the rage, willingly throwing aside all the warnings that the sword screamed into his subconscious mind.

With supernatural speed, the Shogun ran onward, the very earth itself seeming to bend and bow in an attempt at making his passage through easier. No tree branch reached out to grab at him as he ran, and every rock or obstacle appeared to roll out of his way. The wind rose to an almost gale-like force as if to push him toward his enemy.

****

The Stalker slipped out of the trees and into the clearing where Amanda had collapsed, still whistling. His black coat was drenched now, and his dark hair clung to his neck.

He pulled out a long curved knife. Its blade was serrated, and the black pommel fashioned into the likeness of the grim reaper's head with two glittering rubies for eyes. Amanda began to weep uncontrollably when she saw the silver gleaming blade.

"There you are, Amanda. You gave me quite a chase."

"What do you want from me?" she managed to ask through the heaving sobs.

"Want from you?" he responded. "I don't really want anything from you. It's more of what I want to do *to* you."

Amanda cried so hard that she could no longer form a coherent sentence. She tried to plead with her assailant, but her pleas for mercy came out as a muddled stream of croaks and groans and sniffles.

The Stalker bent down until he was face-to-face with her. He rested his arms on his knees, the blade of his knife pointing toward the wet ground. She stared into his icy eyes and knew that this was the end for her. In her few short years of life, she had never seen such dead cruelty in a person's eyes before.

"There, there, Amanda," he said soothingly. "This will all be over soon, I promise."

He stood again and lifted a pair of headphones up and placed them over his ears. Reaching into his coat with his free hand, he activated the music player on his phone, and it began to squawk loudly.

"You are just like me!" the man sang loudly, his eyes closed, rocking his head and torso violently. "You are just like me!"

When the Stalker reached his demonic state, the wind rose up suddenly. It invigorated Amanda, kindling a small spark of hope that her to find enough courage to move.

Noticing that her stalker had his eyes closed and seemed to be lost in his music, she jumped at the small window of opportunity and took off toward the river. The stalker didn't notice her movements until it was too late. He bellowed in protest when he noticed she was gone.

****

The Shogun smiled when he heard the Stalker's howl. He had sent hope to Amanda on that wind, and his attempt at encouraging her had worked. It was not much, but perhaps it would buy him the time he needed.

Hold on a little longer, he mentally urged her.

Pain erupted as something struck him in his back. His concentration faltered, and the wind ceased. He stumbled and fell face-first to the ground. He lay there disoriented, and a large pair of black boots appeared by his head.

He tried to push himself up, but one boot slammed down on his back, shoving him into the mud. His attacker pressed his foot down and, using all his weight, stepped over the prostrate form of the Shogun.

"I guess you forgot about me, mon ami?" the man asked in that familiar French inflection the Shogun had come to hate. "It seems my little friend kept you busy. I should have known it was he you were after and not I. I wish I could say that it did not hurt, but it does."

Once again, the Shogun attempted to push himself upward, but the Musketeer kicked him hard in the side, sending him flying into a nearby pine tree. He hit the large trunk with a sickening crack. It split and bent from the impact, spewing pine needles everywhere.

"Obviously, I had only hoped to distract you earlier. That was my undoing. I should have endeavored to end the game once and for all. If I had, then your elementary ruse would not have worked."

"You exaggerate your abilities, old friend," replied the Shogun, getting to his feet. "You were never that proficient a swordsman."

"That clever wit of yours again rears its ugly head!" the Musketeer chortled. "Oh, how I wish it had come forth sooner."

As soon as the Shogun got to his feet, however, the Musketeer lunged, attempting to end the fight with one swift blow. The Shogun was ready for the attack, deflecting the strike and kicking the Musketeer hard in the stomach.

The Musketeer winced in pain. "You know, despite all your efforts, that girl will die."

The Shogun struck him hard in the jaw with the pommel of his sword, and the Musketeer stumbled backward.

"Well, that was uncalled for!" he growled, caressing his injured jaw. "It is the truth, mon ami, and you know it!"

Furious, the Shogun lashed out with his sword. Their blades clashed again, as they had done countless times before.

Chapter Four

Amanda managed to reach the river, but the hope that had so recently been in her heart had faded. All that remained was an icy cold numbness. She had reached the river and had nowhere left to run. She closed her eyes and exhaled, taking in the sounds and smells around her as she resigned herself to the inevitable.

She could hear the Stalker's heavy breathing as he drew closer. Still in his frenzied state, he tore and fumed through the trees like a wild animal. He broke through the tree line and found her quietly waiting.

He smiled, and she couldn't help noticing that he was handsome. Why she thought of this now was a mystery to her. In a few minutes, it wouldn't matter anyway.

It was then that it hit her. She did know him.

"Why?" she asked incredulously.

He cocked his head to the side, as if considering her question. "Because I can," he answered.

The Shogun saw all that was happening to Amanda and hated himself for his lack of vigilance. In the past he never would have been waylaid by such an obvious trap, but for the last few years, he'd felt his connection to Tzedakah wavering. To the rest of the universe, it was imperceptible, but to him, it was glaring. It was a true sign that the end was near. Deep down, he longed for that end.

He deflected a strike from the Musketeer and followed it up with a few of his own. The dance continued on with neither man able to gain an advantage over the other. The Musketeer swiftly lunged at him, and he parried the attack to the left while continuing his momentum into a downward slash. The Musketeer planted his feet and lifted his blade up, deflecting the blow.

The Shogun hacked repeatedly at the Musketeer's blade, each blow driving his opponent farther and farther down toward the ground. He was not thinking, just reacting, and in his fury, he had left his stomach open. The Musketeer noticed his vulnerability, and before the Shogun could correct it, the Musketeer impaled him with a fierce jab from his rapier.

The Shogun, ignoring the pain, struck down, his blade cutting deeply into the Musketeer's shoulder. Grimacing from the fiery pain in his shoulder, the Musketeer leaned into his own blade, driving it deeper into the Shogun's stomach.

Exerting all his will, the Shogun planted his foot on the Musketeer's chest and shoved him backward, forcefully dislodging both weapons. They both lost their balance and tumbled over.

"Why do you fight on so?" asked the Musketeer. "You are near the end. Soon none of this will matter."

"It matters to Amanda," replied the Shogun.

"Oh, spare me the sentimental hero nonsense!" he spat back, rising to his feet. "She is nothing but a passing flicker in the inferno of life. What does it matter how she is extinguished?"

"It matters." The Shogun got to his feet as well.

"Not anymore." The Musketeer smirked. "I will enjoy ending you, Shogun, but now is not the time for such diversions. I have other matters to attend to."

With that, he walked away, melting into the waiting shadows. "Until next we meet," came his ghostly whisper.

The Shogun could have followed him if he wanted, for there was no place the Musketeer could go that he could not follow. He just did not have the heart for it. Instead, he walked to the river and sat down on its muddy bank. The rain had stopped, and the horizon was beginning to brighten with the coming of day.

The current was strong from the storm, and the water rushed past him carrying a wet bundle on its hurried trek downstream. The river rolled it over and over, battering it cruelly. It struck a large rock not far from where the Shogun sat and hung up there.

It was the broken body of Amanda Pratt. His shoulders slumped and he bowed his head. Death was a part of life, and the Shogun had seen his share of it, innocent as well as wicked. In fact, he had grown cold to it over the years. However, something about this tragic event touched a long-forgotten chord hidden deep within his soul, and he did something he had not done for centuries. He wept.

Chapter Five

The silver Chevy Malibu sped down the highway, weaving in out of traffic like it was on the last stretch of the Indianapolis 500. The window was down, and the throb of the radio's bass created a dissonance bubble that could be heard three cars away. The music vibrated through the driver, unlocking some primal instinct that was lying dormant. He pressed his foot down on the gas pedal harder.

Twenty-eight and already a detective on the police force, Jared Caddret had no worries of ever getting a speeding ticket. Even if some rookie didn't recognize his car and happened to pull him over, he would just flash his badge, and all would be well. Being a cop certainly had its perks.

God, I love being a cop! Jared thought as he passed a brand spanking new BMW convertible that was going eighty. He waved to the driver and winked as he flew by. The red face of the yuppie driving the beamer gave him warm fuzzy feelings inside.

His pastor, who just happened to be his father, told him he still had "issues" which needed to be resolved. Something about harboring hatred toward those kids who used to pick on him when he was in school. Jared, after careful self-examination, came to the realization that his dad was right. He still felt like he was twelve every time he was near someone who fit that adolescent mold of popularity.

That's probably one of the reasons why I became a police officer, he thought. Sure, he loved helping people. Always had. His friends used to say he had a hero complex. But Jared also loved the perception of power the job gave him. He felt like he was somebody whenever he flashed that badge.

All of the usual thoughts flooded into his brain, and he heard his father's voice again. *You are somebody because Jesus died for you.* He knew it in his head because he had heard the sermons a thousand times, but most of the time he didn't feel it in his heart. He loved God and believed in Him, but sometimes it was just so hard to silence the thoughts and feelings that told him he was nothing more than a loser.

Jared sighed and shoved his thoughts back into the deep recesses of his heart and gave himself over to the music and to the speed. None of that mattered right now. All was well with the world and what wasn't, he would deal with later.

The sun was slipping below the horizon in a dazzle of brilliant colors. It seemed as if the clouds were immense puffs of rainbow cotton candy that he could reach out and pluck. He drew in a breath and drank in the crisp air. As he continued to glory in the wonders of autumn in upstate New York, he failed to see the slowed traffic up ahead.

"Oh crap!" he exclaimed when he realized how close the cars ahead of him were.

Gritting his teeth and cursing his lack of attentiveness, he slammed the breaks. They loosed a blood-curdling screech, the sound was not unlike that of a cat being tortured, or his little sister singing, either analogy would do. Thankfully, the car came to a shuddering halt one millimeter from the small red hatchback stopped in front of him.

"That was close," he said with a long sigh to no one in particular.

The line of cars stretched as far as the eye could see. It was five o'clock traffic, after all. Jared turned his radio down, which now just seemed like noise to him, and prepared himself for the long crawl ahead.

Well, I might as well check my cell while I wait here to die of starvation, he thought.

Pulling out his phone, he slid his finger across the screen and quickly checked his text messages. It was then that his world came crashing down around him in the form of one small message: *You have three missed calls*.

"Oh no—Jasmine!" he said grimly. "I forgot again."

Jasmine was his girlfriend of two years. She was twenty-three, buxom, blonde, blue-eyed, beautiful, and the former prom queen of Johnson City High School. She was everything Jared had ever wanted, or so he thought.

Six foot tall and ruggedly handsome with sharp blue eyes and dirty blond hair, Jared had high standards. All of the other women he'd dated seemed to fall short in some way. Jasmine was a bit conceited and high maintenance, but she was a Christian, and that made his parents happy.

He had to admit that he did love her, but who didn't? She was the desire of every guy in her college and even some professors. Not a day went by where she wasn't hit on or proposed to. It made him jealous, but Jared liked having something to be jealous about. He had all but given up hope that he would ever find the right girl, when out of nowhere, she dropped into his life like an angel from heaven. In fact, he had even contemplated asking her to marry him, but something inside always seemed to stop him before he could make that leap.

She was usually a kind person, but she was particularly annoyed by people who were always late. This was the third time this month that he'd forgotten about a dinner date and he was running out of excuses. He had used work as an excuse the other three times and doubted if she'd accept it again.

Jared pulled up her cell phone number but stopped short before hitting the send button. What would he say? He had no idea. The real reason he was late was because he had taken his partner, a woman, home after their shift was up. Jasmine hated Dana. No matter how Jared tried to explain their relationship to her, she never seemed to understand.

Dana was his best friend and his brother-, well, sister-in-arms. He put his life in her hands every day, and she did the same with him. Jasmine could never understand that; all she saw was a rival. She was unwilling, or unable, to understand that they were just friends. Because of this, every time he had tried to talk to her about it, the conversation ended up in a fight.

Jared closed his texts and put his phone back in his pocket. He was not in the mood to deal with this right now. His shift had been a hard one. Some beat cop had found a young girl's body floating in the Chenango River last night. She'd been cut to pieces and dumped.

Murders happened all the time everywhere, even in small backwoods towns like Binghamton, but the murders in this area weren't usually so gruesome. Most of the time they were just the usual shootings or the occasional stabbing, but nothing as disturbing as what he had encountered today. The most disquieting fact, however, was that this murder fit the MO of the New York City serial killer known as the Eastside Stalker.

It couldn't be him of course, because up till now he had been linked to murders in the City and nowhere else. Still, it did fit his profile and that could not be ignored. His bosses had decided it was better not to speculate on the similarities for now. Besides, it was very unlikely the killer had expanded his hunting grounds this far north. Dana, however, had been quite shaken up about it and had asked if he would escort her home so they could discuss the case.

Dana had immediately recognized the girl, whom she identified as Amanda Pratt, a woman she'd known from college. She told him they'd shared a few of the same classes one semester. Dana had also gone to school with his little brother, Steve, and they'd even dated for a year. Amanda was the girl that Steve had shacked up with after he broke up with Dana, but neither of them had had any contact with her in years.

Both officers had talked as they parked in front of Dana's house for about an hour and a half before she finally said good night and got out of his car. He knew for sure that he was going to pay dearly for being a good friend and partner, and he resented that. Sure, he didn't have to drive her home—he could have just called later—but he cared about her too much to just ignore her when she needed him. In all the years he had known her, he had never seen her this shaken up by a crime scene. Well, it was already done and there was nothing he could do to change it now. Jared was just going to have to suck it up and face the music.

The traffic started to move. It wouldn't take him long to reach the restaurant. He thought of all the things he would say to try to put out the inevitable fires that would spring up, and before long he reached the exit that would take him to his doom.

Chapter Six

Jasmine sat quietly scowling into her cappuccino. She had been at the Number Six restaurant for over an hour now and Jared was nowhere in sight. She reached for her cell phone for the thousandth time but then thought better of it.

No, she told herself. *I've called him three times already and I am* not *going to call him again.*

This was the third time in a month that he'd stood her up. It wouldn't happen again. She turned and waved, summoning the waiter. A short, fat, balding man, the waiter rushed to her aid, as most men did when she wanted them.

"Yes, madam, is there something I can do for you?" he said with a smile.

"The check would be nice. It appears that *my friend—*" her tone dripped with such vehemence that the waiter winced, "—is not going to be coming after all."

"Yes, madam, right away." He rushed off to get her check.

Jasmine fumbled with her purse, trying, without success, to free her lipstick. Just when she had managed to get hold of it, she lost her grip on the purse. It fell to the floor, spilling its contents everywhere.

She swore and bent down to gather her belongings. Tears formed in her eyes. Jasmine was upset, more upset than she had been in a long time.

Bending down, she rummaged around, trying to catch her runaway cosmetics and an especially crafty pack of gum that seemed to elude her every attempt to capture it. On one particularly remarkable attempt that had her contorted in a manner not even a world-class yoga instructor could have duplicated, a man's hand suddenly appeared, catching the packet of gum before it could escape her again.

She followed the arm to a very handsome face with mesmerizing blue eyes. He was smiling at her and she grinned sheepishly back. Trying her best to avoid his eyes, she quickly gathered the rest of her things and jammed them into her purse.

"Thank you," she said, self-consciously fixing her hair. "You are a savior."

"You're very welcome," replied the man in a deep, heavily accented voice.

Jasmine's savior was tall, dark, and handsome. The kind of handsome you only find on Instagram feeds and *GQ* covers. He was toned and athletic with long, flowing black hair that hung down to his shoulders. He wore khaki pants, Dockers she guessed, and a baby-blue polo shirt.

"Nice," she whispered under her breath. "Very nice!"

"Excuse me? I did not catch what you said," the man said in that glorious accent—Romanian, maybe? She'd had a crush on a Romanian guy in her first year of college, mainly for his accent.

"Nothing," she said with a timid smile.

"I am sorry to intrude, but I could not help but notice your plight." He smiled at her and handed her the stray pack of gum. "I could not stand by while such a beautiful woman was in need."

Jasmine blushed at the compliment. "Thanks again, sir. I really appreciate your help."

"Please, you may call me Vladimir," he said with a bow. "Vladimir Durgala."

"Jasmine," she replied with a giggle. "Jasmine Lassiter."

Vladimir reached out, and before she could protest, took her hand in his. He lifted it to his mouth and kissed it, giving Jasmine goosebumps. "It is my pleasure to make your acquaintance, Miss Lassiter."

Dumbfounded for a moment, she regained her composure. "How did you know I wasn't married?" She flashed him a cheeky smile.

Vladimir's blue eyes sparkled. "No man, who has the favor of such a beautiful woman like you, would ever allow her the disrespect of having to dine alone. So you must be single. And being the gentleman that I am, I would be lacking in my duty if I did not extend the invitation for you to join me at my table."

"You are quite the charmer, aren't you, Vladimir?" She removed her hand from his. "But I am waiting for my boyfriend."

Vladimir's smiled again and glanced at the table where Jasmine had been sitting. There were two menus but only half-drunk cappuccino. Jasmine realized then that he'd probably been sitting at the table next to hers for quite some time. It would not have taken a rocket scientist to conclude that she'd been stood up.

"Yes, as I said before, I could not help but notice your situation." He glanced back at her and his blue eyes seemed to look right through her. "I am not usually so forward, but it seems to me that you have been here for quite some time with no sign of your absent friend. I am not familiar with your relationship, but it's too bad that he has allowed other priorities to take precedence over you."

Ouch. That hurt. A moment before, she'd decided to turn away, but what Vladimir said struck a chord inside her. He was right, of course. Something was always coming up for Jared. Usually, it was his partner Dana, and Jasmine hated her for it. They could pretend all they wanted, but Jasmine knew the truth.

Dana had become a cop because of Jared. Jared didn't know this of course, and Dana would never admit it, but Jasmine knew better. She'd overheard Dana talking to Jared's dad one Sunday afternoon at a family picnic. She had confessed it all, blubbering the whole time like a five-year-old.

Jared's "friendship" with Dana always seemed to override his confessed love for her. If Jared truly loved her like he said he did, then why did he always seem to choose Dana over her? The reason was obvious for anyone to see, and Jasmine kicked herself for not having seen it before. Jared loved Dana too. In fact, he loved Dana more than he loved Jasmine. There was no other explanation.

Her heart sank, and she thought she would break apart standing right there in the Number Six restaurant. She looked around at the happy couples scattered about the large dining room. Some were laughing, while others just sat together in the quiet familiarity that comes over a lifetime together. All of the restaurant's patrons were sharing moments, moments that would shape the rest of their lives together. Moments that would become memories and memories that would become bonds of love and friendship.

She ached deep inside and it was at that moment that she finally realized how truly alone she was. Jared was the one who was supposed to be there to fill that ache, and he wasn't. She had given her heart to him, had let him into the deepest parts of her soul, and she was still alone. Why was that? It was because he had not let her into his heart, not completely. He'd let someone else in instead. She blinked back tears of anger.

Well, no more. She refused to allow the tears to well up in her eyes and pushed down the lump in her throat. *I deserve better than this.*

"Are you all right?" Vladimir asked, concerned.

They say that a person's life is filled with decisions that must be made. Of these billions of decisions, a select few are of such importance that they change the course of our lives. Jasmine had come to one of these life-changing choices, and the decision she was about to make would change her world forever.

"Yes, I am," she replied, taking his arm in hers and leading him away from her table and her old life. "And if you don't mind, I would like to take you up on your invitation."

Chapter Seven

Jared pulled into the parking lot of the Number Six restaurant, cutting off a little old lady in a hideous orange Lincoln. He brought the car to a screeching halt in a space marked for handicapped people and was out of the car before the engine had time to fully shut down.

The Number Six was an old firehouse that had been reconditioned and modified into a high-class restaurant. It was awfully expensive, and Jared only ate there on special occasions. Jasmine, on the other hand, loved it and tried to coerce him into dining there often.

It had been dark for quite some time, and he knew he was over an hour late. He really hoped that she had not left already. There was a line of people waiting to be seated, and Jared had to nudge through them to reach the entrance. Frantic and desperate, he accidentally bumped a large man in a black sport coat.

"Sorry," he mumbled halfheartedly to the man, who scowled at him, but Jared didn't notice. He was too focused on getting to the front door to be bothered with such distractions. With a little more maneuvering and a few pokes and bumps, Jared made it to the front door and slipped inside.

The host, Joe Caputo, a thin Italian man with slicked-back hair, was flustered by the influx of people. His white tuxedo shirt was untucked, and when he saw Jared, his friend, coming through the door, he grimaced.

"She isn't here," he said, cutting Jared off before he could get a word out. "And I don't have time to sit here and discuss it with you."

"But!" Jared stammered. "Did she leave a note or something? I checked my cell, but she didn't leave me a message telling me she was leaving."

Joe held up his hand and turned to argue with a disgruntled waiter. Irritated, Jared checked his watch while Joe solved the waiter's dilemma. Just when he thought Joe would return, the man passed him by to seat an elderly couple.

Jared's heart was pounding so hard that he thought it would beat right out of his chest. The throbbing in his ears drowned out the loud noise of the busy restaurant, and he almost didn't notice when his friend came back to talk to him.

"Sorry, Jared, I know you're upset, but it's been a madhouse in here tonight," he whispered, taking Jared's arm and leading him back outside.

They walked past the line of people waiting to be seated and around to the back of the building. The host pulled a pack of cigarettes out of his pocket and shook it till one poked out of the top. He offered it to Jared who declined.

"I know you are upset, and I feel for you! I really do!" he said as he lit his cigarette. "But this was the third time this month, man! You can't really blame her for being upset."

Jared sighed and leaned up against the building. "What happened, Joey?"

"Do you really want to know?" he asked, exhaling. "I mean, do you want the truth, or do you want me to make something up?"

"Oh, for crying out loud!" Jared snapped. "Just get on with it already, will you?"

"Okay, okay! Yeesh!" Joe threw up his hands. "Calm down!" He exhaled another stream of smoke. "You're putting me in a tough spot, you know?"

"I get it. But I need to know what happened," Jared replied, trying hard to keep his emotions in check.

"So you can do what? Go give the guy a ticket or something?" snapped Joe.

Jared's face went pale.

Joe winced. "Oh shit! I'm sorry, man, I didn't want to tell you that way."

She had left with another man? How could she have done that? It did not make any sense. He had done everything right, hadn't he? She had left him without even saying a word. No. Joe must have been mistaken. There was no way she would have gone off with some stranger.

Joe reached out to grab his arm comfortingly, but Jared swatted it away.

"How could you let her leave with some other guy?" he growled. "You're supposed to be my friend!"

Drawing back, Joe glared at him, his cigarette dangling from his lips. "I am your friend!" he shot back, wounded. "And it sucks that I was the one who had to be there to witness the result of your stupidity. You didn't really think you could ignore her time and time again, and she'd just accept it, did you?"

Jared clenched his fists. "I never ignored her. My job requires a lot from me. I have no control over that."

Joe rolled his eyes. "It was never your job. That's just what you tell yourself."

What was Joe getting at? Of course it was his job. What else could it have been? He was a cop, and his job required more from him than most. Regular people like Joe, Jasmine, and even his parents never really understood that. Only Dana did.

"What are you saying?" Jared shot back. "If it wasn't my job, then what was it?"

"I think the correct question is, who was it?" Joe took a long drag on his cigarette.

Jared threw his hands up in disgust. "Oh come on! Now you're starting to sound like everyone else! Dana is my partner. Why can't any of you understand that?"

Joe shrugged and took one last drag from his cigarette before flipping it away. He exhaled and the smoke hung in the air in front of him like a cloud. "I think we understand more than you realize. Maybe it's you who doesn't really understand. Or maybe it's just that you don't *want* to understand."

Why did everybody keep bringing Dana up like she was some kind of romantic rival for Jasmine? He simply didn't feel that way about her. Did he?

"You don't understand," he said, but his voice held less conviction than before. "I don't love Dana that way."

"But you do love her," pressed Joe. "More than you realize, it seems. Hey man, I'm not trying to tell you your own heart, but I've seen you in action, again and again. Whatever you feel for Dana always seems to override what you feel for Jasmine. I'm sorry to have to be the one to say this, but what happened tonight was inevitable. It was only a matter of time with the way things were going."

Jared said nothing.

Joe put his hand on his shoulder. "Hey man, I'm not saying these things because I want to be a jerk or something. I am saying these things to you because I am your friend."

"I know," Jared replied softly as he watched a large cloud pass over the moon, causing the small parking lot to feel even more gloomy.

Joe gave his shoulder a reassuring squeeze. "You going to be okay?"

Jared sighed. He felt like he was going to keel over and die, right there on the ground in the alley next to the Number Six restaurant. He wanted to scream, *No, you idiot, I'm not okay.* "Yeah, I guess," was all that he could get to come out of his mouth.

Joe fixed his tie. "I'm really sorry, Jared. I truly am, and I wish I had all night to talk to you, but I have been gone too long already and I really should be getting back to the slave ship."

Joe gave him one last reassuring pat on the shoulder before walking back down the alley, leaving him sitting there alone.

Chapter Eight

Jared collapsed in his car closed his eyes and gritted his teeth. He felt like he was going to throw up, so he rolled the window down to let more air in. The sounds of the city shattered his blessed silence.

Sighing deeply, he wondered if he should roll it back up, but determined that it didn't matter. He was so agitated that he couldn't sit still, so he decided to get out of his car and go for a long walk through the city.

Maybe some mugger will do me a favor and rob me, killing me in the process, he thought as he locked his doors and then slammed them shut.

The night was especially busy, and Jared found it hard to find a place of solitude. So he walked down a nearby alley to get away from the crowds. Just as he passed into the darkness, a nice-looking young brunette propositioned him. He flashed his badge and she flipped him off, telling him where he could stick it. Ignoring her, he kept on walking, too absorbed in his own misery to care.

Jared wandered the dim city streets, passing so many houses that they all began to look alike to him. His thoughts were bleak, his mood depressed, and he soon lost track of time.

Realizing it was getting late and he needed to get home, he checked the street sign of the road he was on. Falkirk Ave. Jared had no idea how long he'd been walking, but apparently it had been for quite some time.

I guess I'd better call someone for a ride. He reached into his pocket to retrieve his cell phone.

What? Damn. He fumbled around, feeling a quarter and some lint, but no cell phone. Panicking, he quickly patted every one of his pockets, but came up empty.

Then he remembered where he'd left it—back in his car on the seat. Jared growled in frustration and decided to take his anger out on a telephone pole, nearly breaking his hand in the process.

Shaking his injured hand, he took in a deep breath and exhaled forcefully in an attempt at calming himself down. He then scanned the area and located a payphone on the other side of the street, which was sitting like a relic in front of a gloomy convenience store.

Reaching for the phone with his good hand, he listened for a dial tone. As he had suspected, the payphone didn't work. Nothing in Jared's life seemed to be going right for him tonight, so why should this payphone be any different? He slammed the phone down and walked over to the road.

After a few minutes of sulking, he noticed a lone figure walking out of the shadows across the street. Something about the man gave Jared an uneasy feeling in his gut. The person seemed to be out of phase with the physical world as if he were a phantom instead of a physical being.

What the heck? He must be more tired than he thought. He rose to his feet, squinting as he did so, attempting to force his eyes to focus. If anything, the action made the effect worse.

"Hey!" Jared called as he cautiously approached the figure.

The man started when he saw him coming toward him and he fell into a defensive crouch. His hand quickly darted for the fold in his black leather coat.

Jared stopped and reflexively reached his own hand behind his back finding the handle of his duty weapon. "Whoa! I don't want any trouble. So just keep your hands where I can see them."

He still could not make out the man's features when a sudden burst of vertigo washed over him.

What the heck is going on?

"Jared?" the man asked. "Is that you?

"Yeah," he replied, shaking his head slightly.

The man relaxed. "Jesus, you scared the crap out of me, big brother," he said with a sigh. "I thought you were a mugger or something."

Before Jared could react, the man stepped out of the shadows and lifted him up in an immense bear hug. As soon as his brother grabbed him, the vertigo ceased, and his vision cleared.

"I gotta admit it's good to see you, but what the heck are you doing so far away from home?"

"Me?" Jared said. "What in God's name are you doing here? I thought you were still in the city."

"I'm here visiting a friend."

"Who?"

"Nobody you know. Just a friend," Steve replied. "Hey, you never answered my question."

"I went for a walk and lost track of time," Jared said distractedly. "I guess I wasn't paying attention to where I was going."

"You are a long way from home, dude. That must have been some walk." Steve put his arm on his brother's shoulder. "What happened? You look like you lost your best friend."

All of the emotions of the day finally got the best of Jared, and he slumped into his brother's arms and wept uncontrollably. His brother held him close, and Jared buried his face in his chest, sobbing like a little kid.

Soon the whole story came out, of how things had been difficult between him and Jasmine. How he'd been late to the restaurant that night again. How he'd lost the love of his life. He told the story in between sobs, but his brother got the picture.

Jared let go of his brother and stood up straight. He sniffed and wiped his nose on his sleeve, forcing back more tears. "She dumped me for some other guy, Steve! How could this happen?"

"That's rough, man," Steve said as he ushered Jared in the direction of his car. "Why don't I drive you home and you can fill me in on everything else that has been going on?"

"I don't want to go home!" Jared responded.

"Okay," Steve muttered. "We can't stay out here all night. I'll take you to Dad and Mom's house, then."

"No. I don't want to go there, either."

Steve sighed. "Then where the heck do you want to go?"

"Dana's house."

"What? You can't be serious!"

Really, him too? Did everyone in his life think he had some secret flame for her?

Jared turned on Steve angrily. "What are you implying?"

"Nothing, it's just that... Well, you know it's kind of odd that you'd want to go see her of all people. I would think she would be the last person on your mind right now."

"She is my fricking partner and my best friend," Jared snapped back. "Why doesn't anyone understand that? You're starting to sound like Jasmine, too."

"Now I understand," his little brother said with that annoying, no-it-all look on his face.

"You don't understand anything!" retorted Jared. "Just take me there and shut up about it. I'm not in the mood for a lecture right now!"

"This explains why you don't want to go see Dad and Mom."

"Just stop talking before I slug you."

"Okay, okay! Stop being so dramatic." Steve laughed. "It's not the end of the world, you know."

"I know, but it feels like it," Jared muttered.

"Come on, Jar. My car is parked just down the road. You can tell me the rest of the sob story as we walk."

They walked slowly down the empty street, Steve listening patiently as his brother continued to relate all of the events of the past few months that had led up to this moment.

Steve put his arm around his brother as they walked. When the two of them stood side by side, the resemblance was so strong, one could almost mistake them for twins.

Both brothers were tall and handsome with bright blue eyes. Steve had long flowing black hair while Jared's short dirty blond hair looked like straw. Jared, however, made up for his unruly hair by being slightly more muscular than Steve.

Jared loved his brother, and he couldn't help but smile slightly as they walked. The mere presence of his younger brother made everything seem better. He had always envied his ability to project absolute confidence. Charismatic and loved by almost everyone he met, Steve, was everything Jared was not.

They talked as they walked, the way only brothers can, and before long they arrived at Steve's car. It was a new black Jaguar. Jared's jaw dropped in shock when he saw Steve pull out a set of keys and use the key fob to unlock the doors.

"When did you get this?" Jared asked. "I knew the band was doing better, but this must've cost a fortune."

Steve smiled and opened the driver's side door. "I wasn't going to tell you until after you were through with your mourning period, but I guess now is as good a time as any. We just signed a major record deal, and this was one of the perks."

Not even registering the slight sarcastic jab, Jared stood in silent awe as Steve got in. The sports car started up immediately, the engine humming to life.

Steve rolled down the passenger side window. "Well, are you just going to stand out here all night, or are you going to get in?"

Jared took one last appreciative look at the car before getting in. "This is really yours?"

Steve winked. "Hope to die, stick a needle in my eye."

"I think I'm in the wrong profession," Jared mused. "You guys wouldn't be looking for a kazoo player by any chance, would you?"

Laughing, Steve threw the car into drive. The tires squealed as the car surged forward, leaving a long black rubber streak in its wake.

Chapter Nine

The night was dark and dismal. The Shogun made his way down the empty street, knowing that he was already too late. He cursed the sudden waves of emotion that had so incapacitated him earlier. The loss of yet another innocent to that maniac was more than his pride could bear. Once, he might have had the strength to deal with such horrors, but not anymore.

He bent to examine a small patch of overgrown weeds that inhabited an alley. The broken body of a young woman with shoulder-length brown hair. She appeared to have been dumped like a bag of garbage, her heavy winter coat tossed not far from her.

The Shogun solemnly picked up the woman's coat and reverently placed it over her dead body. It covered her face and most of her torso but left her legs and arms exposed. It was not a perfect shroud, but it was all he had, so it would have to do. Maybe her family would appreciate the kindness.

A stream of crimson slowly flowed from the blades of grass to form a small pool of blood on the sidewalk. He sat there for what seemed like hours, quietly examining the pool before lifting himself up and away from the lifeblood of the young woman.

"This will not happen again!" he vowed as he walked away from the grisly scene.

The killer was on the move and traveling fast, but not fast enough. It would not take the Shogun long to reach him and reach him he would. The Stalker was now the stalked, and if he had known who it was that hunted him, he would have turned himself into the police long ago.

He had only taken a few steps when two shadows separated themselves from the darkness and drifted into the street, two pools of writhing blackness, with menacing red eyes.

The Shogun recognized them. Terrible beings usually found in nightmares; they emanated an aura of fear that would have caused even the bravest of men to flinch. The demons neared the Shogun.

"What do you want of me?" The Shogun drew his glowing blade from its scabbard. "My quarrel is not with you today."

The spirits hissed at him, "We know you, Ma'at. You have hindered many of us in the past!"

"I know your kind as well and have no time for your games!" the Shogun snapped, the darkness in his eyes seeming to burn with a shadowy fire. "I will deal with you as I have dealt with the rest of your kind, if you do not step aside!"

The shadowy specters shivered and convulsed and howled in outrage. They began to twist and contort until each shadow took on an almost humanoid form with large bat-like wings protruding out of their backs. Each demonic specter held a large shadowy curved sword in both hands, and with a gust of brimstone, their weapons ignited with unholy fire.

"The master has sent us to deal with you, Ma'at!" they growled in unison. "He has grown weary of your interfering in his work."

"Who is your master?" inquired the Shogun. "And why does he protect the murderer?"

"Enough talk!" bellowed the demon on the left. "Let the battle commence. It has been long since I have seen combat!"

"You know full well that you have not the authority to slay me."

"We may not have the power to destroy you, Ma'at, but we can hinder you," hissed the demon on the right. "And that is all we were sent to do."

"Then let it begin. But I can assure you that you will not hinder me much."

Eager and impatient, the demon on the left attacked first, swinging his flaming blade hard at the Shogun's head. The Shogun deflected the blow easily but was forced slightly off balance by the strength of the strike. The second demon attacked then, stabbing at the Shogun's midsection.

With supernatural agility, the Shogun managed to parry the strike while leaping away from his attacker. Before he could land, however, the first demon attacked again, thrusting his blade forward and up, attempting to skewer him in midair.

The Shogun deflected the attack with a spin. His sword whirling like a helicopter blade, he deflected yet another attack from the second demon. Before landing, the Shogun kicked the attacking demon's face, but his foot passed through the shadowy figure.

The demons fell upon the Shogun as soon as his feet hit the ground. Red flames sparked from the clashing weapons as the battle continued. Strike after strike, counterstrike after counterstrike, neither side gained the advantage.

The Shogun could feel the Stalker getting farther and farther away, and he feared that this delay might prove more costly than he had anticipated. If he did not end this confrontation quickly, his chance of catching the murderer would slip away from him.

The Shogun gritted his teeth and kicked one of the demons, managing to hit its leg. The demon howled in pain and fury, and the Shogun turned on the other attacker.

Despite its strength and cunning, without its partner to complement it, the demon was at a severe disadvantage. It was no match for the full power of the Shogun, who attacked it mercilessly. The demon met the Shogun's attack with an intensity of its own that caused it to surpass its usual skill, and it somehow managed to hold him at bay long enough for the other demon to reenter the conflict.

Outnumbered and once again on the defensive, the Shogun realized that he had underestimated these demons. Damn! He felt so weary. Perhaps it was not the demons but rather his own waning power that was the problem. Either way, if he did not finish this confrontation soon, the murderer would escape him yet again. With renewed determination, he gritted his teeth and continued fighting, each moment allowing the Stalker to slip farther and farther away.

Chapter Ten

Dana Campbell peered through the curtains into the dark of night. She thought she'd heard a car pull up, and the noise had awoken her instantly. The events of the previous day had disturbed her, and in response, she'd decided to keep her nine-millimeter pistol loaded and ready in her nightstand.

Holding her gun at arm's length, she pulled the curtains back to get a better look. A black Jaguar was parked directly in front of her house where there had not been one earlier. She tried to recall if she knew anyone who drove a Jag but came up empty.

A handsome man with long black hair popped out of the driver's side. He looked familiar, but she couldn't place him. When the second man opened the passenger side door and practically fell out of the car, she knew instantly he was.

Jared. Her heart leaped in her chest. She closed the curtain so he would not see her, then dashed to her dresser to grab a brush. With a few quick swipes, she smoothed her tangled locks into a ponytail. She knew

Jared probably wouldn't notice her hair, he never did, but she wasn't going to take the risk.

When she was finished, she examined her handy work in the mirror and scowled. Her hair was passable, but the dark circles under her brown eyes had to go. With a few quick dabs, she smoothed makeup over her classically beautiful face and flawless olive skin.

A beautiful young woman, Dana had a body most women would kill for. But even though she was beautiful, she never really dressed the part. Dana just wanted to fit in with the rest of the guys. Except, of course, when it came to Jared.

The doorbell rang and she fumbled with her mascara, dropping it to the ground. To her horror, it bounced twice and then rolled underneath her dresser and out of reach. She frantically dropped to the ground in a desperate attempt at catching it and slammed her head painfully into a slightly open drawer.

The doorbell rang again, and she instantly scrambled to her feet to examine her injured head. A large knot was already starting to form directly in the middle of her forehead and she almost cried when she saw it.

"Great, how do I explain this one?" she whined. "I look like some sort of deranged Hindu!"

The loud persistent knocking interrupted her sulking, and she dabbed more foundation on her mark. After a few more minutes of primping, she decided it was time to answer the door.

It did not take her long to reach the front door and she swung it open just as Steve was about to begin another symphony of knocking.

He stumbled forward off balance when his fist hit only air. She ignored him, even though she had not seen him for some time and locked her gaze on Jared.

"What's the matter? You look awful," she asked, concerned.

"Well, it's nice to see you too," Steve said sarcastically. "I've been good. How have you been?"

"Can we come in?" Jared asked, trying not to smirk.

"What's the matter?" she demanded, checking herself again. It was then that she realized she had neglected to change out of her baby blue cotton nightshirt with the little pink bunnies on it, and her face flushed red.

"Nice shirt," Steve snickered. "Isn't that the same nightshirt you wore to Sandra Hamperton's sleepover party in fourth grade?"

"Leave her alone, Steve," Jared scolded.

Dana ducked behind the door so only her head was visible and waved them both in. "You two make yourselves at home while I go change."

She dashed down the hall to her room as the two brothers made their way to the living room. Dana rented a two-bedroom house in the nice section of town. She liked her privacy and could afford to not have a roommate. Plus, being a single woman alone in such a big house was a good excuse to have Jared over often.

"If you are thirsty, I have some soda in the fridge," she called out. "Help yourselves to whatever you like."

Dana's room was clean and organized, with all the typical things you would expect to find in a young woman's room. A nice bed with a matching dresser and hutch mirror, and a hope chest that was given to her by her father. Pictures of her family and friends littered her room and a rather large jewelry box sat on her dresser.

She quickly stripped off the nightshirt and threw it carelessly into a corner, before rummaging through her dresser and pulling out a pair of green shorts and a white T-shirt. After getting dressed, she did another quick inspection, fixed her makeup a bit, and then took a deep calming breath before heading out to the living room.

Jared was sulking on her brown leather couch, his eyes closed, and his brow scrunched like he was experiencing the migraine of the century. Steve was sitting in the matching leather recliner with his feet dangled over the arm, drinking a can of soda.

The first thing Dana did when she entered the room was smack Steve's feet aside. His drink sloshed.

"Hey, what was that for?" Steve whined, brushing the stain off his shirt. She ignored him and sat down next to Jared, putting her arm around him.

"So, partner, what's going on?" she inquired. "You don't usually show up here so late unless there is something major wrong."

"His little girlfriend dumped him for some other guy," Steve answered for him. "It's got him torn up really bad."

Jared shot Steve a glare that would freeze water, but his brother just shrugged it off and went back to enjoying his drink. Dana did her best to suppress a grin.

"I'm truly sorry, Jared," Dana said, trying her hardest to sound sympathetic. "I know how you felt about her."

"Me too, big brother," Steve echoed with a warm smile. "I know I am being a bit of a jerk about it, but I'm just trying to cheer you up."

Jared sighed and sat back in the chair. "I know and I appreciate it. I just can't believe that she would do that to me. How could she leave with some stranger?"

"I wish I had the answers, Jared, but I don't," Steve said with a sigh. "But I don't think I am the one you should be talking to right now."

"What do you mean by that?" Jared asked. "Who else would I talk to?"

"All I am saying is that I need to take a nice hot shower and get some rest. You two should talk alone. After all, that's why you wanted to come here anyway, wasn't it?" He stood up and stretched. "If you don't mind, Dana, I'd like to use your shower. I've got a long day ahead of me tomorrow, and it's already very late."

"Of course, the guest bathroom is upstairs. First door on your left. There are towels in the closet, and you can help yourself to whatever toiletries you need."

Steve yawned and ambled up the stairs. Just as he was about to put his foot on the first step, Dana called to him, "It really is good to see you, Steve. Maybe tomorrow we can catch up."

"That would be nice," he replied with a tired smile. "You look after Jared for me, okay?"

He winked at her and she realized that he knew more than he was letting on. She had made no secret of how she felt about Jared and had spoken openly of it to Steve when they were younger. Evidently, he hadn't forgotten.

An uncomfortable silence fell over the two and Dana fidgeted nervously. Jared continued to sulk undaunted, absorbed in his own misery.

"Can I get you anything?" she asked, breaking the silence.

Jared looked up as if seeing her for the first time. "I'm sorry, did you say something?"

"I just asked if you wanted anything," she replied, looking him deep in the eyes.

His eyes were such a dark shade of blue that they almost seemed purple. The first time she had looked into those eyes, even though she was only ten, she had fallen in love.

"No thank you," he murmured gloomily, looking away again. "My stomach's a little upset right now."

Not knowing what to say next, the conversation lapsed back into an uneasy silence. She hated seeing him this way and cursed Jasmine under her breath. How could she be such a fool? Dana would give up anything to be with Jared, and she could not understand why Jasmine didn't feel the same way.

Dana pulled her legs up to her chest, hugging them close with her arms. Jared was not only the man she loved, but her best friend and partner as well. But there was nothing she could do for him. She could only wait until he was ready to talk, and she was determined to wait forever if that's what it took.

It wasn't long before Jared broke the silence. "I really appreciate you letting us crash here for the night."

"You know you're always welcome," she replied with a reassuring smile. "But you owe me big time for bringing the almighty rock star here."

Jared chuckled slightly, and Dana nudged him with her elbow. "Is that a smile I see?"

The smile only lasted a second. "I don't know why I asked Steve to bring me here. I guess I didn't want to go to my apartment, and I didn't want to disturb Mom and Dad..."

"So this was the only place left to go," she said. "I understand. You don't have to explain anything to me, partner. Stay as long as you need to."

He gave her another weak smile and grabbed her hand. "Thanks," he said, his voice thick with sincerity. "This means a lot to me."

Her breath caught in her throat, and her heart seemed ready to beat right out of her chest. She knew that he held her hand out of friendship, but she could imagine it meaning more.

"So how did Steve manage to wind up here?" she asked, changing the subject and trying to avoid his eyes. "I thought he was in the city."

"I don't really know. He said he was visiting a friend, but when I asked him which one, he dodged the question."

"That's strange. Why would he need to be vague about which friend he was visiting?" she asked, her brow furrowed.

"I don't know. Come to think of it, he was acting kind of weird. At the time I was too distracted to notice, but on reflection, it does seem rather odd."

"I'm sure it is nothing," she said. "He was probably drinking and didn't want you to know about it."

"That's probably it. I'm sure he was afraid that if I knew, I would tell Dad. Despite all his rebelling, what Dad thinks still matters to him."

The uncomfortable silence returned, neither of them knowing what to say next. It was Jared who decided to speak first, and Dana gave him her full attention.

"I wish there was a way I could talk to her," he said, gritting his teeth. "But she won't answer her phone. If I could just get her to talk to me, then we could work this out."

"I'm sure she'll come to her senses after a while," she heard herself utter, hoping in her heart that she was wrong. "She just needs a little time to think things over."

"You're probably right," he replied. "But you know me. Patience is not one of my strong suits. I have to fix things right away or I go crazy. Steve has already said more than once that I am overreacting."

"There's no quick fix for this, Jared. When it comes to love and relationships, you're just going to have to give her time."

Dana looked back at the clock and groaned when she saw the time. Two o'clock in the morning. Both of them had to be at work at six.

"I can't believe how late it is," she said with a yawn. "Tomorrow's going to be murder on us if we don't get some sleep soon."

Jared reached out and embraced her unexpectedly, drawing her close. "Thanks for being there, partner. You're a real friend. I don't know what I would do without you."

"That's me," she replied when she could breathe again. "The girl next door."

What would happen if she rested against his chest? Dana decided to find out. He didn't try to push her away, so she closed her eyes and listened to his rhythmic breathing. Each second seemed as if it lasted a lifetime and she hoped against hope that this moment would never end.

Then she felt his chest shake with the deep sighs that came from intense crying. She wished she knew the magic words to make his hurt go away. While she was wishing, a potion that would make him fall in love with her would be nice, too. But for all her imagining, she knew it was Jasmine he was thinking of and not her.

Still, right here and now, that did not matter. Jasmine wasn't here. This moment was hers and hers alone. She allowed herself to enjoy the feeling, and before long she had fallen fast asleep, her head still resting on his chest.

Chapter Eleven

The Shogun waited for the two shades to make their move. His torn shirt hung limply, and he felt uncharacteristically spent. Amazingly they had managed to fight him to a standstill. Either these two demons were extremely powerful, or he was weakening faster than he realized. The latter was the most likely answer.

The shade on the right, the impatient one, lunged first. The Shogun parried the flaming blade away, but the shade followed up the thrust by slashing its other weapon at the Shogun's head. The Shogun ducked and the flaming blade hissed by.

The maneuver left the shade's torso exposed, and the Shogun brought his blade forward hard. The blade bit deep into the shade, nearly cutting it in half. The demon cried out in agony, its body held together by a mere wisp of smoke. Crimson clouds of noxious vapor leaked from the creature's wound and the burning red glow in its eyes ebbed. Before long, it dissipated into the shadows.

The other shade used the death of its brother as a diversion, and it struck the Shogun hard from behind with both blades. They bit deep into the Shogun's torso, impaling him and setting his clothes on fire. The shade quickly retracted its blades and slashed them both downward, cutting two wicked gashes into his back.

He stumbled forward, then fell awkwardly to his knees, his clothes still smoldering with dark fire. The shade attacked him the instant his knees hit the ground.

The Shogun, not nearly as injured as he appeared, sprung over the attacking shade, spinning once in midair while hacking at its passing head. His cut split the shade's head in two. It stumbled forward, leaving a trail of crimson smoke in its wake.

He landed in a crouch with his back to the injured demon, his blade held out in front of him. The demon dissipated, and the Shogun relaxed his grip on his weapon.

"I never thought I would see the day when a mere pair of shades could cause you so much trouble," a voice from somewhere behind him said. "It appears that you are weaker than I anticipated."

The Shogun recognized that familiar accent. Standing up, he faced the Musketeer leaning up against a large tree, his arms crossed and a grin on his face. He winked at the Shogun, removed his wide-brimmed hat, and bowed, his long black hair falling into his face.

"Did you miss me? I apologize for having to leave so abruptly before, but I thought it would be best to leave you alone in your moment of grief. Anyway, I was in the neighborhood and thought I would pay you another visit."

The Musketeer returned his hat to his head and slowly approached the wary Shogun. He drew his long slender rapier from its scabbard and playfully swept it through the air. The eerie radiance of the weapon bathed the dark street with an ethereal violet glow.

"Oh, how I do cherish our little contest. And I truly wish that things could be different, but alas, we both know how this must end."

The Shogun bowed his head in acknowledgment but said nothing. His blade glowed with the same extraordinary supernatural light, growing in intensity until it was slightly brighter than that of the Musketeer's. The world around them was awash with streams of violet and blue as the two sources of light vied with each other for dominance.

"It is a shame that you have grown so weak," the Musketeer reflected. "How grand a victory it would have been to have taken you in your prime. It was you who defeated my predecessor, was it not?"

"I did nothing," the Shogun replied. "The sword took him. I was just the instrument it used."

The Musketeer looked away as if he was contemplating some deep revelation and nodded his head. "It is so for us all, my friend. We are mere pawns, servants to their will. In spite of all our differences, you and I are the same."

"I am nothing like you. You serve darkness and have always done so. I, though I have very little will left in the matter, serve the forces of light and have always done so."

The Musketeer sneered at him. "You sanctimonious fool! I know what you have done. All of those you have slaughtered in the name of justice. I have witnessed your deeds, and your self-righteous *judgments*!"

"I am just in all I have done, even if my actions may seem harsh and cruel at times. How can it be any other way?"

"Just?" the Musketeer scoffed. "One man's justice is another man's tyranny!"

"Vain philosophies have no bearing on the truth," he replied. "You know as well as I do that there is only black and white. Gray is a state imagined to justify sin."

The Musketeer rubbed his forehead as if he had a headache. "Why must you bore me with your frivolous lectures? Enough! I have not come here to bandy words with you but to destroy you. Unlike you, I enjoy the power he gives me, regardless of the price I must pay. I have the power to do anything! He has made me a god among men!"

The Musketeer's black eyes writhed with defiance as the light from the sword exploded around him, covering his entire body with a violet aura that emanated pulsing waves power.

"You are nothing but a slave," he responded.

The Musketeer grinned and chuckled. "Maybe so, but I enjoy it nonetheless."

With that said, he lunged at the Shogun, and with the clashing of their ancient blades, the conflict which had begun centuries before entered into its final chapter.

The Shogun's sword arm dropped slightly, and he staggered somewhat off balance. Perceiving his weakness, the Musketeer attacked with animalistic ferocity, attempting to overpower him quickly. The Shogun, his eyes blazing with defiance, met the assault with surprising strength, managing to counter the Musketeer's every strike.

Both men fought with a skill greater than the greatest of master swordsmen, their movements as intricate as a choreographed dance.

"I am pleased that you still have some resolve left in you!" the Musketeer jeered. "It will make my victory all the more satisfying."

The Shogun responded with a wicked combination of attacks that wiped the grin off his face and sent him into a frantic medley of countering maneuvers. The Musketeer was now the one on the defensive; it would be difficult for him to regain momentum now.

The Shogun's arms were a blur as he slashed repeatedly high and then struck low, the Musketeer parrying every blow. Unrelenting, he struck again and again, but the cunning Musketeer knocked each one aside.

"I can feel you weakening," he said between strikes. "It will not be long now."

The Shogun said nothing and continued to fight undaunted, but in his heart, he could feel the fatigue. His eyes suddenly went wide, as the weariness and pain of a hundred lifetimes assaulted him at once. The weight of it took his breath away and he gasped. His hand faltered.

The Musketeer struck. He only scored a glancing blow on the Shogun's sword hand, but the blade that had not left his hand for nearly four hundred years slipped from his grasp. It spun away from him like in a dream before hitting the ground without a sound.

Time stopped, and the world around them stilled. Both men stared at the fallen sword as if the inconceivable had just happened. Then the Musketeer thrust his blade forward, sliding it deep into the Shogun's chest.

He gasped as the cold steel cut unrelentingly through tissue and slid through organs. His muscles would not obey him, and he watched without sensation as his body twitched when the Musketeer removed the blade. He fell backward and landed on the ground, lying in the soft grass and staring up at the night. His life force slipped away; this was the end. All the long years of service were finally over. Now he could rest. The darkness that had replaced his mortal eyes faded, giving way to a brilliant shade of brown. Those eyes once again beheld the stars before they closed for the last time.

The Musketeer stood over him, casting a long shadow over his body. He could no longer sense the presence of the Shogun and knew that his enemy had moved beyond the confines of the mortal world.

"So long, mon ami. You were a worthy adversary," he said with uncharacteristic respect. "May you find rest."

With his final respects paid to the dead, he approached the fallen sword. A baleful hostility vibrated out of it, and while he wore his sword, he did not dare come any closer for fear of what it might do to him.

Theirs was a bitter conflict that was predestined to last until the world ended. The Musketeer turned and walked away leaving the weapon where it lay. Both swords continued to glow in defiance of each other until the Musketeer was out of sight.

When they were gone, the sentient sword lifted itself off the ground and hovered. It bobbed up and down and its glow softened as it made its way over to its former bearer. The weapon continued to hover over him, bathing the dead body with blue light.

Before long, it settled into the Shogun's stiff open palm, and its glow ceased. The weapon rested there in the familiar hand that had wielded it for so long. After a while, it began to contort and melt until it had fashioned itself into a new form, that of a small golden locket with a large blood-red gem at its center.

Here it would rest until another who was worthy of the call would come to claim it. It could sense that the new bearer was near. It would not have long to wait. It never did, because the cycle which had begun at the fashioning of the universe itself would continue until the last light of that universe faded away.

Chapter Twelve

Dana awoke with a start. Someone was gently shaking her and whispering her name. The face that hovered over her was Steve's, and she groaned and placed one hand over her eyes hoping he would go away.

"What time is it?" she asked groggily.

"Five thirty," he said with a yawn. "I made you some coffee, hope you like it strong."

She started to sit up and felt Jared stir slightly from the movement. It was then that the events of last night came flooding back to her with amazing clarity. She could not remember what time it had been when she finally fell asleep, but she knew that it must have been late.

"I heard your alarm going off in your room and after about ten minutes of it, I realized you weren't in there to turn it off," he whispered as he helped her up. "I thought that you might appreciate the wake-up call."

"Thanks," she replied, looking back down at Jared. It touched her that he had stayed with her all night. She was loath to let the moment go, so she just stood there silently gazing at him.

Steve put the cup of coffee on the end table, slipped out of the room and back to bed.

It was late and she had to start getting ready for work, so she bent down and gently kissed Jared on the cheek. "Maybe someday you will love me as much as I love you," she whispered.

Jared stirred as she spoke, and he opened his eyes and stared at her dazed. "Jasmine?" he asked, confused.

"No," she replied, her voice cracking. "It's Dana. You stayed at my house last night, remember? It's about five thirty and I have to go to work. I'll tell the lieutenant that you are sick or something. You stay here and get some rest."

She dashed for the door before she finished with her last sentence, wiping away the tears that now flowed freely down her face.

"Wait! Can't you stay with me?" he called to her. "I don't want to be alone right now."

She ignored him, too choked up to speak, and quickly made her way down the hallway to her room, slamming the door shut behind her. Sobbing uncontrollably, she slumped to the ground and pulled her legs up to her chest, hugging them close.

When she'd heard him say Jasmine's name, it had shattered her perfect moment, breaking her heart. She had no one to blame but herself and she knew it. He had come to her as a friend, not a lover, and she had set herself up to be hurt.

"Get ahold of yourself, girl," she scolded herself. "You have a job to get ready for, and you don't have time to do this right now."

After a few calming breaths, she got changed and made her way into the bathroom to prepare for the day.

Jared awoke to the irritating sound of a phone ringing. His eyes were red and swollen from crying and he wasn't sure where he was. He felt like he had a hangover. It was then that he remembered everything from last night and he sighed deeply.

"Dana," he said dreamily to himself. She seemed upset before and he hoped everything had turned out okay. Jared wondered what could have made her so upset. He could not come up with anything offhand, so he returned to his brooding. The phone continued to ring and after a few minutes of ignoring it, whoever it was hung up.

He walked out into the kitchen, yawning and stretching away the stiffness. He opened the refrigerator door and peered in, looking for anything edible. Nothing looked good, and he didn't feel like eating anyway, so he closed the door, deciding to skip breakfast. Well, at least what he thought was breakfast, anyway. He wasn't entirely sure what time it was.

The clock on the microwave told him that it was nine o'clock and he wondered if Jasmine had tried to call him. If she had tried his cell phone, she would have received no answer and probably would have been infuriated. His cell was still in his car at the Number Six restaurant, so he had no way of checking to see if she had called. He wondered if she'd tried to call his parents as well, but he didn't want to bother them.

Who was he kidding? According to Joe, she had left the restaurant with some other guy. The last thing that she would likely do is call him right now. He had to talk to her, and he had to do it right now. In a panic, he picked up Dana's home phone and dialed the number to Jasmine's cell. It rang until her voice mail picked up and he left a heartfelt message telling her to call him.

A call to her parents revealed that she had left for New York City with her new friend. They felt sorry for Jared but said that they had promised not to tell him where she was staying in the city. He did manage to get the name of the guy she was with, though. Vladimir Durgala. He was apparently a diplomat of some kind and had stopped in Binghamton on his way back to the city.

Jared slammed the phone down and slumped into the chair at the kitchen table. How could this be happening? What a nightmare. One day everything was fine, and then, poof. In one fell swoop, it was all gone. It was amazing how your entire life could be thrown into complete and utter chaos in one moment's time.

The phone rang again, startling him out of his lethargy. He quickly picked it up, hoping it was Jasmine. It was Dana, however, and he did not try to hide his disappointment.

"Jared?"

"Yeah," he responded gloomily. "What's up?"

"Are you up and around?"

"I just woke up," he replied with a yawn. "Is something wrong?"

She did not respond immediately, and he could hear her talking to someone else in the background. When she returned to their conversation, she sounded tired and a bit distraught. "Yeah, we got another one on our hands, and the captain wants you here ASAP."

"Another *what* on our hands?" he asked. "Can't you handle it on your own just for today?"

"Jared, get your head out of the gloomy cloud it's trapped in and listen to me for two seconds," she snapped. "We have another dead girl on our hands, and the FBI has shown up. Since we were the presiding detectives on the other case, the captain wants us both here at the crime scene to assist them in any way necessary."

"Oh man!" he said excitedly, his own problems beginning to seem small in the light of what Dana had just said. "They think we have a serial killer on our hands, don't they?"

"The FBI being here is a good indication, don't you think? We can discuss the details when you get here. Just hurry, okay?"

"I will," he said, getting up from the table and grabbing a piece of paper and pen. "Where are you right now?"

"Twenty-One Falkirk Ave. Do you know where that is?"

"The name sounds familiar." He frowned in thought. "I'm pretty sure it's in our jurisdiction."

"Just on the edge of it. It's not too far from the Number Six restaurant."

Jared's face went pale when he remembered why that street sounded so familiar to him. That was the name of the street he had crossed on his little adventure last night. He was surprised that he remembered it since he had only glanced at the sign once. He could see the sign in his mind as clearly as if he were looking right at it.

"Are you still there?"

"Yeah," he stammered, deciding not to tell Dana until after he had a chance to think it over. "What was the time of death?"

"They are not sure yet," she said. "The crime scene was only just recently secured, and the medical examiner has not yet looked at the body."

"All right. I'll be there in about twenty minutes or so."

"Okay, see you then," she said and hung up.

His head swooned, so he reached out and grabbed the table using it to steady himself. Maybe if he hadn't been so preoccupied with his own worries, he might have been able to help that girl. Of course, he was not sure of what time he had been there. But the knowledge that he might have been able to save her would probably haunt him for the rest of his life.

Jared was still dressed from the night before, so he decided to skip going to his apartment to change before heading directly to the murder site. As soon as he had gotten down the stairs and opened the door to leave, he remembered that he had left his car at the Number Six.

Gritting his teeth, he rushed to the stairs and called up to his brother but received no response. He called again and received the same result, so he decided to go find Steve and wake him up. Upon reaching the guestroom, he found it empty, and the bed made. A note was lying on the nightstand and he picked it up and quickly scanned it.

The note was from Steve. It said that he had left early to do some errands and that he would be at Mom and Dad's later in the day if Jared wanted to see him before he returned to the city. He crumpled the note and threw it into a corner.

"Well, I guess I am going to have to call an Uber," he grumbled as he stomped back down the stairs.

Jared went back into the kitchen, and upon realizing again that he had left his cell in his car, picked up Dana's phone and called a taxi instead. Before long, a beat-up old station wagon painted yellow with a large sign that said "Yellow Cab" on it pulled up in front of the house. He jumped in and had the driver take him to the Number Six restaurant to retrieve his abandoned car.

When they had arrived, he grimaced as he handed more money than he had wanted to the cabby. It was a bit chilly this morning so the first thing he did after getting in his car was put on his black coat. He started up the engine and blew on his hands as he waited for the car to warm.

Jared knew it was a long shot, but he checked his cell phone to see if Jasmine had left him a message. Just as he suspected, she had not, and he tossed the phone onto the passenger seat, disgusted. It bounced twice and then dropped down into the crevice between the seat and door. He ignored it, too annoyed to care, and slammed his foot down on the gas pedal.

Jared reached the area around Falkirk Ave forty-five minutes after his conversation with Dana. He had to park a couple blocks away, thanks to the usual mob of bystanders and journalists gathered there like vultures.

Hurrying, he fought his way through the dense crowd to the taped off area at the corner where he'd met Steve. The officer on watch, an old veteran with short gray hair and a bushy mustache, was a close friend of his and waved him through as soon as he saw him approaching.

"Hey, Sergeant Cotter, how ya doing?" Jared asked the older officer. "Must be some heck of a show going on here with all these people hanging around. Is Endless in town or something?"

"Ha! Ha! Very funny, Jar," Cotter replied dryly. "Where have you been? Dana's been going out of her mind looking for you."

"Overslept," he said, his breath making a cloud in the cool morning air. "You know how it is."

Cotter laughed and rolled his eyes. "Maybe for you girls in homicide. We beat cops never get to sleep in. Think of what would happen if we did. Who would do all the work?"

"Not to mention get the coffee," Jared shot back. "I take mine with two sugars but no cream, thanks."

"Get your own coffee, you son of a bitch!" Cotter retorted with a wry smile. "I have better things to do than babysit you."

"Okay, okay!" Jared said, throwing up his hands and backing away. "I can see you have your hands full already, so I won't take up any more of your time. Say hi to the hottie from action news for me, will ya?"

"No. I think I will keep that one all to myself," Cotter said, turning just in time to see the aforementioned "hottie" standing directly behind him. His face flushed with embarrassment, like a little boy caught with his fingers in the cookie jar.

"This is going to cost me big time, isn't it?" Cotter asked the reporter dejectedly, and she smiled and nodded.

Jared fled down the street toward the area where the body was found before Cotter had time to properly thank him for setting him up. He smiled, his depression forgotten temporarily until he reached the crime scene and saw the expression on Dana's face.

He walked up to her, passing the barely covered body of a young woman, and the gravity of what he saw hit him like a ton of bricks. He could do nothing but stand and gawk at the morbid scene. A deep sense of sadness swept over him, and all his petty troubles were lost in the terrible finality of death's cold stare.

CSI officers worked like archeologists gingerly scouring the area for any clue the killer might have left, while other officers talked to the occupants of the surrounding houses, attempting to gather as much information about the events of the night before as they could. All in all, it was a typical murder scene much like the numerous others he'd been called to investigate.

But this one was different somehow, and he could not fathom why. Deep down in his gut, however, he could sense that there was something disturbing about this particular murder. He could not put his finger on what it was.

Dana walked up to him and stared down at the broken body of the young woman. "Why can't I shake the feeling that there is something strange about this murder?" she asked him softly.

"You and me both," he replied, unable to turn his gaze away from the grisly scene. "It's almost as if this is more than just a murder." He ran his hand through his hair. "I don't know what I am trying to say. Maybe this is the kind of thing that usually happens when dealing with serial killers, but I can't shake this strange feeling of dread."

"Yeah maybe," was all she said. Neither of them bought the hasty rationalization.

They stayed there staring until a large man wearing a brown suit interrupted them. "Detectives Campbell and Caddret?"

"Yeah," said Jared, tearing his gaze away to look at the man who had addressed them. "What can we do for you?"

The man tried not to stare too long at the girl, but his curiosity got the better of him. His face went wan and he looked as if he was going to throw up. "I... um... am Special Agent Johansson from the FBI."

"Is this your first crime scene, Mr. Johansson?" Jared asked. "You look a little nervous."

"Uh... no, not really. I don't know why this one is affecting me this way. Maybe it's how young the girl is. She kind of reminds me of my daughter. I apologize, but I think I am going to need to sit down."

"We'll join you," Jared said, taking Dana by the arm and turning her away from the scene. "The boys from the coroner's office will be here to take her away soon, anyway."

"Yeah," Dana said, shaking her head as if waking from a dream. "I have all the information I need for now."

The trio walked over to a parked patrol car and opened the driver's side door. Johansson sat down and bent forward, breathing heavily. None of them spoke for a while, each lost in their own dark thoughts.

Johansson was a tall well-built African American man with short-cropped dark hair and dark brown eyes. He was in his mid-fifties but looked older, the stress of his job weighing heavily on his features.

"Sorry to have pegged you for a rookie back there," Jared said, breaking the silence. "But I've seen a lot of guys faint when they look shaky like that."

"No offense taken," Johansson said with a gruff New England accent. "I don't know what came over me. In all my years at the Bureau, that's never happened to me before."

"You're not alone, Special Agent," Jared replied. "Detective Campbell and I were just discussing the strange reactions we were experiencing as well."

Dana nodded but said nothing.

"Detective Campbell informed me that you are here to investigate the possibility of our two murders being linked with the ones you have been investigating in the city?" Jared asked. "The Eastside Stalker, I believe."

Johansson stood up gingerly and smiled. "You're a smart detective, and I assume the thought has crossed your mind as well. There are striking similarities between the murders, wouldn't you agree?"

"Yes, but there have not been any murders outside of the city to date," Dana said. "Why should we believe that he has moved from his usual hunting grounds?"

"That's true," Johansson replied. "All of the reported murders that have been linked to him have taken place in the city."

"Then why should we be quick to assume that these two murders, which have not even been connected to each other yet, are connected with the ones in the city? Don't you think you are jumping the gun a bit here?"

"Hey, I'm not the enemy, Detective Campbell!" Johansson said, putting up his hands. "I'm not here to second-guess you guys, but when you get two grisly murders in as many days in a city that only gets about twenty-four in a year, then I'd have to say that this is definitely more than a coincidence."

"I'm sorry. This whole thing has just had me a bit on edge lately."

"Please call me Tom," he said, waving off the apology. "We are all in the same business here, after all, trying to end the career of sickos like this guy."

"If you don't mind me being forward," Jared interjected, "you seemed to be alluding to something earlier before Detective Campbell interrupted you."

"I was," he said winking at Dana playfully, causing her to blush slightly. "I am not really at liberty to tell you, but I'm going to stuff regulations and tell you, anyway. The way I see it, the only way we can effectively work together is if we're all honest with each other."

"We appreciate that, Special Agent Johansson," Jared replied.

"Tom, Detective. 'Special Agent' makes me sound so old and stiff. I am just a working-class guy like you."

Jared nodded.

Johansson leaned in closer and lowered his voice. "These are not the first murders to have occurred outside the city that can be feasibly linked to the Stalker. In fact, I have over twenty known cases that could be linked to him."

Both detectives were shocked. Twenty cases outside of the city being linked to one killer was unthinkable to the small-town detectives.

"If what you say is true, then that would make him one of the most prolific serial killers to date," Jared said.

Johansson winked, making a gun motion with his fingers and a popping sound. "Now you can see why we are taking such an interest in your two murder cases here. The Bureau has been trying to track the killer by, for a lack of a better term, following his trail of breadcrumbs."

"Why hasn't the press gotten wind of this yet?" Dana asked. "It seems like one of those vultures would have put two and two together by now and broken the story to the public."

"Murders happen every day in a thousand different cities. But of course you already knew that. If we don't make a big fuss about them, neither do the newsies. Besides, if it got out that the Stalker was hunting anywhere and everywhere, then there would be a whole lot of people panicking needlessly. It also might alert him to our strategy and cause him to lie low for a while."

"Needless?" Dana said. "If there are as many people dead from this maniac as you suspect, then I would have to say that their fear is warranted, wouldn't you?"

"Touché again, Detective. I'm sorry, I didn't mean it like that. It's just after years of seeing this kind of thing, you start to become desensitized to it. Anyway, I think we can stop this guy before he kills again. We caught Dahmer and Gacy, didn't we?"

"Only after they killed a lot of people."

"Do you have any suspects yet?" Jared asked, breaking up the scuffle and shooting Dana a glare. "It would help us a great deal if you could give us any kind of a lead we can look into."

Johansson sighed. "That's the catch twenty-two. This guy is so good at what he does that, to date, he hasn't left one single shred of usable evidence. No fingerprints, footprints, fibers, or anything else that the CSI guys can use. It's downright bizarre if you ask me."

"So what you are saying is that you have nothing," said Jared.

"Pretty much. I was kind of hoping you'd have some leads in your local investigation here that might be of some help to us."

Dana rolled her eyes and walked away from the two men and their conversation. This whole thing was starting to overwhelm her, and she just needed to be alone for a few minutes to clear her head. She strolled across the street and sat down on the curb not too far from where the crime scene investigators worked.

The sun was getting high in the sky, and it bathed the area with its wonderful light, driving away the few lingering shadows. She basked in its warmth, hoping that it might also chase away the quiet dread she felt.

As she gazed, a tiny glint of sunlight from the grass to her right caught her attention. The strange object piqued her curiosity, so she walked over to see what it was. She found there, barely visible above the overgrown grass, a small golden locket. Realizing that it was out of place, she decided to pick it up to examine it.

It tugged on something as she tried to retrieve it, so she bent down and pulled a little harder. When she saw what it was caught on, she shrieked in horror and fell backward, pulling the locket free.

Jared and Johansson were by her side instantly and they both gasped in shock when they got close enough to see what it was that had startled her. There, lying peacefully in the bushes, was another body. But unlike the first victim, this one appeared to be a male and in some kind of traditional Japanese outfit.

"How in the world could we have all missed this?" Jared fumed. "It's only a couple of yards from the other one."

She had screamed so loudly that all of the hustle and bustle in the area stopped as the other officers looked around. Her face flushed with embarrassment as Jared reached out his hand. She took it reluctantly, wishing she could sink into the ground and disappear, and he helped her to her feet.

After seeing the dead body, Johansson had taken off to get someone to secure the area. He returned shortly with half a dozen local blues and soon had the entire area taped off.

"Are you okay?" Jared asked her.

"Yeah, fine," she replied, disgusted at herself.

"Sorry. I've just never seen you so uptight before."

"I know," she grunted. "I don't know why it freaked me out like that. Just took me by surprise, is all."

Johansson walked over to the two after he had made sure that everything was in order. "You, okay?"

"Yeah. Just spooked," she replied with a forced smile.

"It's very strange that no one noticed the body lying here," Jared said.

"It's just like everything else that is linked with this guy, bizarre!" Johansson murmured. "It's like these people were murdered by a ghost or something."

Jared shook his head in acknowledgment but said nothing. Dana was suddenly very aware of the locket in her hands, and for reasons she couldn't explain, she decided to keep it hidden from the others. She dropped it into her pocket before either of them noticed it.

She stretched and yawned. "There is a lot of work that still needs to be done, so if you don't mind, I think I'll get back to it."

"You two both look exhausted," Johansson said before she had a chance to leave. "I can handle it from here if you two want to take a break or something."

Dana and Jared exchanged glances and he smiled at her. She returned his smile weakly, and he reached out and grabbed her hand, squeezing it reassuringly.

"That would be great," he said. "Give us about an hour and we will be back here to help you clean things up."

"No problem, take as long as you need."

The three parted company, but none of them could shake the uneasy feeling that haunted them. Even though homicide was their job, they somehow knew that this time it was different.

Chapter Thirteen

The rest of the day went off without a hitch and Jared soon found himself parked out in front of his parent's house, exhausted and drained. He had made sure that Dana arrived home safely and was now able to relax.

The small town of Greene, where his parents lived, had not changed at all in the years they had resided here. There was still only one grocery store, and in true New York fashion, four different pizza places. Greene was known for its antiques, and people came from all over to shop in the little stores that lined the small downtown area.

There was one large factory that provided most of the economic stability in the town and gave the people jobs and the few retail stores customers. Greene was small town America at its best, the type of community you'd search for when looking for a place to settle down and raise a family.

Like most of upstate New York, Greene abounded with Colonial and Revolutionary War history. It was said that General Nathaniel Greene of the Continental

Army had founded the town during the American Revolution, and the town was named after him. One of the small houses at the end of his parent's street had once been the residence of the Iroquois princess Go Won Go.

It was near impossible to walk down the small streets of Greene, New York, and not find some government marker designating a historical location. Jared, being an avid history lover and fancying himself a novice historian, admired the area for its vast historical richness.

Yesterday he had vehemently rejected the notion of coming here, and he didn't know why. His parents' house had always been a place of refuge, and now that he was here, the familiar feelings of warmth and security flooded back.

The Caddret house was white with black shutters, of average size with a small garage to its left and a pool in the backyard. Like many American yards, the Caddrets' was in desperate need of mowing, but otherwise, everything looked homey and inviting. It seemed to Jared that the yard was always like this. Now that the two brothers had grown and left the house, no one kept up with the usual lawn care. Pastor Caddret never seemed to have enough time.

He walked up to the small front porch, running his hands along the black ironwork rails. He winced as the porch light suddenly came on when he got close enough to trip the motion detector. Not wanting to go in just yet, he closed his eyes and stood motionless on the steps, allowing the familiarity of it to wash over him.

The familiar smells of his mother's cooking hit his senses and his stomach growled. He knew his mom would most likely have prepared a feast in honor of his brother's unexpected visit, but despite his stomach's protests, he didn't feel like eating. So instead of going in, he sat down on the concrete steps.

He couldn't count how many times he'd sat in this very spot contemplating the universe's mysteries. This house was filled with many such memories, mostly good, and he couldn't help feeling like he was a child again.

It was strange that being here affected him so much. The last time he had felt this way was when he'd left for college. They say that you can never go back again to the innocence of youth, that once a person has left it behind, it's gone forever. The profession he had chosen had certainly taught him that, if it had taught him anything at all.

"Rough day?" a familiar voice asked, startling him out of his reverie.

He jumped and turned, squinting into the shadows to search for his brother, but saw nothing. Jared realized that he had been sitting outside his parents' front door for quite some time. The motion detector, which automatically turned the porch light on, had apparently shut off again due to his inactivity. But the soft gentle glow of his brother's cigarette was clearly visible in the darkness.

"Steve?" Jared asked.

"The one and only," the man replied, exhaling.

"What the devil are you doing out here? And how is it that I didn't notice you when I first walked up, and the porch light turned on?"

Steve flicked away what remained of his cigarette and walked over. Strangely he continued to appear only as a shadowy silhouette until he was standing directly over him.

"Don't know, big brother," he replied with a smirk. "Guess you were just too lost in your own thoughts to notice me."

"Not likely," Jared shot back indignantly. "I'm trained to notice everything, and I am very good at what I do."

Steve shrugged. "Maybe your eyesight is starting to go in your old age. How many fingers am I holding up?"

"Ha. Ha, ha. Very funny!" Jared rolled his eyes. "You must have come from around back after I sat down."

"We will never know, will we? Maybe it was magic."

"Whatever!"

Jared grunted as he stretched, the fatigue from the last few days finally getting the better of him. His body ached all over and all he really wanted to do was go inside, pass out on the couch, and sleep for a week. The light turned on as he rose, the sensor once again detecting his motion.

"I thought you quit smoking," he commented.

Steve opened the front door and held it for his older brother. "I did," he said with a smile. "It didn't take."

Jared shook his head as he walked past his brother. Warmth instantly surged over him as he stepped over the threshold and into the humble dining room. He sighed with relief and the tension and fatigue from the previous few days seemed to melt away.

"God, I love it here," he said to himself.

Their mother hurried out of the kitchen and threw her arms around her eldest son. "How are you doing?" she asked. "I heard about Jasmine. What happened? Everything seemed to be going so well."

Jared returned his mother's hug but shot Steve an annoyed glance as he did so. Steve threw his hands up and mouthed, "It wasn't me!"

Their mother went back into the kitchen, saying over her shoulder, "She called here sometime last night trying to reach you. She mentioned something about not wanting to call your cell phone and said she was sorry if she'd hurt you. She seemed to be in quite a big hurry and asked us to tell you not to try to reach her as she would be going out of town and had no idea when she would be returning to the area."

Jared groaned as the emotions he had been suppressing throughout the day came flooding back. He plopped down into the nearest chair.

"Did she happen to mention where she was going?" he asked miserably.

"Sorry, honey. We were at church last night counseling and missed her call. She left the message on the answering machine."

"If you want, you can play it back," Jared's father yelled from his perch by the computer in the living room. "I haven't erased the messages yet."

Jared's head shot up. He desperately wanted to run into the living room and play that message just to hear her voice again, but he fought the urge. Steve, who was now sitting down across from him, eyed him curiously, interested in how he was going to react to this new revelation.

"No thanks, I'll take your word for it," he said, his mood turning sour. "I don't think I can handle hearing her voice right now."

His dad came into the room and he rose to give him a hug. The two men embraced, and Jared's dad held him longer than he usually would.

"You sure you're all right?" he asked.

"Yeah, Dad, I'll be okay. It may not feel like it right now, but it's not the end of the world."

His dad was a short stocky man in his late fifties with salt and pepper hair. Even though he was balding, he was handsome and distinguished, with a well-trimmed beard and sharp blue eyes.

He did, however, have a distinct aura of authority that he naturally projected when he came into a room. His father said that it was the anointing of God on his life. God or not, for Jared it was because his dad was his hero. To this day, he still felt the same awe for his father that he'd had as a child.

Steve fidgeted at the display of affection between the two. When they had finished, he stood up and quickly walked out into the living room and toward the steps that led upstairs.

"Don't go anywhere," his mother called after him as she entered the room carrying a plate of piping hot roast beef. "Dinner is just about ready."

"I have to take a piss," Steve said as he lumbered up the stairs.

"Steven James! You know I don't like that word."

"Sorry, Mom," he shouted from somewhere up the stairs.

"I swear, that boy says things like that just to get under my skin," she complained to her husband. She placed the dish on the table and headed out into the kitchen to get the rest of the meal.

"He says things like that to prove that he is his own person and no longer bound to our rules," his dad replied. "That's also why he continues to smoke. I used to think it was just another one of his rebellious phases and that he'd grow out of it, but now it has become a matter of independence for him. I don't understand why he fights so hard against what he knows to be right."

Ever since they were kids, Steve's nonchalant attitude had always made Jared smile. He didn't care what anybody thought about him or whether they approved of what he was doing. Steve lived his life on his own terms and never did anything simply because it was customary or expected. Much to his parents' dismay, at times he went to the extreme to prove he was his own person, a man not bound by society's rules.

Jared sometimes wished he could be more like his younger brother and not so uptight, but no matter how hard he tried, his conscience always got the better of him. It had been that way even when they were children, Steve never showing that his parents' disappointment bothered him and Jared never able to let the sun go down before he'd confessed all his transgressions.

The two distinctly different personalities were also apparent in the types of careers that they had chosen. Steve was drawn to the risqué lifestyle of a rock star, while Jared had gravitated to law enforcement. But despite all their differences, Jared and Steve were the closest of friends and had been since childhood.

His mother brought the remaining plates of food out and set them on the table. The aroma caused Jared's stomach to grumble. He hadn't eaten all day and only then realized how hungry he was.

His mother sat down across the table from his father who always sat at the head, and the three of them patiently waited for Steve to return from the restroom. He didn't come of course, and Jared's dad sighed. They waited a few minutes longer, but his dad's patience had run out, and he was ready to eat.

He grunted. "If we wait any longer for that boy to get down here, the entire meal will be cold. Let's just bless the food and start without him. If he wants to eat a cold meal, he can. But I am not."

They all held hands as his father blessed the food, and as usual just as the prayer was coming to an end, Steve came barreling down the stairs.

"Sorry, everyone," he said with a smirk as he popped down in the chair next to Jared. He gave him a playful nudge, and Jared returned the favor by kicking him hard in the leg under the table. "Did I miss anything?"

His dad grumbled something under his breath as he reached for the bowl of mashed potatoes. He scooped out a heaping spoonful and plopped it on his plate.

It seemed to Jared that since his brother had grown up and gone out on his own, all the meals that they shared together as a family started out this way. Why his brother was so set on irritating their father was a mystery to him. He knew that they did not always see eye to eye, but Steve's constant testing seemed a bit much. After all, Steve was twenty-seven years old. It was time for him to grow up.

"So Steve, how long are you going to be in the area?" his mother asked cheerfully, attempting to diffuse the situation. "It's not often that you get up this way anymore. Judy will be sad if she misses the opportunity to see you."

Their younger sister, Judy, was nineteen and in her first year of college. She had opted to go to a nearby Christian university, following in her parents' footsteps. This, of course, was a matter of great contention with the two boys, especially Steve. They both loved their sister dearly but disliked the fact that she'd always been their parents' perfect little angel.

"Sorry, Mom," Steve said, taking the corn from Jared. "Just till tomorrow. The band and I were returning from a gig down south, and I thought I'd make a quick stop up here to say hi to everyone. But I've got to be back in the city by Monday to work on our new project."

"What's the name of your band again?" their dad asked curiously between mouthfuls.

"Richard Cranium," Steve mumbled through his roast beef.

Jared tried to suppress a burst of laughter but managed to spew some food out onto his plate, anyway. He covered up the outburst with an ambiguous fit of coughing.

Concerned, his mother asked, "Are you okay, honey?"

"I'm fine," Jared said gruffly. He drained his glass. "Just went down the wrong tube."

His dad glared at him, unconvinced, then turned his piercing gaze on Steve. His eyes bored intensely into him as if they would burn right through him.

"Do you think that I am stupid?" he asked evenly, his voice not betraying the obvious anger that he felt. "You may think that I am too old or Christian to get the joke, but I have news for you, I do."

The room went silent, Jared and his mother not daring to interfere with the running conflict between Steve and his father. Steve shifted in his seat uncomfortably.

"It's just a name, Dad," he finally said. "What does it matter anyway?"

"What does it matter? Don't you think that you are talented enough not to have to resort to such vulgar and obviously childish antics?"

"Dad, it's just a name!" Steve snapped. "I'm sorry that you don't approve of it, but we are not a Christian band, you know, and *Richard Cranium* is just as good a name as any other!"

His dad huffed, rolling his eyes. "That's not what I am saying, Steve! Why do you always react to everything I say as if I am judging you?"

"Because you always are," Steve growled back. "Nothing I ever do is good enough for you. When I was a kid and I grew my hair long, you didn't approve. I was a heathen when I moved to the city and started singing in bars, and now the name of my band is offensive to you. So, tell me, Dad, why would I think you are judging me? Huh? Why?"

His father fell silent, and the reticence only added to the tension in the room. Jared and his mother picked at their food, occasionally glancing up at each other, hoping the fight would end soon.

Neither of them had seen the two go this far before. Steve usually did an adequate job of holding his tongue and his father tried to avoid any deep confrontations. Tonight, however, the strain that had been brewing over the last few years finally exploded.

"It's not that I think you are a heathen, Steve. It's just that you have strayed a long way from what we raised you to believe," his dad said sadly. "You can't imagine the pain I feel when I think that there is even a slim chance that one of my children would not spend eternity with me."

Steve continued to stare at his plate, refusing to meet his father's eyes. The room once again fell back into an oppressive silence as Mr. Caddret watched his son expectantly. He had revealed to Steve his greatest fear in hopes that the revelation would help the young man understand how much he genuinely loved him.

Steve heaved a sigh and put down the fork he'd been using to prod his food. He placed both hands on the table and pushed himself to his feet. Everyone at the table stared at him hopefully.

"I know you love me, Dad," he quietly said. "You would still love me even if I were the most horrible murderer to prowl the earth, because that is the kind of person you are. But no matter how much you love me, I know that you will never approve of the lifestyle I have chosen to live."

A lone tear traced down their father's cheek. "Steve, I will always love and accept you, no matter what you do. You have to know that."

"I know that, Dad. But being a Christian is not high on my list of things to do right now. I love being free of the oppressive constraints of religion, and I know that that is something you can never accept. Don't get me wrong, I do believe in God, I just don't want anything to do with Him."

His dad said nothing in response, but sat there staring at his youngest son, the tears flowing more freely now. His mother's expression was one of utter heartbreak, and Jared wanted to jump up and slap some sense into his younger brother. How could he deliberately hurt their parents like that?

Steve turned away from his wounded family and walked quickly to the front door and open it briskly. Before he could make it outside, his dad called out to him.

"Steve, no matter what you may think, I still love you and am very proud of you," he declared, choking back his tears. "I may think you are wrong in rejecting what you know to be true, but you will always be my son. Nothing can ever change that."

Steve stepped out into the cold night air, and the door thudded shut.

Chapter Fourteen

The city morgue was a place for the dead and those who tended to the dead. None of the living seemed to be comfortable there. In truth, people only came to the city morgue when something tragic and terrible had happened, and most people found it disturbing and sometimes frightening to come face-to-face with their own mortality. For this reason, even the police and emergency responders disliked coming here.

The small waiting room in the front of the morgue was closed for the evening, and the room was dark except for a faint light emanating from the door that led deeper into the inner sanctum where the medical examiners performed their grizzly work. It glowed softly but was not strong enough to chase away the shadows that filled the small room. The soft light was barely holding on to life as if it too would soon be overcome by the encroaching darkness.

Just when it appeared that the darkness would finally prevail, a brilliant flash of blinding light burst into the room. The darkness was no match for its radiance, and it fled instantly before the light. This was no ordinary illumination, however, and it revealed more than what mortal eyes could see. All around the room, the hiding places of demonic beings were exposed. The demons winced and writhed in pain and screeched in protest at the intrusion of the painful light.

The blinding glow shivered and contorted, coalescing into an angelic being. The demons shielded their eyes and thundered protests as it passed by them. Ignoring their insults, the angel made its way deeper into the morgue. The demons that were wise fled before it, but those that were foolish enough to defy it were sent screaming back to Hell in explosions of white flames.

The angel had come to this small forgotten town for a reason. He had been sent here, in fact, to perform a very important task for the Most High Himself, and there was no power in any realm that could hinder him. To the mortal world, the angel appeared as nothing more than blindingly bright light, but in the realm unseen, he was a powerful warrior adorned in bronze armor and brandishing a massive flaming sword. Standing well over seven feet tall and, true to most angelic depictions, he had large feathered wings neatly folded behind him.

Before long, the angel stood in front of a closed door that read *AUTOPSY*. Beyond the door, the angel could make out the silhouette of the coroner. A drill hummed; the coroner lost in his work. Then the man quietly dictated what he'd discovered into an electronic recorder that sat on a small table next to the gurney.

"The official report from the investigating detective states that the body, which appears to be that of an Asian man about fifty years old, was found this morning around ten a.m. Time of death is currently unknown, but the cause of death appears to be from a puncture wound to the chest made by a sharp object. The wound is clean, and the blade seems to have passed directly through the subject, leading to the conclusion that it was most likely made by a sword or very large knife."

The angel passed through the door as the man dictated his findings. The coroner was a short balding man in his late fifties with a slight paunch. He wore the usual lab coat of a doctor and it was covered by a blood-speckled plastic poncho. The goggles he had been wearing to protect his glasses sat next to him on the small rolling table he used to hold his instruments. The man seemed bewildered, and he ran his fingers repeatedly over his scrunched forehead.

"Note: I'm not sure if I am just overtired, but I cannot observe any of the usual signs of death. Rigor mortis should have already set in, but the subject's muscles are still supple and relaxed. Moreover, there are no signs of algor mortis either, as the subject's body temperature has not dropped even one degree since it was brought in. It is as if the body has been placed in a state of suspended animation. Of course, that is not scientifically possible."

The angel smiled, lighting up the antiseptically bright room even more, and he reached out and rested his massive hand on the little man's shoulder. A wave of serenity washed over the man and he exhaled, visibly relaxing.

"It is time to take a break, James," the angel whispered.

As if on cue, the man stood up. "I think I'll take a quick break. I'm sure things will make more sense after I get a snack and a quick rest for my obviously tired brain."

He turned to the cadaver on the table. "Now, you don't go getting up and walking out on me, okay? Unless, of course, you are a vampire. Then feel free to get up and leave at your leisure. But if you are not one of the undead, then I promise when I get back, I will do my best to find some clue that will lead us to whoever did this to you."

Turning away from the body on the gurney, the coroner gingerly pulled the poncho up and over his head and walked right through the angel standing behind him. Being a creature of the spirit, the angel, though able to affect the physical world, was unseen and incorporeal to most mortal beings, so the man felt nothing as he passed through him. He hung up the poncho near the room and left the angel alone in the room. Well, not entirely alone.

The body of the ancient warrior was naked and covered by a white sheet. The angel, whose eyes saw everything in both the physical and spiritual worlds, inspected the body searching for anything out of the ordinary. After a few minutes of careful scrutiny, the angel determined that the relic was not there. It had most likely transformed itself and captured the attention of a new bearer. There must have been a worthy successor in the proximity either during or directly after the battle, and the relic had already passed on. Either way, it was gone.

No matter, the angel had come for the Shogun and did not have the authority to tame the ancient power, anyway. The Lord in His great mercy had allowed him to come for his friend. Let the Blade Tzedakah be about its own business; the angel only cared about Sakanoue.

"Sakanoue no Tamuramaro," the angel boomed, his voice resounding like a trumpet's blare. "Rise."

Immediately the body on the table sat up, and the white cloth fell away. Blinding light burst from the man, engulfing the small operating room like an exploding star. When the light receded, where the lifeless corpse had been sat a handsome young man. He glowed with ethereal light, no longer naked but clothed in brilliant white robes. Gone were the nightmare black eyes that had been his duty and his curse for so long. Gone was the darkness, the nightmare over.

Sakanoue looked up at his friend for the first time in ages with his own sparkling brown eyes. He attempted to blink away the tears that flowed freely down his cheeks. The angel lifted the small man up from the gurney and pulled him into a massive bear hug.

"Saka, oh how I have missed you, my friend!" he said. "As soon as the news of your passing had reached heaven, I petitioned the Almighty for the honor to be the one to come and retrieve you. Of course, it was granted to me."

The newly awakened man smiled for what felt like the first time in a thousand lifetimes. His smile was broad, and he laughed heartily as he hugged his dear friend back. After a long moment, the angel returned the ancient warrior to the ground and he placed his massive arm around him. "Come, Saka, Heaven awaits us where there will be feasting and joy beyond measure."

Saka didn't move but stood still his face scrunched in confusion. "Michael, it is strange. I can barely remember anything past that one fateful night. I know that I have walked in shadows for centuries, but it's as if it was merely a nightmare that has faded away upon waking. I remember you. I remember my children. I remember my wife and I remember all of the joy that I found in this life, but for the life of me, I cannot recall anything else."

The angel laughed softly and smiled. "That is by design. The Most High has washed away any memory of grief or pain and left you with only that which has brought you joy."

He reached out and opened a tear in the fabric of time and space. Pure light streamed from the opening. Saka squinted into the blinding light, trying to see what lay beyond it, but it was impossible.

"Come, my friend, this life has ended and the burden you once bore has been lifted from your soul. Let us now pass together into eternity."

With that last statement echoing in the air, both men stepped into the light and vanished.

Chapter Fifteen

He stumbled down the corridor, his katana dragging noisily on the tile floor. Royal guards lay scattered throughout the palace, dead or dying. They had fought honorably and would be remembered well in the halls of their ancestors. He had no time to stop and mourn for them; he must reach the children's bed chamber. It was all that mattered now.

His foot struck the wayward spear of one of the dead guards; he stumbled and fell. He hit the ground hard, knocking the breath from his chest. He could not breathe but choked on the blood flowing up from his damaged lungs. He struggled to rise but found that his arms no longer held strength. He was dying. So close! He was almost to the room of his youngest son. Please, just a few more feet!

He could hold back the tears no longer, and he wept, coughing, and spitting up blood.

It was too late now. Death would take him. He had failed them, failed them all. So close yet not close *enough. He closed his eyes in resignation and relinquished himself to death's icy grip.*

As he slowly slipped into unconsciousness, he was sure he could hear death's mocking laughter. It came to him softly as if he was hearing it in a dream. Then a scream snapped him back from the paths of death. He surged back into awareness as another scream split the air around him. He knew that scream as any father would. It was the cry of his sixteen-year-old daughter, Jade.

He bellowed and, with a strength born of desperation, lifted himself off the ground. The laughter he'd heard had come from the intruder who'd slain his men. It stopped when he'd shouted, and his daughter cried out instead.

"Otōsan!"

He pushed past the door. Light flooded into the dark room, revealing a man cloaked all in black and hooded standing over the still body of his youngest son, Yashimi. He held a blood-streaked katana in his hand. Jade cradled her brother, her arms hacked to ribbons and one hand severed at the wrist. She had thrown herself over her younger brother in a desperate attempt to protect him.

The Ninja glared at the wounded man. "Are you still alive? Shogun, you surprise me with your resilience. You are as hard to kill as a cockroach. No matter. You are mortally wounded and no match for me." He turned back to look at Jade. "When I am through with your pathetic excuse of a father, I will return to finish with—"

The Shogun leapt, swinging his sword downward in a vicious chop. The Ninja put up his own sword to parry the strike, but to his surprise, the

Shogun's blade went completely through his own and cut deeply into his chest. Metal clanged as his sword broke at the hilt and clattered to the floor.

Confused, the Ninja managed to gurgle, "How?"

The Shogun growled and thrust his sword forward until half of it was sticking through the assassin's back. The Ninja coughed and spat blood as he tried to scream. The Shogun yanked the blade out and then, with a heart-wrenching scream, hacked the injured assassin to death. That did not slake the Shogun's wrath, however, and he continued striking the lifeless body until all of his rage had been spent.

When he was finished, he painfully stood and faced his children. Gasping for breath, the Shogun could barely stand. Blood and gore covered his armor from head to toe, making him look more like a demon than a man.

His daughter hunched over her brother, bleeding, pale, unmoving. His rage now spent; he fell to his knees. He crawled over to her and held her in his lap. She still breathed, just barely, so he brushed the damp hair from her face and kissed her brow. Her warm brown eyes opened.

When he looked into her eyes, he did not see the young woman she had become but the little girl she had been. "It's okay now, Jade. Daddy is here," he said through his tears.

"Daddy?" she asked weakly. "I tried to save Yashimi, but I could not." Tears spilled down her cheeks, and it broke his heart.

"No. No. My little bear, you did well. Your brother only sleeps. It was all just a bad dream. All is well now, my little one. Go to sleep, and everything will be fine when you wake. You will see. Tomorrow you will run together in the mountains you two love so much."

His daughter went limp in his arms, and he wept hard, painful tears. He pulled her close to his chest and buried his head in her hair, rocking her still form.
"I love you, my little bear."

****

Dana awoke, tears streaming down her cheeks. This was the third time tonight she had had the same dream, and on every occasion, she awoke weeping violently. Each time the dream became more and more vivid. What did it all mean? Nothing like this had ever happened to her before.

She was covered in sweat, her covers kicked off the bed. She sat up with her head in her hands. What was happening to her? Was she losing her mind? The dreams were so vivid, it was as if she was reliving lost memories. But whose memories were they? They certainly weren't hers. If she believed in reincarnation, she would attribute them to past lives, but she was a Christian and Christians did not believe in such New Age philosophies.

"Get yourself together, girl." She ran her hands down her face. "There has to be a logical explanation for this."

She was exhausted, almost as if she had just run a marathon. She hoped that this would be the last time tonight she would have the dream. She needed to get at least a few hours of uninterrupted sleep before work in the morning. Which was... She looked over at the clock and groaned. Five twenty-nine a.m., almost time to get ready for work. Five thirty. The alarm clicked on and chirped. She groaned again and slammed her hand down hard on the alarm clock, hitting the snooze button.

But, no. If she fell back to sleep again, it would do her more harm than good. So she got up and started the day. At least she'd have time to make coffee before she had to take a shower. The thought of a cup of steaming hot java finally gave her the motivation she needed to extricate herself from her nice warm blankets and climb out of bed.

She yawned, stretched, and groggily stumbled out of her room and into the hallway. As she walked, her hand gently brushed against her chest and she abruptly stopped. A surge of panic washed over her, and she stood frozen in place, too afraid to look down at her hand.

When she finally mustered the strength to look down, her eyes went wide in horror, because what she saw dangling there was a small golden locket. The same small golden locket she had compulsively taken from the crime scene the day before. Her head swam with thoughts of losing her job, or worse, jail time. What had possessed her to remove evidence from a crime scene? In all her life, she'd never done anything so reckless and stupid.

Calm down, girl, she told herself. After a couple deep breaths, she removed the locket from around her neck and examined it.

The locket was small and circular, gold with a large red gem embedded in its center. She ran her fingers along the edges and felt raised markings. She tried to make out what they were; it looked like some kind of ancient writing. Upon further scrutiny, Dana discovered that there was a small button on the side of the locket fashioned in the shape of a tiny sword hilt.

She pushed the button and the locket popped open. Inside was a photograph—faces she recognized. Unthinking, she threw the necklace across the hallway. It landed face upward against the wall, exposing the portrait of a middle-aged Asian man and two young children. The same man and children who had haunted her dreams.

She took another deep breath and closed her eyes.

Calm down. Get your head on straight and think rationally here. There is no way that the family in your dreams and the picture from the locket are the same people. Even if they are, you must have simply opened the locket before you went to bed and seen the picture. Right? There's always a rational explanation for everything.

Of course, she knew deep down in her gut that she had not even noticed the locket since she had pilfered it from the crime scene yesterday. She hadn't opened it or even inspected it until now. Dread washed over her. If she had believed in such things, she would have sworn that the locket was either haunted or cursed.

Come on, girl. You are a freaking police officer, for crying out loud. Pull yourself together. You know that there is no such thing as ghosts. Curses are just the stuff of fairy tales and children's stories.

With that, she gathered her courage and approached the small locket with the same careful caution that a trainer would use when facing a dangerous animal.

She reached down and picked it up. At first, she was afraid to look at the picture and simply held the locket at arm's length. Before long, however, her curiosity got the better of her and she drew the small piece of jewelry up to eye level so she could get a closer look at the small picture.

Her heart thumped so hard, it felt like it would beat right out of her ribcage. This time she was certain it was the same family from her dream. There was no mistaking the faces of the two children. She had seen them murdered repeatedly in her nightmares last night.

What the hell is going on?

Grief, not fear, washed over her as she gazed on the faces that had been seared into her heart. Tears spilled down her cheeks as the overwhelming emotions from her nightmares came rushing back.

She slid down the wall until she was sitting with her knees up against her chest. The locket dangled from her fingers. She buried her face in her legs and sobbed until all her grief was spent. What was happening to her? What the hell was happening to her?

She knew she had to tell someone about the locket, but who? She could not trust the FBI investigator. He would probably lock her up and throw away the key. If she told anyone else on the force, it would put them in a compromising position, so that was out. Who else could she tell? There had to be someone.

With a sudden clarity that caused her to shoot straight up, she knew exactly who she should go to for help. Jared, she could tell him anything. He'd had her back since they were young, and she knew that she could trust him with anything, no matter how serious.

She put the locket back around her neck and returned to her normal morning routine. She was strangely calm as if the entire ordeal had never happened. In fact, she thought to herself, *maybe it really was nothing more than a dream*. What was she worrying about, anyway? As she quickly got dressed and styled her hair for work, she did not notice the low, steady glow of the small gem at the center of the locket, nor that her eyes shared that very same red sheen.

Chapter Sixteen

When Dana finally arrived at work, she found the entire precinct in a state of panic. Officers were scurrying about; the usual disciplined morning routine of the agency having given way to chaos. As soon as she walked through the entrance's metal detectors, she was approached by a tall officer she didn't know very well.

"Detective Campbell?" the man asked, extending his hand.

"Yes," she said, shaking it firmly.

"Sorry to bombard you, but Agent Johansson and Detective Caddret asked me to look out for you and to take you to them as soon as you arrived. Follow me, if you would."

That's strange, she thought, following him off toward the stairs. *Why would he take me to the stairs and not to one of the conference rooms?*

"Officer?"

"Steveson."

"Officer Steveson, why are we going downstairs? If Jared and Agent Johansson are waiting for me, then wouldn't they be somewhere on the first floor?"

"Sorry, ma'am. I know this seems strange, but they are both down in the morgue."

Dana's mind raced. She was certain that whatever had happened in the morgue was most likely the cause of all the commotion.

The scene that Dana beheld when she walked through the doorway was like something out of a television crime drama. CSI techs could be found in every corner of the room, peering into all of the nooks and crannies with all the instruments and devices that they had in their respective toolboxes. She quickly spied Jared talking to Agent Johansson in one corner of the small room. Even with the two cups of coffee he was holding, he still managed to wave her over.

"Glad you could make it to work, sleepyhead." Jared's eyes were still bloodshot and swollen.

Did he even sleep last night? she wondered.

He handed her one of the coffee cups and took a long sip from the other. "It seems that there is a strange series of events happening here in upstate New York."

"Are these strange occurrences why the science nerds are out in force this morning?" she asked curiously, blowing on her coffee.

"A very keen deduction, my dear Watson," he said with a wink. She smiled in spite of herself. It was good to see some of his normal playfulness returning. Of course, it was a horrible time for him to be joking, but Jared had bad timing in most things in life.

"Okay, now that we have established that you have a dark sense of humor, what exactly happened last night that has everyone in the entire building so riled up?"

Agent Johansson spoke first. "Well, it's the strangest thing. You know that body we brought in yesterday? Well, it's gone and gotten itself lost, right under the noses of an entire police precinct and the coroner's office."

Dana stopped mid-sip and just stared at him. She glanced from Jared to Johansson. "You're serious?"

"As serious as the Bambino's curse," he replied. "Well, I guess more serious than that, since we kicked that curse to the curb in 2004."

"Wait. I mean, just how the heck is that even possible? Don't we have cameras and a friggin' security system? With all of the equipment we have here in this building, it's just not possible."

"Well, sweetheart," said Jared in his worst Humphrey Bogart impression, "apparently the universe doesn't give a damn, because the corpse just simply vanished into thin air."

Dana rolled her eyes. "Just shut up already. And for the record, it was Clark Gable who said that, not Bogart."

He grinned as he took another long swig of his quickly cooling coffee. "Well, on a serious note, impossible or not, the body has simply vanished. We already checked the security cameras for the only time last night that Dr. Strayhand was out of this room and we found nothing."

"What do you mean by nothing?"

"What he means by that, Detective," replied Johansson, "is that nothing out of the ordinary is on the security camera footage. Nadda. Zilch... absolutely nothing. The tech guys are going over the video feed as we speak, but from what I could tell, there does not appear to be any tampering with the video. One minute the body is there and the next minute, abracadabra, it's gone. Honestly, I've never seen anything like this in all of my years with the Bureau, and I have seen a lot of strange shit in my time. We may actually have a bona fide unsolvable mystery on our hands."

"I am still not buying this." Dana frowned. "There has to be a rational explanation that we haven't yet considered. I am sure after more careful examination we will be able to solve this mystery."

"Don't think so," Jared said. "I don't know why, but I can't shake the feeling that something supernatural has or is happening here."

"Seriously, Jared? Supernatural? Like angels and demons or whatever? Have you lost what's left of your mind? You and I both know, and I am sure Agent Johansson here will attest, that there is always a rational explanation for everything. I may believe that God is real, but God didn't come down from heaven just to take a dead body from a morgue. There has to be an explanation other than ghosts and demons."

"All I am saying is that it feels... strange to me. Otherworldly. And no, I don't think God came down from heaven for this corpse, but I can't shake the feeling that this whole situation is far more than it appears."

"I agree with Jared," interjected Johansson. "But I also agree with you, Detective Campbell. There is more going on here than just your normal run-of-the-mill murder, but I do think that there is a rational explanation that we just haven't stumbled across yet."

"Rational explanation or not, what does a body disappearing from the morgue have to do with this case?" Dana asked. "Has this happened before?"

"Not to my knowledge. In fact, I can't think of one instance where an entire body has simply up and disappeared. Well, not unless the mob was involved.

Even in those cases, it was never a corpse that disappeared, but rather a live one. Of course, that body was most likely not going to stay alive for very long, if you get my drift."

"So, this is an entirely unique occurrence then?" Jared asked.

"Yeah, I would have to say so, but 'occurrence' is putting it mildly. If this had happened in New Mexico or Nevada, I would simply chalk it up to aliens, but we are nowhere near Area 51."

"Really?" Jared asked excitedly. "Is Area 51 an actual thing?"

"Of course not, I was just joshing ya. Everyone bites at that, though."

"All right, enough jokes, we need to get back on track here. What did the coroner say when he was interviewed?" said Dana. She was still exhausted from not sleeping, and the time that the two men were wasting was starting to get on her nerves.

"The doctor saw nothing," Jared replied. "He stated that somewhere around one or one thirty in the morning, he got hungry and decided to go to the break room for a snack. He said he was there for around fifteen minutes, and upon returning to the examination room, he found the body missing. He immediately reported the incident to the officers on duty, which then went about treating the lab as a crime scene. As you already know, up to this point the investigation has turned up nothing."

Johansson said, "The real question in all of this is not just how, but why? Why this particular body? The coroner did have time to examine the body before it disappeared and the wounds on the man are not consistent with the same type of weapon that killed the other victims. The murder weapon usually preferred by the Stalker, and the one that killed the other two victims, was a large serrated hunting knife. This one, however, is clean and seems to be made from something more precise, like a surgical instrument. That being said, out of all of the victims that this bastard has left in his wake, what makes this one special?"

"Other than the victim being killed by a completely different type of weapon," commented Jared, "he is a man and not a woman. That's not usual for the Stalker. Maybe the man was killed because he stumbled on the Stalker killing the girl. A case of wrong place wrong time."

Johansson nodded.

An officer walked up and handed Dana some paperwork. She casually looked it over as she listened to Jared and Johansson talk. After reading it, she knew one more thing that made the missing corpse special. "Well, actually there is another thing that makes him stand out," she said, handing Jared the papers. "Out of the three victims we have here, he is the only one that could not be identified."

"You mean we couldn't verify his name or where he lives?" Jared asked.

"I mean, that upon investigating him, we found nothing. As far as we can gather, he has never been arrested for a crime and his fingerprints are not on file in any database we have access to. He has no birth certificate that we can locate, and no one has come forward yet looking for a missing person of his description. Agent Johansson may have access to more information than us, but as far as our investigators are concerned, he's a ghost."

"That is strange," said Johansson. "It is possible that he's from another country. I'll run him through the agency's database and let you know what I come up with. Most likely he is a foreigner who is not registered with any local agencies. Honestly, I would not worry about it. It may be strange, but I am sure we will find a rational explanation for the disappearance."

Dana scrunched up her forehead slightly and squinted her eyes. "If you say so, but I have been a cop for a long time, and I have never heard of a body disappearing from a morgue."

He shrugged her concerns off with a smile. "True, but this guy was probably just some immigrant who was at the wrong place, wrong time. Don't worry, though. I will look into it and let you know if I find anything."

Dana was still unconvinced, but she let it go for now. As she thought, her hand gently brushed up against her chest, and it took everything in her not to freeze in panic when she felt the small locket underneath her shirt. Instantly the events from this morning and the night before rushed back to her and she balked visibly.

"You okay, Detective?" Agent Johansson asked curiously. "You seem like you are about to lose your coffee."

Dana composed herself quickly and physically waved away Johansson's concern. "I'm fine. Just tired, is all. I didn't sleep well last night, and I think I just need something a bit stronger than coffee to get me fully going today. I will be fine, but I do need to go over a few things with my partner here before we get the day started."

"Okay..." Johansson replied. "Well, I have to go make a few calls and go over a few emails, anyway. I will be forwarding whatever your tech geeks found to my people in NYC, and I'll bring you both up to speed as soon as I do."

Jared also was unconvinced, and he watched her with concern as Johansson walked away, already talking loudly on his phone. He noticed that Dana was absentmindedly playing with something through her shirt and he wondered about it.

"You good, partner?" he asked. "I know how you act when you are overtired, and you are not that grouchy yet. In fact, you are not even as mean as usual."

"Well, if you want, I can be even more of a bitch," Dana snapped, her hand never leaving the place on her shirt.

"Whoa," responded Jared, putting his hands up. "Dang, Dana, I'm just concerned. You are visibly shaken by something and it has me worried. I know this case has taken its toll on you, but I can tell that something else has gotten under your skin. Honestly, I haven't seen you this shaken up in years."

Dana sighed. "I need to talk to you about something, but it has to be in private. I think it may have something to do with the murders, and it has me... spooked, for lack of a better word."

"All right," he said. "Let's get out of here and go to the coffee shop around the corner. That should be private enough and you can tell me this big secret of yours there."

"I never said anything about a secret."

"You don't have to," he replied with a smirk. "As I said, I know you and I can tell when you have something you need to get off your chest."

"Well, you got me."

And in more ways than you know, she thought.

Chapter Seventeen

The two detectives talked casually as they made their way to the small coffee shop just around the corner. Dana sat down at a table outside away from prying eyes and ears, while Jared went in to get their coffees. Her mind raced as she tried to figure out what she was going to say.

How in the world was she going to explain everything that had been happening to her? She went over it all again in her head, but every time it sounded even more and more insane. In fact, after her little speech back at the morgue about everything having a rational explanation, how could she give any credibility to her feelings at all?

She was a detective and her whole adult life had been about finding the truth, and that truth was always found in the rational world. Even when she was a kid and her parents had taken her to church, she found it hard to believe in something she could not see and reasonably prove. She would never admit this to Jared, but she was not even sure as an adult that she believed one hundred percent that God existed.

Jared returned with two cups. He placed one down on the table in front of her. She looked up at him and saw the concern on his face and blushed. She was honestly touched by it, even though she wished that it meant more than it did. After all he had been through over the last forty-eight hours, he was making the effort to be more concerned about her than his own pain.

Jared was the first to break the silence. "So... what's going on?"

She glanced down at the warm cup in her hands. "Well, I guess there is no good place to start, so I will just rip off the Band-Aid and go right to the bad part. I took something from the crime scene the other day."

"You did what?" Jared coughed, spilling coffee.

She still couldn't look him in the eyes, not only because of her guilt but also for fear of her strong feelings for him. "I took something from the crime scene the other day," she softly said.

"Okay," he said, calming himself. "What did you take—and better yet, why did you take it?"

"It was a locket. I found it lying beside the Asian man whose body disappeared. As far as why I took it, I have no earthly idea."

Jared was at a loss. Dana was his rock and the one person that always seemed to make the right decisions. It was simply inconceivable that she could have stolen evidence from a crime scene. Something was seriously wrong, and he had no idea what it was.

Dana mistook his silence for anger. "I really don't have any memory of doing it, Jar. I am so confused."

Her eyes pleaded with him for understanding. He was sure she was mistaken. Maybe she had dreamed about taking the locket and was confusing real events with fictional ones. But if that was the case, then more was wrong with her than mere fatigue. That scared him more than a simple act of bad judgment.

He noticed her anxiety growing the longer he stayed silent, so he forced a smile. "All right, just calm down. I am sure there is a rational explanation for this. After all, if you have no memory of taking the locket, then how do you know you took it?"

Her eyes gave way to the fear gripping her inside. "Jared, I know I took it, because I'm wearing it."

Jared was shocked speechless.

She reached into her blouse and pulled out the small locket. The chain was still around her neck and her hands shook slightly as she held it for him to see. She could no longer hide the fear that was slowly overcoming her resolve. Tears welled in her eyes.

"It gets worse."

"Really? Worse than theft and tampering with evidence?"

She took a deep breath but still could not calm herself. "Yes."

Jared heard Dana speaking, but what she was saying was barely registering with him. He could not tear his gaze away from the locket. It was as if the rest of the world had faded away and no longer existed. All that remained was this locket. The red jewel in the center of the ornament began to glow ever so slightly, its beauty filling his consciousness. He did not know why, but he desired it. In fact, he desired it more than anything he had ever sought before.

"Jared! Are you listening to me?"

He shook his head and blinked like he was waking up from a dream. "Yeah. Yeah, I was. I was just lost in thought."

Dana misinterpreted his laps as more melancholy about Jasmine, and that made her even angrier. "Seriously? I am spilling my friggin' guts here and you are still fixating on that woman! Jasmine is gone, Jared. Gone, and she is not coming back. Get over it already. I am here and I need you."

Jared's face looked as if she'd just slapped him. "I am sorry, Dana. I..."

When Dana realized what she had just said and done, she was mortified. "Oh God, Jared. I am so sorry. I am just really frightened. I have no idea what is happening to me. I barely slept last night, and I am so tired and confused."

Jared smiled and placed his hand on hers. He wanted to be mad at her but seeing her like this drove all the pain and sorrow he had been feeling over the past few days from his heart. It likewise broke the strange grip that the locket seemed to have on him. "No, I'm sorry. You obviously needed me, and I've been emotionally lost lately."

His touch and concern took her breath away for a moment.

"It's okay."

"No. No, it's not. Honestly, I thought it was just the nature of the case that had you so spooked, but now I see that it is something else entirely."

She shook her head. "None of what's been happening to me makes any sense."

"Well, why don't you start at the beginning. What happened after you took the locket?"

"As I said before, I don't remember taking it. Well, at least I don't remember it clearly. It's almost like waking up from a vivid dream—it simply fades away and there is nothing more than vague impressions. I know I took it, and I can almost remember doing it, but I can't... if that makes any sense."

"It does. So, you don't know why you took it?"

"No. I have no idea what possessed me to do it. In fact, 'possessed' may actually be a good description of what has and is happening to me."

"I don't follow," he said, confused.

"Ever since I took this damn thing, I have not been able to sleep. In fact, I've had the same terrible nightmare every time I close my eyes. It just keeps repeating over and over again."

"What is the nightmare about?"

She took another calming breath and held her coffee with both hands. "A man. Japanese, I think. In fact, the very same man we believe was killed by the Eastside Stalker and whose body disappeared last night from the morgue. And this same man's face is also inside the locket I compulsively took from the crime scene yesterday."

"Are you sure?" he asked. "Maybe, with all that has been going on, and being the officer who discovered the body of the Asian man, somehow sparked something in your subconscious that caused you to dream about him."

She looked him right in the eyes as he spoke, and he saw in her eyes a fear he had never seen in her before.

"That is what I rationalized as well, until I saw the picture that was in the locket," she said unsteadily. "The portrait is not only of our victim but also his children. The same children I saw viciously murdered every time I closed my eyes."

Jared didn't know what to make of that. "You must have looked at the picture sometime before you went to sleep."

"No. I didn't. Jared, there is no rational explanation for what has been happening to me. In fact, I had strangely forgotten the whole thing even occurred until I touched the locket at the precinct. As soon as I did, the whole series of events came flooding back to me like it had just happened. I am so confused!"

"It's okay. Tell me what you can remember about the dream."

What Dana could remember was every intricate detail of the nightmare she had been forced to experience the night before. Right down to the metallic smell of the children's blood. Jared was surprised at how much of her dream she was able to recall. Quite frankly, it was near medically impossible for her to have such a lucid memory of a dream. Perhaps if she had just awoken, it would be possible for her to remember it, but not hours later.

"And that's all I remember," she said, her face flushed and streaked from crying. "Honestly, it was more like I was reliving a memory from a past life than having a dream. It was so... real."

Jared sat looking at her quietly for some time before he spoke. "Well, dreams can be strong like that, but they're usually linked to a memory, experience, or emotion a person is trying to repress."

She grimaced and took another sip of her coffee. "Thank you for the analysis, Dr. Phil. I already knew all of that. Don't you think psychology would be the first place I would look to try to make sense of all of this? There is nothing, and I mean nothing, in my past or present that could possibly cause my subconscious to create such a horrible event. I mean, they murdered my children! Er, his children. Oh God, I can still hear their little voices."

She began to cry again, and Jared knew it was time to let her off the hook. "It's going to be okay, Dana. It was just a dream, I'm sure of it, and it's over with now. Probably the whole thing is just your subconscious making you feel guilty about taking the locket."

She looked at him dubiously, but he did see a glimmer of hope in her eyes. He was lying to her and he knew it, but he also knew that she was a practical person by nature, and he'd given her something rational to latch on to.

"Come on, partner," he said with a wink. "You know full well that you can't handle guilt. As I recall, every time we did something even remotely sketchy when we were kids, your conscience got the better of you and you ratted us both out. I am sure this is just your mind's over-reactive way of forcing you to come clean."

She smiled slightly and brushed a stray strand of hair away from her face. "You think so?"

"I am certain of it," he said smiling encouragingly. "Hey, let's try this. I'll take the locket from you right now and put it with the rest of the evidence we collected yesterday. Once you no longer have it in your possession, I am sure your guilty conscience will be sated, and these intense feelings will fade. I'll just tell the sergeant on duty that I forgot to log it in."

"Are you sure? What if Johansson finds out?"

"He won't, and after I have logged it in, we can both take it to Johansson and see what the FBI can find out about the people in the image. Sound good? Maybe this is the key to identifying our missing John Doe."

"Okay," she said, taking the locket off. "Honestly, I was beginning to think I had lost my mind, but what you're saying makes sense."

She handed him the locket and he slipped it in his pocket. Dana sighed as if she was freed from some heavy burden. "I really appreciate this, Jared."

"Of course, what are partners for?" he said, putting his arm around her and guiding her back toward the precinct. "Of course, my new nickname for you is going to be Klepto."

She stuck an elbow in his ribs. "Like heck it is."

"Oh, you are never living this down, partner," he said with a mischievous grin.

As the two detectives slowly walked away from the coffee shop, they were unaware of the man scrutinizing them from the shadows. He chuckled to himself, ignoring the people passing by.

"So Tzedakah has already chosen another bearer," he said, "and so soon after the death of the Shogun. Well, he always was a fickle master, but to have chosen the detective, now that is an interesting development, no? Perhaps we shall stay around for a while and see how this develops. Maybe I will have the pleasure of killing two bearers before my time is done."

The Musketeer smiled a wicked smile and preened his mustache as he watched the two detectives. When they were gone, he sighed. "I think I will get a croissant, or at least what passes for one in this century," he lamented and faded into the busy crowd of people around him.

Chapter Eighteen

Upon arriving back at the precinct, Dana and Jared were met immediately by Agent Johansson. He was leaning up against the wall directly next to the front door, smoking a cigarette. He smiled and waved them over exhaling through his nose as he did. He casually flicked his cigarette away as they approached.

"Crazy day, huh?" he asked with a slight groan. "It's not every day you get a serial killer and a missing corpse all in one swoop."

Jared nodded and Dana casually avoided Johansson's gaze. She noticed Johansson glancing at her out of the corner of his eye, and she tensed up a bit, clearing her throat. He grunted but gave no other indication that he had noticed the anxiety she was trying to hide.

"Well, my fellow gumshoes, the Bureau has officially come up with squat. It's like the guy simply popped into existence to die and then, bam, he's gone again. Honestly, it's the strangest thing I've ever seen. Sucks too because this was the first real possible clue that this bastard left behind. Every other victim has been a woman, and upon further investigation, there's always evidence of the killer stalking them before he finally murdered them. But this guy, he was definitely more of a wrong place at the wrong time kind of killing."

"Well, hopefully, the CSI guys can find something that will help break this case open," Jared replied. He yawned and his hand drifted to his pocket and to the locket he had hidden there. Dana noticed the movement and her face went pale. Jared was going to tell Johansson about the locket before he had time to secretly put it in with the other evidence they had collected.

Jared removed his hand from his pocket and she visibly relaxed. No, he wouldn't do that to her, and she knew it. Regardless of whether he felt the same way she did, he was still her partner, and he would not betray her trust that way. She knew, however, that someone had to tell Johansson about the locket, even if it got her into trouble. Particularly if the locket was the key to this case.

"We have some new evidence," she blurted.

She blushed and Jared stared at her incredulously.

"Are you sure?" he asked.

"Just show him already!" she snapped. "We need to just get everything out and on the table in order to get this guy before he ruins someone else's life. And besides, it was eating me up, anyway, and you know full well I would not have made it more than a few more minutes before I confessed."

Johansson smiled. "You two are like a friggin' TV show over here. Seriously, have I stepped into prime time or something? Anyway, all drama aside, let me see what you got."

"Okay, but just so you know," Jared said watching Dana out of the corner of his eye, "I forgot to log something in yesterday. No one was trying to hide anything from you or anything like that, it was just a brain fart on my part."

"Oh, for God's sake," Dana huffed. "Just show him the stupid locket already."

Jared scowled at her and removed the locket from his pocket and held it out for Johansson to see. Johansson reached out to take it from him, but Jared flinched back. The FBI agent noticed the movement but reached out and took the locket.

For some strange reason, everything inside Jared was screaming for him not to let Johansson take the locket. It took every ounce of discipline he had to not snatch it back from the man before he'd had a chance to examine it.

The agent scrutinized the small piece of jewelry curiously. He flipped it over a few times, taking in every inch of detail, before finally pushing the small button and opening it to reveal the portrait inside. He stared at the small, faded picture.

"This is our missing John Doe."

"Yes. That's why we thought it might be the missing piece of the puzzle that could break this case open for us," Dana said.

"I am not going to ask why this is not in evidence right now," he said, his brow furrowed, "but from now on, no more surprises, okay?"

Both detectives nodded.

"I have decided to trust you here, and I need to know that you two are going to afford me that same level of trust. If not, then you two can go back to your desks, and I will find some other schlep that will. Got that?"

They both nodded again.

"Okay. Now that we have got that unpleasantness out of the way, what do you two think about this little trinket you found?"

"Well," Jared said, his eyes still fixated on the locket, "it is definitely a picture of our missing victim and we thought that maybe it could help us to identify him. We assume that the two children that are with him in the picture are his. They might also be a help in identify him."

Johansson returned the locket to Jared. His hand trembled slightly as he reached for it. It took all of his internal fortitude not to swipe the locket from the older man's hand.

"Okay. Why don't you two take that thing down to the lab and have the CSI geeks see what they can get off it? Also, make a copy of the picture and send it to me so I can give it to my people to see what they can dredge up on the two kids. I want to warn you both, though—this is still most likely another dead end."

"Copy that," replied Jared as Johansson turned to walk away.

"You're not coming with us?" Dana asked.

"Nah, I need to make a few phone calls and check in with the big wigs back in NYC. I trust you two can handle this without daddy watching over your shoulder. Just make sure it gets there this time, okay?"

Johansson pulled out his phone and left the two detectives to their task.

Jared turned to Dana who still appeared a bit shaken. "Well, that went better than I thought it would."

"Yeah," was all she said as she watched the FBI agent walk away. Her face was still pale, and her eyes were sunken in from lack of sleep, and she looked as if she'd just lost her best friend. The truth was, however, that she felt like there was something off about Agent Johansson. She couldn't put her finger on it, but she was sure he was hiding something from them.

Jared smiled and gently nudged her on the arm, and his heart skipped a beat as he touched her. He stared at her out of the corner of his eye and for the first in his life, he allowed himself to notice just how beautiful she truly was. "Come on, let's take this down to Brad and see what he can find."

Chapter Nineteen

It took a few hours for Brad Henderson to get back to the two detectives on what his CSI team had been able to discover from their inspection of the locket. Thankfully, he did not ask any questions about why he was just now getting the item, or why the chain of custody forms had not been filled out properly.

Dana and Jared caught up on paperwork while they waited. They called Johansson as soon as Brad had notified them, he was done with his preliminary examination of the locket. All three investigators headed down to the CSI lab.

Brad, a blond man with a paunch and two-day-old scruff, was hunched over examining something when they walked through the lab door. He did not look up to greet them but simply waved them over.

"What have you got?" Jared asked curiously.

Looking up, Brad blinked to give his eyes time to adjust. In front of him on the table was the locket perched under a large lighted magnifying glass.

"Well, in all honesty, not much at all."

Jared grunted. "Really?"

"I can see it's incredibly old. The writing on it, from what I can gather, is some form of pre-cuneiform script."

"Pre-cuneiform?" Dana asked. "From what I remember from my Humanities class in college, cuneiform is the oldest form of writing we know of. How could this be pre-cuneiform?"

"Well, because it looks like cuneiform, works similar to cuneiform, but is not cuneiform. And just to be clear, there are other forms of ancient writing that are considered possibly to be older in other regions of the world, such as from South and Central America."

Dana rolled her eyes and grimaced. "Okay, so this locket is over five thousand years old?"

"Well, as far as scholars can tell, cuneiform came into prominence somewhere around 3500-3000 BCE and this is most likely older, so from the writing alone, we can assume that the locket is somewhere around five thousand five hundred to six thousand years old."

Johansson whistled in amazement. "Holy crap."

"Holy crap indeed. There is just one problem with that assumption."

"And what is that?"

"Either this locket was kept in a vacuum chamber for the last six thousand years, or it is not really that old. In fact, it is in such pristine condition that I would've assumed it was made yesterday."

"What did the carbon dating turn up?" asked Dana.

"That's another problem with this locket's enigma. We couldn't get any readings from carbon dating."

"How is that possible?" she asked.

"Well for starters, it takes at least a day to determine how old an object is through carbon dating, and moreover, it requires a piece of the material to use in order to determine how old the object is."

Dana groaned. "Okay, so when will you get the results back from the lab?"

"As far as I can tell, never," he said flatly.

"Never?" asked Jared incredulously.

"Yup." Brad replied matter-of-factly. "One other bizarre feature of this mysterious little piece of jewelry is that the material strength of the metal is so strong that we have not been able to cut it with any tool we have here in this lab. So, that rules out it being gold, which of course is what it appears to be made of. Moreover, the jewel—which looks like a ruby—is harder than a diamond. This little trinket really is a conundrum."

"Okay," Johansson said. "I guess I can take it to the lab in NYC to see if they can have any luck with it there."

"Unless they have a plasma laser, I am betting that they won't."

"You're probably right about the laser, but the tech geeks there do have a whole lot of toys to work with," Johansson said with a smile.

"What about the picture?" Dana asked Johansson. "Has the Bureau gotten back to you on that?"

"Not yet, but it usually takes a while and I just sent the image to them a few hours ago, so I am not expecting anything for at least a few more hours."

"Sorry I couldn't be of more help," Brad said apologetically.

"It's okay. Keep us posted if anything else sticks out to you," Jared said, reaching out to retrieve the locket.

Johansson caught his hand. "Wait a minute, Jared. Even if the CSI guys didn't find anything, this is still the only piece of evidence that this guy has ever left, and I am going to need to take it back to NYC for further examination."

"I agree," Jared managed. The compulsion to hold and possess the locket had suddenly become overwhelming again. He slowly backed his slightly trembling hand away from the it.

"Okay. It's all yours then," he said. "But is there any way that we can be the ones to transport the locket?"

Dana glared at him as Johansson stroked his beard. "I don't see why not—if it's okay with your boss, that is. I wouldn't want to step on anyone's toes here. That's not my style."

"I have some vacation time that I can use, and honestly, I think it'll do me some good to get out of the area for a while," he said, trying to hide the relief he felt. "What do you think, Dana?"

Dana blinked at the sudden proposal. "I guess I'm down for it, but I am not sure how the chief is going to feel about us leaving during two ongoing murder investigations."

"Well, this locket is the only real piece of evidence we have for *our* murders, as well," Jared said. "The chief will most likely be in favor of us partnering up with the FBI in order to help solve our homicides at home. At least, it could be a good PR play for him."

"Okay, then it's settled," interjected Johansson, bringing the conversation to a conclusion. "Don't worry about transportation. I'll get the Bureau to foot the bill."

Dana was still uncertain about the whole endeavor, but she trusted Jared's judgment. And she could use a change of scenery, too. She managed a weak smile as the two men discussed the details of their expedition to the big city. No matter how hard she tried, though, she could not shake the lingering feeling of dread.

Chapter Twenty

It was late by the time Jared finally pulled up in front of his modest apartment. It had taken a whole lot longer than he had anticipated to convince the chief to get on board with the New York City excursion.

A loud rap on the driver's side window jolted him, and he reached for his sidearm.

"Hey, big brother."

Steve was bent down and peering into the window. "You gonna shoot me?"

Jared's face flushed when he realized his duty weapon was resting on his lap with the barrel pointing up at his brother. He growled as he replaced it in its holster and gingerly stepped out of his car.

"How long was I sitting there?"

"For a while. You seemed lost in thought, so I decided not to bother you."

"Scaring me half to death is what you consider not bothering me? Seriously though, I could have shot you."

"Maybe, maybe not."

"What the heck does that mean?"

Steve smirked. "Never mind. Why so jumpy? Something happen at work today? Get dumped by another girl?"

Jared glared at his younger brother. "You're an ass."

"Too soon?" Steve smiled a big puppy dog smile as he threw his arms out for a hug. "Oh, come on now. I'm just screwing with you."

Jared pushed past his brother, ignoring the proffered hug, and slogged up the stairs to his apartment. Steve fell in line behind his brother, pulling out a cigarette as he walked. He stopped to light his cigarette, flipped his lighter closed, and took a long drag.

Jared turned about halfway up the stairs. "You coming?"

Steve exhaled and smiled. "Only if you have something to drink up in that bachelor's mess you call an apartment."

"Sure, I have soda, water, and milk."

"You got chocolate milk and juice boxes too? I mean something for adults, Jar, not kindergartners."

Jared rolled his eyes and continued up the stairway. "I am too tired to be annoyed by you right now. Come back in the morning and I am sure it'll be easier to get under my skin then."

Steve took one more long drag off his cigarette before flicking it away. "I can't believe you still don't drink. Honestly, if I'd had the kind of last few days you've had, I would've been drunk by now. Of course, who's to say I'm not?"

Jared reached his second-floor apartment, and his hands shook causing him to drop his keys. "Seriously? Frickin' crap."

"You even swear like a kindergartner."

Jared bent down to pick up his wayward keys, grunting as he did. "Just shut up already, or I really will shoot you."

Steve chuckled as his older brother finally got his apartment door open after several tries. Jared held the door open for his younger brother, who walked in and plopped down on the sofa.

Jared's apartment was a one-bedroom, one-bath with a small kitchen and dining area. He dropped his keys down on the kitchen table and grimaced as he removed his jacket.

Steve watched his brother as he gingerly moved about the small kitchen. "You okay? I know I gave you a bit of a hard time, but I was trying to cheer you up a bit since I know this week has been a tough one for you."

"You want coffee?"

"Sure. Can you put a bit of bourbon in it for me?" Steve said then grinned at Jared's audible sigh from the other room. "Cream and sugar will do just fine."

After a few minutes, Jared returned to the living room with two mugs of coffee and handed one to Steve. He took a quick sip of the black liquid and then sat down next to his brother. Neither man spoke as they sat and sipped their beverages.

Steve was the first to break the silence. "I am going back to NYC tomorrow. I have a concert the day after tomorrow and I need to get back in order to get ready."

"That was a quick trip."

"Yeah, I was only planning on staying up here for a few days to tie up some loose ends. Honestly, if it wasn't for our illustrious sister not being able to keep her big mouth shut, then I could have avoided Mom and Dad altogether."

Jared's eyes bored into his brother. "It would have been better if you had. You were quite the jerk the other night. What the heck has gotten into you? I know Mom and Dad aren't perfect, but what the hell, man?"

"Whoa, an actual adult swear word. I guess I'm in real trouble now."

"Don't think I won't whip your butt like I did when we were kids, Steve. You were way out of line. The smoking and the alcohol I can overlook as a phase, but how you acted the other night, that was just asinine."

Steve's careless facade cracked. "Asinine? Me? How about how they act? My whole life they have chastised me and judged me for not being like them and their God. Well, news flash, big brother, I don't believe, and I never will. And we both know that they will never accept that, and that means they will never accept me."

"What are you talking about? Of course, they accept you. They love you. They are Mom and Dad; they will always love you."

"Love and acceptance are two completely different things, man, and you know it."

Jared shook his head and groaned. "Perhaps Mom and Dad aren't the intolerant ones here. Maybe it's you. Since you were fourteen years old, you did literally everything within your power to hurt and disappoint them."

"No, Jared, they have simply not been able to accept who I am and who I was becoming, and they're unable to accept me now. I can't help it if who I am does not fit into their world, and that 'hurts and disappoints' them."

Jared rubbed the bridge of his nose. "Just because you don't agree with Dad and Mom's philosophy doesn't mean you have to run recklessly in the opposite direction. Do you ever think that, maybe, you being so extreme is what they don't accept and it's not you yourself?"

Steve cocked his head and chuckled. "Extreme? Honestly, Jared, maybe I am not the problem here. Maybe it's all of you. You claim to be believers, but you don't even practice what you preach, and I am not talking about your antiquated moral code. You see me as being extreme because you don't truly understand what it means to believe. If you really believe something, it dictates every area of your life, from your thoughts to your actions, and there is no compromising that. Something is either true or it is not. There is no in-between. You all only see me as extreme because I live the way I *believe* I should, and not the way you all believe I should."

Jared slouched lower in the chair and closed his eyes. He was tired. No, weary was a better term. Weary of the endless conflict between his brother and his parents. Of having the same argument over and over again, never getting anywhere with either party. He was weary of Jasmine and weary of his job. He was just... weary.

Jarrod noticed his brother watching him, most likely anticipating an argument. Usually Jared would have scolded his brother for his earlier behavior, but he didn't have the energy. Instead, he simply sighed and got up from his chair and made his way back into the small kitchen.

He poured himself another cup of coffee. "You want a refill?"

"No, I still have half a cup."

Jared returned from the kitchen but didn't retake his seat in the big comfy chair. "I don't know where you planned on staying tonight, but you are welcome to crash on the couch. I know you won't go to Mom and Dad's, and there's no reason for you to shell out the money for a hotel when you are leaving tomorrow. Either way, there are clean sheets and a blanket in the linen closet if you're sticking around."

Jared started down the small hallway to his room. He was too tired to argue with Steve tonight, and with all the death he had witnessed over the last few days, he did not want to, anyway. He loved his brother and was just happy that he'd gotten a chance to see him while he was up visiting.

"Oh, and I forgot to mention," he said, looking back at his brother. "I'm going to NYC tomorrow, as well. I would say let's carpool together, but it's a work thing and I can't. It would have been fun, though. We could have listened to audiobooks the whole way like we did when we were kids going on vacation."

Steve smiled. "Yeah, those were good times. Remember the vacation when we drove out to the Grand Canyon? I think you threw up the entire way from here to Kansas. I never saw so much puke."

Jared leaned against his bedroom door. "Too bad we had to grow up. Life was so much simpler back then. So much more... happy."

Steve did not respond right away but smiled slightly at whatever he was thinking about. He sighed and looked up at his brother. "Hey Jar, you want to come hang out while you're down in the city? I know the style of music I play is not your thing, but I'd love it if you'd come check us out. If you have the time, that is."

Jared thought about it. "You know what, I would actually love to hear your band play. I hope they are better than that band you used to play with when you were fifteen. God, they sucked. Seriously, man, you guys were awful."

Steve laughed. "Yeah. Yeah, we were. No, we are much better than that, although the lead singer is still the same. You think you can handle that?"

Jared grinned and decided not to throw another verbal jab at his younger brother. "I will ask Dana tomorrow if she wants to go and we will see. Most likely she'll say yes."

"Oh. Dana's going too. Really?"

"It's not like that. She's my partner and we're going on business."

"I see, *business*. Well, whatever you kids call it these days. In all honesty, bro, she loves you, man, and she is great. If I were you, I would let go of that waste-of-space Jasmine and grab ahold of her with both hands and not let go."

Jared just shook his head and opened the door to his bedroom. "Good night, Steve," he said, closing the door behind him.

"You can ignore me all you want," Steve hollered. "But you know I'm right."

Jared stood with his back against the closed door, thinking about what Steve had just said. After his conversation with Dana at the coffee shop earlier, he could not deny that he was beginning to see her in a new light. God, her eyes were beautiful.

He shook his head and stumbled toward his bed, too tired to take his clothes off. He flopped down on the sheets and buried his head in his pillow.

Dana was his partner and his best friend; he didn't want to mess that up. Then again, maybe Steve was right. If he was truly honest with himself, he had to admit that he really did love her. Jasmine knew it, Steve knew it, and his parents knew it, so maybe it was time for him to admit the truth.

Well, he thought as he turned over and closed his eyes, *I am too tired to think about this right now, anyway.*

Smiling, Steve fell back on the couch and stuck both his arms behind his head like a pillow. He found immense gratification in being right about how his brother truly felt about Dana. He knew he was right about their parents, too. Even though he had allowed Jared to have the last word, Steve knew that it was the true victor of that argument. The truth was, he would go to whatever lengths were required to prove he was right, no matter how extreme the measures.

A small knock on the door dragged Steve away from his thoughts. He sighed and hoped that if he ignored it, whoever it was would simply lose interest and go away. The knocking persisted and grew louder. Steve groaned and reluctantly rolled off the couch and walked over to the door.

"What the hell do you want at this time of..." Steve stopped in mid-sentence when he saw the person who had disturbed his evening. A gorgeous blonde woman in her early twenties, wearing nothing but tiny night shorts and a tight pajama shirt, stood in the doorway staring up at him doe eyed. She started when she saw him, surprised to see someone other than the usual tenant open the door.

"I am so sorry to bother you so late, but I work afternoons and just got home," she said.

Steve waved off her apology and put his arm up on the doorframe and leaned in closer to the young woman. "No problem at all, miss. What can I do for you?"

The woman blushed. "Nothing really." She brushed a stray strand of hair away from her face. "I was just making some eggs for dinner and realized I had forgotten to stop and get bread on my way home.

I was just wondering if you had a few pieces you could spare so I could make some toast."

Steve's blue eyes twinkled. "Of course, my lady, mi casa es su casa. But I have a better idea."

"And what would that be?"

"Well, I make the absolute best omelets in the world, at least on the east coast, and I would love to make you one. So, why don't I grab my entire loaf of bread over here and I will match it with your eggs, and then I will make you the best omelet you have ever had. How does that sound?"

The young woman bit her lower lip as she considered Steve's proposal. Somewhere deep in her subconscious, her brain was raising its concerns about the man in front of her. The other half of her brain, however, was very attracted to the stranger and was intrigued by his proposal. She knew that her neighbor Jared was a police officer, so she reasoned that he would most likely never allow someone to stay in his house that was dangerous.

"Okay," she said. "But on one condition."

"And what would that be?"

"You only stay until we are done eating, okay? I have to work a double tomorrow and I need to get to bed sometime tonight, or I will be dead tomorrow."

"Deal," Steve said, a twinkle in his eyes.

He left her standing in the doorway and grabbed bread from the kitchen. When he returned, he put his arm around the young woman and led her outside, closing the door behind them.

The two made their way to the door across the hall from Jared's. "I'm Steve, by the way."

"Tammy."

"Nice to meet you, Tammy."

"Nice to meet you too, Steve," she said as they reached her apartment door and went in. "How do you know Jared?"

"Oh, I'm his younger brother."

Tammy smiled at the revelation, glad that he wasn't some kind of murderer or rapist. She turned and walked into the kitchen. "Wow, I didn't even know Jared had a brother. Of course, we really don't talk much. Just the usual 'Hi, how are you doing' in passing, is all."

Steve's smile darkened as he closed the door to the small apartment, locking it as he did.

Chapter Twenty-One

Jared awoke to an empty apartment. That was not surprising since his brother never seemed to stay in one place for awfully long. He had thought that Steve would've slept in due to how late it was when they had finally turned in for the night.

Where does he get all that energy? I am not that much older than he is, and I can barely stay up past eleven, Jared thought.

Not having any time to waste dwelling on his brother's absence, he pushed his questions to the back of his mind and started his morning routine. He glanced down at his watch and realized that he only had about twenty minutes to get to the station and meet up with Dana for the long drive to the city. Not wanting to be late, he kicked himself into second gear and was done with his morning routine and out the door in five minutes flat. A new record for the usually slow-moving Jared.

He arrived at the precinct a few minutes later than he anticipated and was met by a very annoyed Dana.

She was tapping her foot and looking at her watch as he stepped out of his car. He knew by the redness in her face that she was angry. He couldn't help noticing how beautiful her fiery brown eyes were, even though she was using them to launch daggers at him. Being that she was on the short side, she looked like an angry little pixie. Fierce but cute.

Jared approached her slowly and cautiously, like he was about to wrangle a dangerous animal. "Sorry, partner. Steve stopped by last night and I didn't get to bed till late."

She rolled her impossibly large brown eyes, and no matter how hard he tried, he could not stop his heart from skipping a beat. What was happening to him?

"It's okay, but we really need to get going. Johansson went on ahead of us and I have the locket right here," she said, holding it up.

Jared could not take his eyes from it and hesitantly took it from her. She watched him curiously as he stared at it.

"You okay?" she asked.

"Yeah," he replied dreamily.

"Well, if you are through staring at the pretty locket, we really need to leave, or we are going to be late and make Johansson look like an idiot in front of his superiors."

"All right, partner, I get it. We don't want to look like upstate hick cops to the sophisticated city folks." Jared crossed his eyes and gave her a big goofy grin.

Dana couldn't help laughing. She hit him hard on the arm and pushed him playfully. "You are such an idiot."

"I know. But you love me anyway. Don't worry, partner, we will get there with plenty of time to spare. I am positive that no one could ever mistake you for a hick."

Dana blinked a few times and looked up at him. He had never given her such an obvious compliment before without immediately offsetting it with a sarcastic remark. Their eyes met and they just looked at each other. Neither of them said anything or averted their gaze. Dana did not want to get her hopes up, but for the first time in her life, she felt as if Jared really saw her. Not as the childhood friend and partner, but as something more. Before the feelings could take hold, she shook her head.

She cleared her throat and turned away from him. "We really need to get moving. I'll drive. My car gets better gas mileage, plus you drive like a maniac."

He watched her walk away from him, and without thinking, took the locket out of the plastic bag it was in and placed it around his neck. As soon as it touched his neck, he instantly forgot it was there and went back to watching Dana. He could tell she was flustered, and for the first time since he'd met her at the ripe old age of ten, he hoped he was the reason why.

Dana was his best friend and had been ever since they were kids. He told her everything, every joy, and every hurt. In fact, whenever anything happened to him, no matter how mundane or significant, Dana was the first person he thought about telling. Maybe his brother was right. Maybe he did love her.

They drove for about three hours, talking and laughing about everything and anything. Of course, the case was always at the forefront of both of their minds, and for Jared, the locket as well. No matter how hard he tried, he could not shake this almost obsessive desire to touch it. Not wanting to come across as crazy he kept the internal struggle to himself, and for obvious reasons, did not mention it to Danna.

If he told her about the powerful effects the locket was having on him, it would only upset her more than she already was. The last thing he wanted to do was give more credence to the disturbing events she had experienced while it was in her possession.

Once they had left behind the rolling hills, quaint farmhouses, and green forests of upstate New York and entered more urban terrain, they both knew that it would only be a few more minutes before they crossed the outskirts of greater New York City. Dana was a bit fatigued from so much driving, and they decided to make a quick pit stop while they were still in the relative comfort of the suburbs.

They pulled off at the next exit and found a little mom-and-pop gas station with a tiny coffee shop attached to it. Jared got out to stretch his legs and decided to fill up the car while Dana went inside to use the restroom. He was finished pumping gas before Dana returned, so he went inside to get them both some coffee for the last leg of the drive into the city.

Jared grabbed himself a bear claw, paid for the beverages, and was back out in the car before she returned. As she approached the small sedan, he couldn't help but notice that her hair looked a little different. Her shoulder-length auburn hair hung down and wavy instead of tied up in the ponytail she usually sported.

God, she's beautiful.

He just stared at her thunderstruck when she got back into the car. He was still holding the two cups of coffee and the bear claw was dangling from his lips. Dana noticed him staring at her and became self-conscious.

"What?" she asked.

He mumbled something unintelligible as he fumbled with the bear claw in his mouth, trying not to spill the coffee in his hands. He handed one of the cups to her and removed the pastry. "Nothing. Just..."

"What's the matter? Why are you looking at me like that?"

Jared stammered a bit but couldn't remove his eyes from her. "I just... I've never seen you wear your hair like that before."

"You don't like it?" she asked, blushing.

"No. No. It looks... wow," he stammered, feeling his cheeks flush. He turned away and faked a cough. "We should get going if we don't want to hit the bridge at rush hour."

Flabbergasted, Dana held the cup of coffee he'd handed her. She was confused by the new signals he was giving off, and she didn't know what to make of them. If she hadn't known better, she would have thought he was attracted to her. Of course, he'd made it clear over the years that he wasn't interested in her that way. Had something changed?

"Jared, what the heck is going on with you?"

He pretended to examine his coffee cup. "What are you talking about? Nothing is the matter. I'm just in a bit of a hurry because I don't want to get stuck on the Tappan Zee at rush hour."

Dana's brown-eyed stare bore into him like hot pokers. "Really? That's what you're going with? Rush hour on the bridge? You can't even look me in the eye. You know me well enough to know that I don't let anything go and I am not going to let this go. Why are you acting so strange?"

Jared tried to say something, but nothing came out. He just shrugged and did his best to look confused. "I don't know what you are talking about."

She rolled her eyes and put the car into gear. "Okay, partner, have it your way."

The tires on her little hybrid sedan squealed as they surged out of the gas station and back onto the road. She was so flustered by Jared that she did not see the old pickup truck passing the little gas station. Thankfully, the driver wasn't in a hurry to get wherever he was going, so he was driving about ten miles under the speed limit. Dana narrowly missed smashing headlong into the front panel of the little pickup, and the driver laid on the horn as she sped off down the road and back toward the highway.

Jared gripped the armrest. "Seriously, Dana? Slow down—you are going to get into an accident or worse."

Dana glared ahead, anger heating her pretty face. "I thought you were worried we were going to get stuck in rush hour on the Tappan Zee? Make up your mind already. Do you want to get there fast or not? Of course, you can't seem to decide what the heck you want anyway, so why should this be any different?"

Jared looked at her, bewildered. "What is the matter with you?"

"What is the matter with me?" Dana fumed, taking her eyes off the road for a split second. "God, Jared, you are the most frustratingly indecisive person I have ever met. One minute you're all broken up about your blonde bimbo of an ex-girlfriend and the next minute you seem to be... flirting with me. Of course, you can't possibly be doing that, because in all the years I have known you, you have never ever done that. That is what's the matter with me."

Jared's eyes softened. "Pull the car over."

"What?"

Jared sighed and stared deep into her brown eyes. He saw pain and confusion there. Pain that he was causing her. "Please pull over."

"Here? On the highway?"

"Yes."

Dana slammed on the breaks, causing him to lurch forward in his seat. Thankfully, he was still clutching the armrest and braced himself as they came to a sudden, jarring, gravel-flying stop on the highway shoulder.

Dana crossed her arms over her chest and glared at him. Her face was flushed, and tears brimmed in the corner of her eyes. She didn't say anything but just looked at him and waited for him to speak.

Jared looked directly into her eyes. "You want the truth?"

"That would be nice. I may be a detective, but this is the first time in all the years that I've known you, that I have no idea what the heck is going on with you. You come to my house and cry on my shoulder, and I am there for you. I know you are not so dense that you did not know that it was tearing apart my heart to do that for you, but I did it anyway. How many times have I done something like that for you, Jared? How many? I think at the very least you owe me the truth."

Jared shook his head. "Okay, the truth is... I never really felt all that bad about losing Jasmine. Did it hurt? Yes. But no matter how much it initially hurt, and no matter how much I overreacted about it, after a day or two, all I felt was relief."

Dana blinked and a single tear slowly made its way down her cheek. "Relieved?"

"Yeah. I can't really explain it, but after I spent the night on your couch and talked to my idiot of a brother, I realized something."

"And what was that?"

"I never really loved her. In fact, I didn't even like her all that much, that's why I was always subconsciously finding ways to get out of being with her. From what I've been told, everybody noticed it. Everyone that is, except me."

Dana swallowed as more tears welled up in her eyes. Jared finally turned and looked at her. He smiled that stupid crooked smile that always melted her resolve.

"After that, I did some soul-searching, and I realized there was only one person in my life that I never wanted to avoid. In fact, no matter what life threw at me, good or bad, she was always the first person I wanted to talk to about it."

As he gazed into her beautiful brown eyes, he saw a spark of hope there.

"She?" Dana asked tentatively.

He shook his head in affirmation again. "Yes, she."

Tears streamed down Dana's cheeks and he gently reached out to brush them away. She closed her eyes and placed her hand on his. She was afraid that this was a dream and that when she awoke, the moment would be gone, and their relationship would return to the same state it had always been. When she finally did open her eyes, she found him still there holding her face and staring at her with that look she had so desperately wished to see but never thought she would.

"Just in case you were wondering," he said with a wink, "that 'she' is you."

He brushed another tear away with one hand as he held her face with his other. Dana stammered not knowing what to say at this revelation. She had been hopelessly in love with him since she was old enough to know what love was, and she had no idea how to act now that he finally saw her as something more than just a friend.

"I..." she stammered. "I don't know how to respond."

Jared laughed and removed his hand from her cheek. "Well, that's a first."

She scowled and hit him hard on the shoulder. "I am serious, jerk. I don't know what to say. I have been waiting my whole life to hear you say this and I just don't know what—"

Jared interrupted her by taking her head and gently kissing her on the mouth.

He kissed her with a passion he had never kissed anyone with before. Dana closed her eyes and lost herself in the moment, savoring the kiss. When it was finished, he sat back and whistled. "Holy shit."

Dana laughed because he seldom swore, and it took her by surprise. "That good, huh?"

He just sat there staring ahead. "Better than good."

She blushed and bit her lower lip. "We could do it again."

Jared's eyes shined with anticipation. "Oh, we will, but we really do have to get to the city and now we are definitely going to get stuck on the bridge."

Chapter Twenty-Two

On April 17th, 1897, the remains of former president and Union general Ulysses S. Grant were entombed in a red granite sarcophagus and placed in a newly built mausoleum near the banks of the Hudson River in the city of New York. To this day, it is one of New York City's most visited historical monuments.

Less than a mile down the road, however, and unbeknownst to anyone who is not from the greater metropolitan area, resides another monument. The memorial is small and plain and could be easily missed if you did not know it was there. Sadly, the small tomb was almost lost to the great upheaval that the construction of Grant's Tomb caused, but thanks to the overwhelming support of the people of New York, it was saved.

The small grave is known as the Tomb of an Amiable Child and is believed to be the grave of a five-year-old boy who, sometime in the late 1700s, possibly fell to his death from the cliffs lining the Hudson

River. The small marker is made of gray marble and is carved into the shape of an urn resting on a pedestal. A black wrought iron picket fence encases the tiny monument protecting it from the ever-encroaching city and her occupants. Serene and beautiful, it is a testament to a life lost too soon. Tonight, however, the tranquility was defiled.

Crimson blood, looking almost black in the early morning light, stained the ground around the child's grave. A man in a black jacket and hoodie stood over the lifeless body of a small child. He held a long knife covered in so much blood, it dripped over his hands and down his arms.

The child was a young boy with blond hair, blue eyes, and a cherubic face, about five years old. His blue eyes were open and fixed, his face contorted in fear and pain, his mouth open in a silent scream. This was his death mask and would be the last haunting thing his parents saw when they came to identify their little boy's body.

With a grunt, the man lifted the body up and slammed it forcefully onto one of the iron fence pickets. Hanging like a scarecrow, the boy's body drooped forward, his hands dangling by his side. Then his head fell forward too. Growling, the man reached up and pushed the dead boy's head backward so the expression on his face was clearly visible.

After all, he mused, *art like this should not be hidden but be open and available for everyone to enjoy.*

From atop the nearby gothic cathedral of Riverside Church, a giant warrior watched the scene unfold. He shifted the royal purple cloak that shrouded him, revealing shining golden armor and a jeweled crown upon his head. Power radiated from him and streams of golden light poured into the night air, illuminating the rooftop.

The warrior scowled as he watched the horrific scene. *Humans*, he thought. *It never ceases to amaze me the horrors they are capable of.*

As if the man below him heard his words, he canted his head in the direction of the massive church. He grinned at the watching warrior, his eyes wild and enraptured. The man did not speak a word but stared upward, his eyes fixated on the roof of the church.

The warrior's eyes flashed with anger and the glow around grew in such intensity that he appeared to be a miniature star resting atop the church.

"Moloch!" he bellowed.

The man below dipped his head in affirmation and chuckled, the grin never leaving his face. Red glowing eyes glared up at the angel and the ethereal shadow of a large demon erupted around the man. He opened his arms out wide and bared his teeth. "Come now, Sanctuary," the man roared in a powerful deep guttural voice. "Have you forgotten what day it is? Well, I have not. It is a pity, though. You are too late, just as you were then."

Sanctuary surged from the rooftop like a comet, a streak of fire in his wake. He was upon the man in the blink of an eye, and he grabbed him with one arm and hurled him into a nearby tree with such force that the tree cracked and bowed. Every bone in the man's body shattered. Coughing and wheezing, he gasped for air, spitting up blood as he did.

His eyes burned with hate as he fixed them on the angel. "Now now, Sanctuary, you know that killing this vessel will not stop me. I see your rage bests you even now, just as it did then. Tell me, warrior, did the man who killed the Amiable Child scream as you gutted him?"

The warrior grabbed the possessed man by the throat and slowly lifted him up into the air. He glared defiantly into the eyes of the crippled killer, looking through them to the horror inside. With a small flex of his hand, the warrior crushed his neck, and with a flick of his wrist, hurled him back across the small road. The body landed crumpled and broken at the feet of the hanging child.

The man chuckled a soft breathy laugh that reverberated in the air. The chuckle did not dissipate but grew until it became a deep, throaty, bellowing laugh. A smoky silhouette rose out of the killer's corpse, materializing into a massive, black Minotaur. Even though the demon was nothing more than a shadow of itself in this realm, Moloch the Defiler projected the power and menace of a demon lord.

"What would your precious God of love think about what you have just done?" the demon asked. "After all, even wretches such as this man are His children, are they not? I will never understand how He could love such weak and pathetic beings. All I had to do was push this man but a little in order to manipulate him into performing the most unspeakable things. The smallest nudge awakened what was already inside of him."

Moloch smiled and cocked his head as he relished in the memories of what he'd inspired the man to do. "I do miss the old days when whole nations would bow down to me and offer up their children as sacrifices in my honor. Now I must skulk around in the shadows, murdering children in secret. Of course, I do grow fat on the screams of all of the children murdered in the womb in the name of convenience and selfishness."

The angelic warrior growled, "Enough of your prattling already! The humans will be out soon, and I have other matters to attend to. Begone now, in the name of the Lord of Hosts, and murder no more children here."

The demon hunched down in defiance and appeared as if he is going to pounce upon the waiting warrior. Before he could strike, the warrior spoke the hidden name of the Lord and the demon writhed with agony. Chains of pure light rose from the ground and wrapped themselves around the demon, scorching his skin painfully. He howled in anger and raged against the chains that ripped into his incorporeal form. Before the demon dissipated, however, he made one last parting shot.

"You were more right than you knew when you said that you have much to attend to, angel. The Shogun is dead, and Injustice rises... chaos is upon you." The voice faded into the wind, leaving the warrior alone with the two dead bodies.

"No," He breathed. "I must find the sword before *he* does. If Moloch knows about the passing of the Shogun, then so do others. How could I have been so blind?"

As he stood contemplating, the sun began to rise, and the citizens of New York began to awaken from their nightly slumber. He heard someone scream as the body of the dead boy was discovered. He regretted that there was no time to remove the boy from his horrible perch, but time was of the essence. He must locate the sword and help it find a new bearer to minimize the havoc that the forces of darkness were no doubt already performing. Without Tzedakah to keep him in check, the Musketeer would run rampant, after first killing the fledgling bearer before he had time to bond with the blade.

More and more people flocked to the grisly scene. A young woman in a pink jogging suit noticed him standing nearby and pointed him out to the growing throng of people. Someone shouted for him to stop where he was, and he realized that it was time to leave. With a flash of blinding light, he disappeared as police car sirens wailed in the distance.

Chapter Twenty-Three

It was around midday when Dana and Jared finally arrived at 26 Federal Plaza. Just as Johansson told them to do, they pulled around to the back of the building where the gate for employee parking was. A guard signaled for them to stop as they approached and motioned for Dana to roll down her window.

The guard, a tall African American man dressed in a blue and black uniform, bent down to look into the car. He examined the two of them thoroughly before speaking.

"How can I help you today?" the man asked with a smile. His eyes, however, did not project the same friendliness.

Dana and Jared both lifted their badges so the officer could see them. "We are detectives from Binghamton. Agent Johansson said that you would be expecting us."

The agent examined the badges, then asked to see their IDs. They both handed them to the officer, and he examined them with the same intense scrutiny he had examined their badges.

"Wait here," he said curtly as he turned and walked back to the small guard shack where another officer waited. Before long he returned with their IDs and two badges. He handed the items to Dana, who in turn removed Jared's ID and one badge and handed them over to him.

"You can park to the right. That's the visitor's area. My partner already notified Agent Johansson of your arrival, and he will meet you both at the north entrance over there." He pointed to a large set of double doors directly across the parking lot. He smiled then and this time it was genuine.

"Thank you very much," Dana said returning his smile.

"You're very welcome, ma'am, and have a nice day."

Dana rolled up the window and pulled the car through the gate. It did not take them long to find a suitable parking space not far from the entrance the officer had pointed out.

Dana unbuckled her seatbelt and started to get out of the car when Jared suddenly grabbed her arm. "Do you think they have any real-life aliens in there?"

She sighed and rolled her eyes. "Seriously, Jared? Why would they keep perfectly good aliens here? I bet if they're anywhere, they're at Langley." She shot him a mischievous smile. "Of course, this is the city, and given the people that live here, nothing would surprise me."

They shared a laugh as they exited the car and headed across the parking lot. "Did you ever think when we were kids that we would be here at FBI headquarters in New York City?"

"Not on my most imaginative day. Of course, when I was a kid, all I dreamed about was..." She broke off and never finished her sentence, embarrassed at what she'd almost said.

Jared smiled but did not press her. He knew full well what she was about to say. The sudden change in their relationship was all too new and he did not want to say anything that might jeopardize it.

They both walked in relative silence across the parking lot and were surprised as the door suddenly swung open. Johansson smiled and waved for them to enter.

"How was your trip in?" he asked as he ushered them into a small waiting room. A large desk with a security officer was all that adorned the rather unremarkable room. "I hope you didn't get stuck on that damn bridge. I know this is supposedly the 'greatest' city on the face of the earth. I swear, the longer I stay in this damnable city, the more I miss Boston."

Jared and Dana shared a look. "It was... an amazing trip in," Jared said. "No problems at all."

Dana never took her eyes off Jared, and Johansson saw the twinkle there. "Well. Anything you two want to share?"

"Nope," Dana replied, forcing her gaze away from Jared. "Did you find anything out about our John Doe?"

Johansson gave her a look that said he knew there was more to the story to hear, but he'd let it slide. "Well, I wish I did. But we got nada."

"Nothing at all?" Jared asked.

"Nope. As far as I can tell, this guy is an honest-to-God ghost. My first guess was that he was a spook or something, but my buddy at the CIA said he didn't recognize him. He could be lying of course, but I doubt it."

Jared grimaced. "Well, that sucks. At least we still have the locket."

"Absolutely. I will get it into the hands of the geek squad immediately so they can examine it," Johansson said, reaching out his hand.

Jared put his hand into his pocket to retrieve the locket and hesitated.

"You didn't forget it in the car, did you?" Dana asked, noticing his hesitation.

"No, sorry, I've got it in my other pocket."

No one noticed the slight blue glow in his eyes as he pulled the locket out of his other pocket and handed it to Johansson, who took it gratefully. Unbeknownst to everyone, even Jared, the locket he had handed to Johansson was a fake that the sentient sword had created. The real locket rested safely around Jared's neck, right where it wanted to be.

Leaning against the wall, Johansson said, "Thank you very much. I could give you a tour if you want. Not the shitty tour we give to the public, but the kind of tour you can only get from an agent. Whaddaya say? At least you will get your money's worth for coming all this way."

Jared brightened at the thought and he turned to look at Dana. She was staring at him with a goofy look on her face, blushing slightly.

"You interested, partner? Want to take a tour of Willy Wonka's chocolate factory?" he asked.

She bit her lower lip and crossed her arms in thought. "Well... I have a better idea. Not that a personal tour of FBI headquarters New York wouldn't be fascinating, but we hardly ever get any time off, and

I'd love to just walk around the city and be a tourist for a day."

Johansson feigned being hurt and clutched his chest. "You wound me to the core, my lady."

They all shared a laugh.

"Eh, you're not missing much," Johansson said. "The tour is nothing special, anyway. Now, if we were at Langley, then I could show you all the really cool shit. Shit that would blow your mind and give you nightmares for weeks."

He ushered them back to the door. "Now you two country bumpkins from upstate run along and enjoy your day off in the big city. Try not to get into too much trouble."

He held the door open for them and they walked back outside. "Actually, I take that back. Trouble can be fun. If you want to know the best places for it, I can help you out with that."

"You know you're welcome to join us if you would like," Dana said.

Jared nodded his agreement even though the look on his face said otherwise. "If you are not too busy, that is."

Johansson gave him a wink. "Naw, this old fart has too much work to do. Besides, who will catch the bad guys while you two gallivant around Manhattan? Go and have fun. We can catch up later."

Jared nodded his thanks to Johansson and turned to follow Dana who was already a few steps ahead of him. Johansson smiled knowingly back and winked again before turning to head back inside the large building. He stopped just before the door closed on him and pushed it back open a few inches. "Hey, you two, I will keep you posted if any new developments happen to pop up."

Dana turned and waved to Johansson in acknowledgment, as the two officers reached the small car. "Thanks again for all your help."

"Yeah, and for not being the usual FBI douche bag," Jared interjected with a laugh.

Johansson waved off the insult and chuckled as he allowed the door to close behind him. The smile on his face, however, disappeared as soon as the door closed. He pulled out his phone as he watched them walk away and pushed the call icon.

"We have the locket," he said to the person on the other end. "No, I am pretty sure that I was able to dissuade them from any further interest in it. Either way, we will cross that bridge if we come to it. For now, I will continue to keep them at bay and hopefully looking in the wrong direction."

He closed his fist around the tiny locket and breathed deeply in and out through his nose. In spite of himself, he liked the two detectives and wished he could tell them more; but the less they knew, the safer they would be. This locket was dangerous, and the sooner it was locked away where no one could ever get to it, the better.

Dana was already in the driver's seat with the car running when Jared finally got in and buckled his seat belt. He turned and gazed at her, admiring her profile and the way her bangs fell across her face, and smiled appreciatively. She noticed him looking at her out of the corner of her eye.

"What?" she asked.

"Nothing. I just can't stop thinking about how long it took me to finally see you."

Her blush deepened and she turned away, brushing her rebellious bangs out of her eyes. She was quiet, then softly said, "I waited a long time."

"I know," he said apologetically. "But at least the waiting is over."

"So, Mr. Better-Late-Than-Never, where do we go from here?"

"Wherever we want," he replied with a smile.

"Okay, so where do we *want* to go?"

"Well, I always wanted to see Manhattan. I know that's pretty cliché and touristy, but I think it would be fun. Plus, if I remember correctly, Steve said he had a show tonight somewhere on the island. Maybe we could go."

She thought about it, then brightened. "Yeah. That sounds absolutely wonderful, as long as you promise to make your brother behave himself. You know how he can be."

"Well, the best I can do is to promise that I will try. Plus, I'm not sure I want to behave myself tonight."

She blushed again as they pulled out of the small parking lot and into the waiting traffic of New York City. "You'd better watch yourself or I will break something important."

He laughed. "I have no doubt you would."

Chapter Twenty-Four

In New York City, there are many dark alleys that a person may hide in or, if one is so inclined, commit any heinous act one can contrive. In one such nondescript alleyway, a writhing cloud of darkness appeared. Like a miniature black hole, it seemed to absorb and destroy the light it encountered.

A slight wind blew around it, stirring up the contents of the small alleyway. With a burst of dark energy, a lone figure stepped out from the darkness. As soon as the figure emerged, the portal dissipated and collapsed in on itself.

The Musketeer removed his large-brimmed hat and brushed away a few particles of dirt. Replacing the hat, he slid his hand along the brim with a flourish.

He closed his nightmare black eyes. His breathing slowed as he reached out with his senses. He did not have to search long. "There you are, mon ami," he said.

Before the Musketeer opened his eyes, however, he sensed another presence approaching his location. A large man—no, two men—quickly drew near. His smile broadened into a wicked grin. "Lady Fortune favors me today."

The two men entered the alleyway just as he turned around to face them. Upon seeing the dark figure, the two men slowed their pace and fanned out, attempting to block the opening to the street. The larger of the two men pulled out a knife.

"Well, well, what do we have here, Pedro? Looks like one of those Comic-Con geeks has wandered too far from his nerd herd."

The other thug, a slightly smaller man wearing a red, white, and blue bandana with a star on it, laughed mirthlessly at the joke while tapping his shoulder with a large Louisville slugger. "Looks like it, Dante," he replied.

Before the two men could make a move, the Musketeer guffawed. "Oh, idiots, this is so—how do you say? —so wonderfully cliché."

"What did you say?" the massive man asked, his smile turning cold.

"Oh, and stupide as well, mon ami. How delightful this is. Here I thought I was going to have to wander around this ugly city for hours before you finally found me."

Pedro scratched his head and scowled. "What he talkin' about, Dante?"

Dante, his eyes now menacing slits, clenched his knife. "Seems this honkey thinks he really is some sort of knight."

"Honkey? What is this honkey you speak of? And I am no knight. How dare you insult me so, monsieur!" He spat on the ground at the man's feet. "I am one of Cardinal Richelieu's finest. A knight indeed! I spit on such idiocy."

"Whatever you are, I think it's time I teach you some respe—" Dante attempted to say before his sentence was cut off. A look of profound bewilderment crossed his face and he stood transfixed, staring straight ahead, his eyes unfocused.

"Dante?" Pedro asked in surprise. "Are you..." His words caught in his throat. As he reached out to shake his partner, both his arms tumbled to the ground.

He gaped soundlessly as his friend's head slipped off his torso and fell with a splat. With nothing left to keep it upright, the rest of Dante's body toppled.

Pedro stammered; his mind unable to comprehend what had just happened. He looked back at the lone figure that they thought they'd trapped. The sword that had been sitting on his hip only seconds before was now unsheathed and casually resting across his shoulders. Pedro let loose a blood-curdling shriek.

The Musketeer cocked his head. "Ah, I see that your pathetic little brain has finally managed to catch up to the present."

Pedro stumbled and fell in his attempt to flee, but with no arms to brace himself, he hit his face hard on the unrelenting pavement, breaking his nose and knocking himself unconscious.

The Musketeer sheathed his rapier and strolled over to where Dante lay. He knelt on one knee, picked up the decapitated head, and studied it.

"Can you see me, mon ami? Ah, I forget you cannot raise the dead, can you? Well, if any of your servants are lurking in the shadows observing, know that I am not here to bring you trouble. I am merely here on a small errand. Of course, if you feel the need to interfere with me, I will end you the way I just ended your, how you say, honkies. I assume that this word suffices, but if not, you will understand the message, nonetheless."

He stood and tossed the head over his shoulder where it bounced a few times before halting in the dust. Brushing himself off, he sauntered over to where Pedro lay. Blood pooled from his arm stumps; red streams trickled into the street.

The Musketeer debated putting the man out of his misery, but given the fact that blood no longer spurted from his wounds, he surmised that the man was already dead. He dusted himself off quickly and then tiptoed around the corpse to avoid staining his boots as he left the grisly scene behind. Just before he turned the corner, he glanced back and winked into the shadows, acknowledging the thing that had been spying on him since he had first arrived.

As soon as the Musketeer was out of sight, a small shadow creature stirred in the alleyway. It moved out to where the two men lay dead and hovered over them. Two tiny red glowing orbs appeared out of the folds of shadow and stared down at the corpses.

The master will not be pleased that the Musketeer has come into his territory, it thought. It knew that it must return quickly in order to relay the message that he left, which was obviously for his master. With a shudder, it dissolved and faded away into the waiting darkness.

Chapter Twenty-Five

Dana and Jared sat talking together at the Starbucks in Times Square. The sun was partway below the horizon and the foot traffic of the city increased as the people of New York left their jobs for the day and headed home. The two watched quietly as crowds of people hustled by. Soon the streetlights blinked to life, signaling the coming of night.

Dana swallowed her last sip of coffee and took in a deep breath. "Do you ever wonder what it would be like to be a cop here in the City?"

Jared shrugged. "Not really. At least not now, anyway. When I was a kid, it was all I could think about. Not only was it where all the action was, but it was where all the superheroes were, as well. I mean, what kid wouldn't want to have the chance to fight crime alongside the heroes of New York?"

Dana chuckled. "Don't lie. You still want to be a superhero."

"What are you talking about? I *am* a superhero." Jared winked as he downed his last sip of coffee.

He stood up and winked before taking Dana's empty cup over to the wastebasket. "You ready to head over to Angels and Kings?"

Dana rose and pushed in her chair. "I guess. You know I am not much for clubs or bars, but since we have tomorrow off and your brother is playing there, I figure we might as well take advantage of the nightlife here in NYC."

Jared turned and put out his arm for her. Unable to hide the blush and the girly smile, Dana accepted his arm. He smiled right back at her and then bent down and kissed her lips. They happily exited the outside seating for the coffee shop and headed out into the busy street.

"Honestly, I don't drink, and if my parents knew I was going to a club, they would have my head, but I really do want to see Steve play. No one in my family has been incredibly supportive of his music since it is in the secular world, and not the Church," he said as they walked. "But since I'm here in the city for a change, I'd like to show him some support."

Dana snuggled up closer to him as they turned down a side street. "You are such a good brother."

Jared snorted. "Well, it isn't because I think his band is any good, that's for sure. It's because the tickets are free and so are the drinks. How could I pass that up? A night like that in NYC would usually cost a fortune."

She punched him on the shoulder but never let go of his arm as they continued down the street. They passed buildings of every kind as they walked. Skyscrapers that jutted so far into the stratosphere that you could not even see the tops from below, as well as brick apartment buildings huddled together.

It was so different from the rural farming communities they were used to. There were so many people and so many things to see and do. At this time of the day in Binghamton, even the small shops and restaurants would be getting ready to close. Here in the Big Apple, you had the feeling that everything was just getting started.

As the two turned down yet another side street, a tall man wearing what appeared to be a musketeer uniform slowly approached them. Upon seeing the man, Jared stepped in front of Dana protectively. The man was probably just an actor promoting his theater group, but Jared's cop senses were going crazy. By the way Dana stiffened up behind him, he could tell she felt the same.

The man smiled warmly and bowed to them as he approached, his face overshadowed by a large, plumed hat.

"Monsieur and madame, how are you on this fine evening? My name is Renault."

Jared could not put his finger on why this man bothered him so much. It was obvious he was just another street performer, but dread ran its cold fingers up his spine. For some strange reason, his hand went to the locket, which had grown inexplicably warm.

"Is there something I can do for you?" he asked.

The man put a finger to his lips in thought. "Hmm... Well, I am not sure. It is possible that you might be able to help me with some amusement. However, now is not the time for such, how you say, enjoyment."

"Excuse me?" Jared frowned at the odd man. "I'm not really sure what you are talking about, and while I don't mean to be rude, we have to be going."

"Ah, you are not rude, mon ami. I only wished to introduce myself at this present time and to see you for myself. I have now done that, and I will be moving on to other endeavors."

Neither of them relaxed until they were a good way farther down the street. Dana turned to look back at the man, but when she did, he had vanished.

Odd, she thought. *How could he have turned the corner so quickly?*

Jared was still frowning as they hurried away.

"You okay?" she asked him.

"Yeah, I'm fine. For some reason, that crazy Shakespeare guy put me on edge. I'm sure he was just some guy trying to promote some play, but something about him just took me as... off. Oh well, I guess that's the city for you. The crazy people where we're from are just of a different caliber."

They both shared a laugh as they continued walking down the busy street, neither one noticing the dark shadow that followed.

Dana slipped her arm around Jared's. She couldn't believe this was happening. It was still so surreal to her, and she was afraid of messing it up somehow. A little voice warned her that this was all a dream, and when she woke up, everything between her and Jared would go back to the way it used to be. She pulled his arm closer to her chest.

Jared, feeling the renewed pressure on his arm, looked down and smiled at her. "Penny for your thoughts?"

"Yeah, I was just thinking, is all."

"About what?" he asked, scanning the road ahead of them.

"Nothing really. Can I ask you a question?" Her voice was small.

"Of course. Anything."

"I have pretty much known you and your family my entire life. Heck, your parents are more like an aunt and uncle then just family friends. But, in all the years I have known you, I have never really understood why there is such a disconnect between Steve and your parents. I mean, your parents are two of the greatest people I've ever met. In fact, there were times when I was a kid that I wished they were my parents. They always seemed so perfect."

Jared mulled that over. "My parents are... complicated. And they'd be the first to tell you they're far from perfect. Don't get me wrong, I love them to death, and I could not have asked for better parents, but just like all people, they make mistakes."

Dana frowned. "Well, all parents make mistakes, but I never saw any evidence that your parents did anything that would warrant such outright hatred from your brother."

Jared shook his head. "Don't judge Steve too harshly. Things happened when we were both very young that we have never really talked about. It happened before our sister was born, and I am not sure if she even knows about it. The incident scarred Steve so bad that he was never able to move past it. I think he blames God for what happened more than he blames my parents, and that makes the divide between them even larger."

"What in the world are you talking about? What incident? I have known you since I was ten, and I don't remember anything like that ever being mentioned about your family."

"It was before we moved to Greene," he said, looking away painfully.

She could tell that thinking about it was difficult for him. She wanted to know what he was talking about, but she hated to see him so distraught. "It's okay, you don't have to talk about it right now."

"No, it's okay. I haven't thought about it in such a long time. My family never talks about it for fear of my sister finding out. That, and I think on some level, neither of my parents have truly forgiven themselves for what happened."

"They are ministers. Surely they know God has forgiven them."

"Of course. But it is one thing to accept the forgiveness of God, and another matter entirely to be able to forgive yourself."

Dana bit her lip. "What could possibly have happened that was so horrible that the ramifications of it are still affecting you all today?"

Jared's eyes looked haunted. "When my parents were still young pastors, my Dad was very... intense about his duty to the house of the Lord. He didn't ignore us or neglect us, but at times, he would be gone for what seemed like days. When Steve and I were about five and seven, my mother became pregnant. Since the church was still very young, it required a tremendous amount of work and faith to keep it going. My dad was there all the time, working and dealing with everything that's required for starting a new church, and he did not have a lot of time to help my mother with Steve and me. Since we had moved three hours to the south, we didn't really know anyone yet. Sure, there were a few families that had started following my dad on the radio that joined up right away, but overall, all of my mother's close friends and family still lived up near Syracuse.

"Soon the baby came, and it was a little girl. My parents named her Hope. She was adorable and Steve took to her almost immediately. Honestly, I was surprised since he'd always been such a brat to me. I figured he would fight hard against being replaced as the baby. But Steve loved her so much that all he wanted to do was be around her and help Mom."

"I didn't know you had another sister," Dana said softly. Her heart sank in her chest as she imagined what must have happened to this sister she'd never met.

"There was a crisis at the church right after Hope was born. Dad was gone all the time. My mother did her best to take care of us all, but, though we didn't know it at the time, she was suffering from severe postpartum depression. We didn't understand what was going on, just that Mommy was acting strange and being very mean at times. I think my mom tried to talk to my dad about it, but at that time, postpartum depression wasn't a thing."

He stopped talking and did not look at her as he choked down his grief. Dana's heart broke for him. She wasn't sure that she wanted to know what came next. When he spoke again, his voice cracked.

"One night my mother was giving Hope a bath. Steve and I were playing in the living room while watching cartoons on television. I remember thinking that it was suddenly so eerily quiet. You know how kids get when everything goes quiet? Steve and I felt restless. Before long we were fighting, and Steve ran off to tell Mom about something I'd done. Honestly, I think it was just an excuse to go find Mommy, not really because he was all that mad at me.

"It was then that I heard the most horrible shriek I've ever heard in my life. I ran into the other room to investigate and found Steve soaked to the bone and holding something in his arms. He was crying and screaming, and I was afraid that maybe he'd hurt himself. I was so shocked that my mom had not come running as soon as the shouting began. It was then that I noticed what was in his arms. It was Hope. She was soaking wet and very blue."

Dana gasped. "Oh my God."

"Yeah. Once the shock finally wore off, I went in search of Mom. I found her unconscious on the bed. She had taken some pills to help her relax and they had knocked her out instead. The effects hit her when she'd gone into the other room to get Hope some fresh clothes. She'd only meant to lie on the bed for a minute but fell asleep. I tried to wake her, but I couldn't.

"Since this was before cell phones, we had no way of contacting Dad. All we could do was sit there and pray. Steve prayed so hard for God to bring Hope back to life, while I cried. I have no idea how long it was before Dad finally came home. To us, it felt like a lifetime. My brother was never the same after that night."

Dana was speechless. She thought she knew everything about Jared and his family, but this revelation was far beyond anything she could have ever imagined. It did, however, shed some light on the underlining strain in relationships she sensed whenever she visited the Caddrets. It was so sad that this tragedy had torn them all apart.

They rounded a corner, and the club came into view. Jared forced a smile and wiped his eyes with his sleeve. "Well, anyway, here we are. Are you ready to have some fun? I sure am. I think I might even let down my hair a bit and try a beer."

"What?" Dana said incredulously. "I'm pretty sure you will hate it."

"You think so? I have always wondered what all the hubbub was about. I mean, it smells like piss, but a lot of people seem to like it."

Dana crinkled her nose in disgust. "Well, trust me, it tastes like it smells. I took a sip of my dad's once when I was a kid and I nearly threw up. As soon as it touched my tongue, I spit it out onto the living room carpet. I thought for sure he was going to yell at me, but all he did was laugh and ask me if I wanted another sip. I've never had a desire for it again."

They continued talking as they approached the club's entrance. The building was painted all black including the windows, giving the club a grimy appearance. Posters plastered the wall around the small ticket window next to the door. A large neon sign prominently displayed Steve's band, along with two other names Jared and Dana didn't recognize. To their surprise, the front of the building was packed with people waiting to get in.

Jared pushed through the crowd toward the ticket window, Dana gripping his arm as they made their way through the throng. The line was not too large, so it didn't take them long to get the tickets and passes Steve had left, and muscle their way through the doors. Inside, the club was painted black, the rooms lit only with an eerie purple glow. Before they even entered the main auditorium, Dana could hear the loud thumping of drums reverberating. The beat moved through her in pulsing waves of energy that rattled her bones and exaggerated the muffled music coming from within. As soon as they opened the main door, the music burst through the opening like a living thing that had been struggling to break free.

Jared winced at the sudden assault of noise as the two of them made their way into the crowded auditorium. The concert seemed to already be well underway and Jared feared they may have already missed Steve's set. The space was much more expansive than it appeared on the outside. It was crowded but not so crowded that they could not move around freely. They found their way through the throng to a table.

As soon as they took a seat, a pretty redheaded waitress wearing short black shorts and a low-cut black T-shirt came over and placed a napkin in front of each of them. She smiled at them and pointed to the menu on the table. Jared smiled back and pointed to the picture of a glass of soda. The woman nodded and turned to Dana who pointed to the word water. The music was so loud that small talk was nearly impossible, so the waitress did not stick around after taking their orders.

Jared's fears were proven to be unfounded as the band currently playing ended their set and cleared the stage for the next act. A burly African American man covered head to toe in tattoos with dreadlocks that hung below his waist strolled out onto the stage.

He flashed a wild smile as he grabbed one of the microphones that had been left on the stage. "Let's give a good round of applause to Killing Lincoln!"

The crowd went wild in either appreciation or drunkenness, Jared couldn't tell which. Either way, the atmosphere was both electrifying and terrifying. Maybe it was his cop senses acting up, but to him, it seemed that just underneath the excitement was a sense that the crowd could erupt into something more dangerous. He looked over at Dana and saw her tensing up. He smiled—you could take the girl out of the precinct, but you couldn't take the police officer out of the girl.

Back on the stage, the curtain had been closed, leaving only the slick-suited emcee hyping up the crowd. Then he held up his hands. "Okay, everyone, give it up for... Richard Cranium!"

The lights dimmed and the curtains pulled apart. In the darkness, an electric guitar wailed loudly and angrily. The crowd roared, an amped-up human tide jumping, thrashing, dancing to the music. In a dazzling light display, Steve appeared on stage. He grabbed the microphone in one hand and the stand in the other, swinging his head to the thundering drumbeat. Jared smiled and saw Dana smiling too. Sure, this really wasn't their type of music, but he couldn't deny the concert's power and excitement.

When the intro ended, Steve began to sing the first song. Jared couldn't help but be proud of his brother. He wished his sister could've been there to share this moment. Of course his parents would never come, and that saddened him a bit. At least Dana and he were here, and he was sure that that would be enough.

Before long the concert was over, and Dana and Jared made their way through the rowdy crowd to the edge of the stage where the doors to the dressing rooms were. Two large men stopped them before they could enter the door. Both men were well over six feet tall and looked like they could be professional wrestlers. The one to the right put out his hand and stopped Jared in his tracks. "No one gets by here without a pass."

Jared smiled up at the man as Dana quietly scrutinized him. "We have passes." He reached into his jacket and pulled out the lanyard he had hanging around his neck. "See?"

The man examined it before looking up. "What about her?"

Dana pulled her lanyard out for the man to examine as well. He did so, and when he was satisfied that they were legitimate, he waved them both through. Once they entered the small door, they were immediately assaulted by the noises and smells of a large party. People were everywhere, doing every kind of vice imaginable. The two detectives found it difficult to suppress their cop nature and ignore the obvious breaking of the law that was not so subtly being performed around them. It did not take them long to find Steve's bandmates among the chaos. Steve, however, was not with them.

It took them forever to find someone sober enough to know where Steve might have gone, and as soon as they did, Dana left to go to the restroom. Jared was directed to a door in the corner of the large room and he headed for it. He shot Dana a text before pushing through the door, so she would know where to find him. The door slammed shut behind him with a bang. He stood staring at a long maintenance hallway that led from the dressing rooms to the rear exit doors. The lights were dim, and a few flickered in the dark.

He made his way down the hallway, passing a few other doors and the occasional straggler. One couple was pretty much having sex against one of the dirty walls, and to Jared's great relief, they ignored him as he hurried past. He eventually came to the door marked "exit" and pushed through it.

"Steve, you out here..."

His words caught in his throat when he laid eyes on his younger brother. Steve was hunched over the prostrate form of a young woman. He jumped, startled by the sudden interruption, and his head snapped up, his eyes wild. The woman on the ground was covered in blood. So was Steve.

Disoriented only momentarily by the scene before him, Jared snapped to life as his training took over. He took in the scene before him as his mind came into complete focus, running through every possible scenario. First, he went to the girl on the ground and checked for vital signs. She was completely covered in blood. If she wasn't already dead, she would be soon. He looked up at his younger brother who had moved away from the body and was now resting up against the wall. He was covered in blood, staring at his hands.

"I... I... found her this way, Jar. I tried to save her. Oh God, I tried to save her, but there was so much blood."

He slid down the wall to the ground.

"Steve," Jared said, leaving the body and walking over to his brother. "We need to call 911 and make sure no one else contaminates the scene."

His mind was now in full-blown detective mode, and he knew he needed to lock down the scene and call the local authorities.

"Oh God," Steve moaned as he put his head in his hands, smearing blood into his hair and all over his face. "What am I going to do? Jared, what am I going to do?"

Jared moved to where his brother was sitting and knelt beside him. "It's going to be okay, Steve, I promise. But right now, I need you to calm down and think for me. Did you see what happened?"

Steve looked up at his brother, his face stained with tears. "No, I came out to have a cigarette and I found her like this. I tried to help her, you know, give her mouth to mouth or something, but nothing I did seemed to work."

"Okay, just relax if you can. You did the right thing in trying to help her." Jared put his hand on his brother's back. "Just try to remember what you saw. Any detail, no matter how insignificant, will help the police in their investigation."

Steve quieted down a bit. He looked over at the dead girl. "I just came out to get some air and I found her like this. After I saw her, I panicked."

"I understand, that's natural. At least you were able to... Wait, I thought you came out to smo—" His words came to an abrupt halt as he no longer had the breath to continue talking.

His vision blurred as he looked down and saw the hilt of a knife sticking out of his side. He gurgled and coughed up blood as he lost feeling in his legs. He stumbled and started to fall. His brother rose with supernatural speed and caught him, holding him like a limp rag doll. Jared tried to move, but his body refused to obey him.

Steve leaned in and whispered into Jared's ear. His voice was strangely calm. "Sorry, big brother, I really wish you had not caught my little slipup. I want you to know that it isn't personal, nor do I hate you. I truly do wish you had not come out here tonight.

"Mom and Dad are going to be heartbroken. I thought you had caught me in upstate that night when you stumbled into me. I kept waiting for you to try to arrest me. I thought for sure you knew what I was. It really is bad luck that you did not stop me then. If you had, then you would not be dying here today in this dirty alley so far from home."

Recognition brightened in Jared's eyes at Steve's confession. It all made sense to him now. How could he have missed it? It was so obvious. The murders in upstate New York coincided perfectly with Steve's sudden arrival. He knew his brother had been acting strange that night, but he had shaken it off. Had he not been overreacting to his breakup with Jasmine, he would have seen it.

Steve drew the knife from Jared's side, and he jerked involuntarily in pain. Steve released his grip on him, and he flopped unceremoniously to the ground.

He could neither breathe nor speak. His brother had known exactly what he was doing when he stabbed him. He had slid the knife precisely into his lung, collapsing it and making it impossible for him to cry out for help.

Jared gaped like a fish out of water, and he spat up blood as he futilely attempted to draw in air. The world around him spun and his vision blurred. He grabbed at his throat in a desperate attempt to... do what? His lungs were filled with blood and he was choking to death.

He swooned and fell forward, limp. Steve caught him and settled him down on his back. His eyes were sad as if he regretted what he'd done.

No sooner had Steve set him down than the door to the building swung open. Steve's head snapped up and his eyes went wide when he saw Dana emerging cautiously into the alleyway. Her face went white when she saw Jared lying on the ground. She ran to where he lay.

"What happened?" she asked. She slid to a halt next to Jared's now convulsing body. She clenched her fists as she cried, "Jared! Oh God no!"

"I don't know what happened." Steve rose to his feet. "I found them both like this. I am going to go get help. You stay with him, okay?"

He bolted off toward the door, shouting for help as he ran. Dana was so distraught that she barely heard him. Jared's eyes were unfocused, his body convulsing from lack of oxygen as she tried to lift him into her lap. She was crying so hard she could barely speak.

"It will be okay. Just hang in there. Steve went for help."

At the mention of his brother's name, Jared's eyes flared to life. He grabbed her head and with all the strength he had left, pulled her close to his face. His mouth moved but all that came out was unintelligible gurgling.

He accidentally spit blood onto her beautiful face, and he attempted to wipe it off, but his hands no longer obeyed him. She just stared down at him with those beautiful brown eyes that were now stained with tears and sadness. He wanted to warn her, to tell her about his brother, but he was too far gone.

God, she is beautiful, he thought. He regretted that he had not seen it sooner.

"Jared," she sobbed, her tears falling onto his face. "Please don't leave me. Not now, not when we finally found each other."

Jared's eyes rolled back into his head and convulsed one last time and went limp in her arms. Steve came barreling through the door. He stopped dead in his tracks when he saw Dana with her head down holding Jared's lifeless body in her lap. Her face was contorted into such a look of anguish, that even his dark heart was moved. She looked up at him shattered by grief and let out a guttural wail of pain. Dana held Jared's head in her hands and rocked back and forth and wept. It was not a girly or cinematic movie cry, but a hard and ugly heartbroken cry.

Steve really was sad that this had to happen. He never wanted to kill his brother, but Jared had forced his hand. It had told him he would have to, but he had never really believed It. In the end, It was right. It was always right.

He sighed and moved closer to Dana. He put his hands on her shoulder and knelt beside her and his brother's body. Sirens wailed in the distance and first responders would arrive soon. He did not worry that he would be caught; It always made sure he wasn't.

The only wild card that he could think of was Dana. What did she know? What had she heard or seen? Had Jared managed to warn her before he died?

"Dana," he said, "I know this is hard, but did Jared say anything before he... before he passed away?"

She did not look at him when he spoke, but kept her face close to Jared's. They sat there quietly for what seemed to Steve to be an eternity. The paramedics came around from the street out front, directed by bystanders to the alley. One EMT bent down to check the girl Steve had killed, while the other came over to where Dana was still holding Jared's body. Steve stood and went over to him. They talked quietly and then walked over to where Dana was sitting holding the body.

He bent down and put his hand on her shoulder. "Dana honey, the paramedics need to take him."

She shook her head and pulled him closer. "No. Not yet."

Steve sighed and looked up at the waiting paramedic. He turned back to her and tried again. "Dana. We need to let the paramedics see if there is anything they can do."

She looked up at him with tear-stained eyes, pleading. She knew she had to let go, but she couldn't. How could this have happened? It was so unfair; he had finally seen her, had finally loved her. After all these years, he loved her, and now, he was gone.

She held on to him for a few minutes longer, before finally releasing him to the paramedics. She felt hollow inside, as they took him from her and checked his vitals. Steve reached down and gently lifted her up off the ground.

As he led her away, she saw the paramedics shaking their heads and checking their watches. Dana had been to enough crime scenes to know what that meant; they were recording time of death. One paramedic walked over with a large black sheet and handed it to the man who'd been checking his watch. He laid it over Jared's lifeless body, and with that, Dana knew he was gone.

Chapter Twenty-Six

I t was late and the normally swamped city streets were barren of any semblance of human activity. But not dead. Night was when the nocturnal denizens of the metropolis came out to play. These were the creatures, both human and otherwise, who wandered the streets at night, as either predator or prey. They all stayed safely hidden in the shadows, watching as the Musketeer made his way toward the club where Jared had been murdered.

The area around the club was quieter than it should have been, and he noticed that the entire region was closed off by yellow crime scene tape. The scent of death and tragedy hung heavy in the air, keeping most creatures away. The Musketeer, however, reveled in the glorious aroma.

Rishut glowed brightly as the Musketeer ducked under the police tape and made his way down the small alley to where the violence had taken place. Two outlines, one of a man's body and one of a woman's, were drawn out on the pavement and bloodstains were still visible in many places. He bent down and touched the ground, feeling for the spiritual echo that had been created by the severity of the violence. He smirked, his nightmare black eyes darkening as the reflection of the tragic events that had taken place here played out before him. He ignored the death of the woman since she was of no consequence to him and fixated on the point where Steve had plunged his knife into Jared's body.

"Oh, what sweet irony," he murmured as he watched Jared's body fall to the ground. "I knew this would be interesting, but I never imagined that it would be so amusing. Oh, Tzedakah, you are black-hearted."

He started to rise when he saw Dana's specter come rushing to Jared's side. "Oh, what is this?" He stopped in his tracks as he observed her weeping and holding him as he died. The echo of Jared vainly trying to tell Dana about Steve. Dana bursting into tears, unable to save the man she loved. The futility of it all was sweeter than the sweetest of wines.

The Musketeer was so entranced by the scene, he did not notice his blade glowing brighter. By the time the warning registered, it was too late. He turned in time to see a fiery blade surge toward his head, and just barely got his own blade up to block the strike.

Even though he had managed to fend off the blow that surely would have removed his head from his body, the force of it sent him sprawling hard into a concrete wall. The wall cracked; cement particles rained down on the Musketeer's head.

He rose to his feet, removed his large-brimmed hat, and brushed off the debris. "I was wondering when you would show up, mon ami."

Nonchalantly he replaced the hat. The entire alley was bathed in a fierce glow that emanated from the blade of his assailant. The extremely dangerous

Sanctuary stood at the mouth of the alley with his weapons at the ready, blocking his retreat.

The angel growled and raised his sword to strike again, but this time the Musketeer was ready for him. The Musketeer was lithe, and he moved with frightening supernatural speed. He was on the angel before he even had time to react. His blade was thin and quick. But despite the fact that Sanctuary's blade was large and clumsy, he still managed to deflect each well-placed rapier strike.

Sparks of arcane energy and tongues of supernatural flames exploded with each blow, showering the small alleyway with color. The Musketeer jumped over a low swing from Sanctuary's fiery blade and ran along the wall, his body horizontal with the ground. He leaped over another fierce cut from Sanctuary and landed behind the warrior. He thrust his rapier forward, attempting to drive it through the angel's exposed back, but Sanctuary was already one step ahead of him, and bent backward, his back nearly reaching the ground, and batted the blade away.

The Musketeer used the energy of the parry to send himself into a full cartwheel, and with catlike reflexes, he flew into a backflip to evade yet another strike from Sanctuary. As he flew past the overextended angel, the Musketeer managed to strike a glancing blow to the warrior's exposed head. It was not a killing blow, but it did knock him off balance.

That was all the opening the Musketeer needed. As soon as his feet hit the ground, he brought his rapier down in a wicked slash that struck Sanctuary in the back. The angel staggered from the strength of the blow and fell forward. Sanctuary, however, was a skilled and experienced warrior, and he used the momentum from the force of the blow to send him into a forward roll. The maneuver took him far enough away from the Musketeer's second strike, that it whistled passed him, just barely missing his neck.

Sanctuary ended his roll too close to one of the building's walls. He tried to slow his momentum but slammed into it harder than he would have liked. He grunted in pain, but none of the wounds he had suffered were life-threatening. The Musketeer did not move to press his attack but stood a few paces away, his blade at the ready.

"Are you done, monsieur?" he asked. "I will admit this little diversion was fun, but we both know it will only end in a stalemate."

Sanctuary glowered up at him but knew what the Musketeer said was true. He might be able to hinder him, but even at his full power, Sanctuary doubted he could kill him. Likewise, the Musketeer could not completely destroy him. Even so, he needed to know what the Musketeer was doing here. If he had killed the new bearer before he had a chance to bond with the sword, then he needed to know. He himself could not wield Tzedakah, but he needed to make sure that it was not hindered or imprisoned by the Musketeer.

Sanctuary staggered to his feet and braced himself against the wall. "Why are you here, Renault?"

The Musketeer raised one eyebrow. "I always wanted to see the great city of New York, so I decided to come here on, how you say, holiday. Why, would you like to show me the sights?"

"Don't mock me, dog! I know why you are here in the city, but what I don't know is if you killed the man who died here last night."

"Ah." The Musketeer smirked. "Do you mean Tzedakah's new bearer? No, angel, I did not. I did follow him here, but I was merely curious, that is all."

"Don't toy with me, faithless one," he spat back. "I know you are here for more than just curiosity. Where is Tzedakah and his new bearer?"

At the mention of the name, the Musketeer's sword blazed angrily, and he hissed in disgust. "I have no idea where it is, and at this current moment, I don't care. You are worried that I came here to kill the little bastard, but what fun is there in that? I like a challenge and killing a fledgling bearer would be as much sport as, how you say, hunting fish in a barrel."

Sanctuary drew himself up to his full height, glowing in intensity. "If you are lying to me, I will rip you apart right here and now."

The Musketeer sighed and shook his head. "You have not changed in the hundreds of years I have known you, mon ami. You are still all intensity and fire. Let me give you a word of advice. You should try to enjoy what you do. Well, if that is possible for a being such as you. Perhaps He will not let you have fun. No joy, only duty for the ever-vigilant angel."

Sanctuary growled at the blasphemous statement, but he managed to somehow keep his cool. "Sorry if my idea of pleasure is not murdering women and children."

"To each his own," the Musketeer replied, not missing a beat. "Well, this has been enjoyable, but I must bid you adieu."

He turned away from Sanctuary and walked toward a nearby shadow cast by a large tree. As soon as he reached the darkness, he began to melt into it.

Before he had completely dissolved, he looked back at Sanctuary. "You are right to worry, mon ami. The new bearer is in danger, but not from me. Not yet, anyway." He said this last statement with a wicked smile, then faded into the darkness.

Chapter Twenty-Seven

The atmosphere in the small funeral home was somber. So many people had come out for Jared's funeral that they could not fit them all into the small sanctuary. Every pew was filled, and the walls were lined with people. Most of the attendees were police officers or those who had, in some capacity, worked with Jared. Old college friends had also come, as well as acquaintances from high school and younger.

The small room was decorated with flowers and pictures from his life. At the front of the room, the coffin rested, a large American flag draped across it. The viewing had been the day prior, and his parents had requested that the casket be closed for the actual funeral ceremony.

In the front row, Dana sat with Steve, resting her head on his shoulder. He hugged her close, the image of brotherly comfort. Her tear-stained face was red from crying, her slightly tattered hair veiling her eyes from curious glances.

She had barely spoken since the incident in the city and Steve was worried. He was not, however, worried for her, but rather worried about what Jared might have said the night he died. Even though she was acting polite, there was always the possibility that she was toying with him, waiting for just the right time to spring a trap. Either way, she was a loose end. He did not like loose ends.

Steve did not hear much of what was said by the endless stream of family and friends who pattered on about his dead brother. It was not that he did not love his brother; he had loved him as much as he loved anyone. It was just that it was physically painful for him to sit here and pretend that he cared. Steve wondered if he had been born this way or whether the circumstances of life had fashioned him into the monster he had become. That was, however, a philosophical question for another time. Today, he had to do his best to bring out the waterworks and solemnize the death of a loved one.

He really did feel bad that he'd had to kill Jared. Deep down he had never held any ill will for his older brother. In fact, he had liked him. Even loved him. At least, he had stronger feelings for Jared than he had for anyone else in his immediate family.

Beside him, Dana shuddered. He stroked her shoulder with his fingertips, coaxing her to relax.

Dear Dana. What should he do about her? Should he kill her? Certainly, it would most likely come to that, but it was too dangerous to kill her now. One dead cop could be survived, but two dead cops in a week's time, now that would cause too many people to take notice. So, for now, Dana lived.

She laid her head on his shoulder. He could feel her sobs rack her body. He held her tighter. Such a sympathetic friend.

It was mentally exhausting for him to be around so much emotion and grief. For years now, he had felt nothing when it came to normal human interactions. He knew what he was supposed to feel; he simply didn't.

Anyway, the dark-haired woman beside him was beautiful. The thought of seducing her was not unappealing, but he did not have any feelings for her other than simple lust. Oh well, maybe he would toy with her for a while before he killed her. At least to find out what Jared had told her in the last moments of his life. Certainly, if she knew it was him who'd killed Jared, she would have had him arrested already. Right? The not-knowing was driving him crazy.

He squeezed her shoulder hard, and she pulled away from him.

"What the heck? Why did you do that?" she whispered harshly. Her red-rimmed eyes were angry. "That hurt, Steve. God!"

She rubbed her shoulder and turned away to bury her face in his mom's chest and cry some more. Mrs. Caddret shot Steve an angry glance and mouthed for him to *be quiet*. He shrugged in mock confusion and turned away. He hunched over and placed his head in his hands, masking his anger with grief.

Someday he would kill his mother. He took solace in the fact that at least he'd taken her perfect son away from her. Yes, he may not have hated Jared, but by killing him, he had hurt his parents. That made him happy. He peered through his fingers at the casket and his father who was leading the service. So solemn.

Oh yes, his parent's pain was glorious. After all, they deserved it for what happened to Hope.

"I know it hurts when loved ones are taken from us before their time, but we must always remember that God is good. This was not His plan for Jared, but I have to believe He will use it for His good," Pastor Caddret said to the congregation. You could tell he was fighting back tears, but as always, his usual mask of pious conviction remained on his face.

His words infuriated Steve. God is good? What a joke. If God was so good, then why had He allowed Hope to die? If God was so good and all-powerful, why hadn't He showed up when Steve had prayed those many years ago?

He had grown up on stories of how God waited to deliver people from evil, but when he had really needed God to show up, He had not. In fact, if his father had not been so preoccupied with *God's* business, then perhaps he would have been home where he should have been, and Hope would not have died.

But for all his hot air, his father was right about one thing. It had not been God's plan for Jared to die; it had been his. *I guess God is not so powerful after all.*

Dana looked over at Steve. His long hair hung down over his face, but she could still make out one eye. She felt sorry for him and could only imagine what kind of grief he was dealing with. If she felt survivor's guilt, how much more must he? After all, he had been the first one on the scene. It must have deeply affected him. How could it not? As a homicide detective, she was used to seeing the terrible things people did to each other, but for someone who did not do what she did for a living, it must be absolutely life changing. He turned his head slightly to look at her and she blanched. The one eye she could make out was glowing a faint angry red.

She blinked and looked again. This time there was no glow, only the sad eyes she had seen earlier. It must have been her imagination. The grief getting to her. He smiled mournfully. She reached out her hand in comfort. He gave it a light squeeze. At just that moment, Pastor Caddret asked everyone to stand for the ending prayer. They released their hands and stood with bowed heads.

"Dear Heavenly Father," Pastor Caddret said, his voice thick with emotion, "we know that Jared is with You now, and we thank You for Your Son who came and died to make that possible. We know that death is not the end, and that it is no small comfort for those of us who are left behind as Jared leaves this mortal realm and enters eternity with You. Though we may miss him, we know that we will see him again. The Holy Spirit comforts those of us who mourn this terrible loss. Be with us as we walk through this dark time. Thank you, God. We love You and thank You for the time we did get to spend with Jared. In Jesus' name. Amen."

Jared's favorite worship song played softly over the speakers as the pallbearers came forward and took their places next to the coffin. All of them were police officers save Steve, who was positioned near the rear on the right side. As they walked, he passed his mother, sister, and Dana. Upon seeing his mother's tears, he smiled ever so slightly. Everyone was to overcome with grief to notice his smirk.

Everyone, that is, except Dana.

Chapter Twenty-Eight

Once Jared's casket had been placed in the hearse and all the attendees had retreated to their cars, the procession left the small funeral home and headed toward the cemetery. It was a long procession, and police officers on motorcycles went before the cars, blocking streets and making sure that the way was clear. Before long, the procession wound its way to a large cemetery sitting on a series of hills just outside the town.

As each car parked, passengers got out and made their way up to Jared's casket. Old Glory was draped over the casket and three officers waited with their rifles at the ready as the family and friends took their places near the gravesite. Chairs had been set out for the family, but Steve declined his seat next to his parents, offering it to Dana instead. She graciously accepted and took her seat. Steve took his place standing behind his parents as Dana watched him out of the corner of her eyes.

Had she really seen him smirk earlier? No, she must have been mistaken. Why would he smile like that? She shook her head ever so slightly at the thought. After all, she was sure she had seen his eyes glowing red during the service earlier. No, her grief was affecting her more than she realized, and it was causing her to see things.

Steve noticed her glancing at him, and stiffened. Why was she watching him? Did she suspect something was amiss with him? Maybe he had not been careful enough in his play-acting grief.

Calm down, Steve. Keep your head about you or you really are going to slip up and give something away. How do people act sad in movies? Just do that.

He lowered his head and brushed away imaginary tears. *Relax!* he told himself. No one knew anything and no one suspected. As always, it had removed any evidence that Steve may have left at the scene. There was nothing to worry about.

Gunfire cracked as the color guard fired off a three-volley salute. When had the order been given to fire? He cursed his inattention.

Had Dana been watching him just now? No matter, his quiet reflection could very easily be construed as grief. He sighed heavily, attempting to release the tension that had been building up inside. Steve continued watching as Dana held his sister as she sobbed. His father's head was down, and he had one arm gently resting on his mother who wept inconsolably. A lone officer lifted a bugle to his lips and the strong, lonely notes of "Taps" flowed. There was not a dry eye to be found as his brother's casket was lowered slowly into the ground.

The rest of the burial was a blur. He was glad when it was finally over. Feigning sorrow was exhausting, and he had a headache. Close family and friends were all gathered in his parents' small house, eating and reminiscing. The place was packed. Steve desperately wanted a beer, but the fridge was a dry zone. The strongest drink he'd find here was soda.

He was just thinking that he'd spent enough time hugging people when he spied Dana quietly slipping out the front door. Great, he needed a break too. His parents were busy talking to some obscure relative and no one noticed him quietly step out to follow her.

It was getting dark, and Dana was nowhere in sight. Angry at missing her, he kicked the ironwork railing that framed his parent's porch. "Fuck."

"Watch your language," came a voice from around the side of the house. "You know your mom would be upset if she heard you talking like that."

He bent over the side of the railing and found Dana resting up against the house. She had her legs pulled up to her chest and a small wisp of smoke meandered up from a half-burned cigarette.

"When did you start smoking?" Steve asked. He put his hands on the top of the railing and vaulted over it, landing next to Dana.

She looked at the cigarette in her hand, shrugged, and took a drag. "I don't."

Sitting down next to her, he reached for the cigarette. She handed it to him, and he took a long drag and exhaled, reveling in the relaxing effect it had on his brain. He handed it back to her, but she ignored him. He shrugged, took another drag, then flicked the butt onto the driveway. "You gonna be okay?"

She hugged her legs tighter. More tears welled up in her already red eyes. "I doubt it."

Steve felt a twinge of pity for her. That made it a bit easier for him to feign concern. He knew that he had to pretend to care long enough not to arouse her suspicions. He placed his arm around her and drew her close. She resisted at first but eventually gave in, letting her head come to rest on his shoulder. Steve said nothing for a long while as he sat there holding her. When he finally felt that he had shown enough concern, he brought up the subject of Jared's death.

"I still can't believe he is dead."

Dana said nothing but continued to sit quietly next to him.

"It all happened so fast and the whole night is still a blur to me. Any word on what the police found out?" he said, doing his best to keep the anxiety he felt out of his voice.

"I don't want to talk about it, Steve," she said, pulling away.

Shit, he'd moved too soon and now she had closed up. He decided to take a different approach.

"I just wish I could have spoken to him one last time before he died. You know, to tell him I love him and all."

She sighed heavily. Another tear tracked down her cheek. "Yeah."

Steve waited for her to add to that sentiment, maybe tell him what he needed to hear. He didn't want to spook her a second time by asking too many questions too quickly. But he was getting impatient.

"You were the last person to speak to him. Did you get to finally tell him how you felt?"

Dana turned on him angrily. "I said I didn't want to talk about it!" She jumped up to her feet. "He died in my arms, Steve. I watched as the light left his eyes." Her voice cracked and she began to cry again, like women do.

Steve stood up and put his arms around her, pulling her close. "I know, I know. I am sorry. I just miss him."

She sobbed in his arms as he held her. Damn, she was too upset right now for him to get any definitive answers from her. It was okay, he had time. When everything finally calmed down, he would try again. At least he had a believable excuse to stay upstate. No one would question why he stayed, and his bandmates would understand his prolonged leave of absence. He could stay up here as long as it took for him to get the information he needed. He would find out what his brother had told her right before he died, and if she even had a hint of what had really happened, he would kill her too.

Chapter Twenty-Nine

All there was, was darkness, complete and total. It was like nothing he had ever known or believed possible. Not darkness as in night or a shuttered room, for even in those places there was some small measure of light. Here, it was as if light itself had never been.

Had he ever known light, or did he just imagine it? The darkness smothering him was all he knew. It swirled around him, pressed in on him, a dank sea threatening to drown him. Just when all that he knew had nearly faded, a glimmer of hope sparked in his heart. It was faint and barely noticeable, but it was there, nonetheless. He grasped at that hope, refusing to be consumed.

The oppressive darkness suddenly shook and raged around him as brilliant tendrils of illumination tore through it, obliterating great swaths of blackness. The light was nothing more than a glimmer, no brighter than the faintest of stars in the night sky, but it shone with such power and force that the darkness fled from it. In the complete blackness, all he could see was that light. It grew in intensity and chased away the shadows and the despair that had almost claimed him.

He reached out to it, grabbing hold of it the way a drowning man reaches for a life-preserver. He knew he had to reach it before the darkness claimed him. He knew it with every fiber of his being. If he did not, he was sure that everything he was, had been or ever could be, would be lost. With an internal fortitude that he never knew he possessed, he pulled himself from the clutching coils of the writhing darkness and embraced the tiny star.

His eyes opened to... darkness.

But it was different.

His senses had returned. Even if he couldn't see his surroundings, he could feel them. Before, there had been nothing, as if he were floating in a formless void. But now his fingers touched silk. His hands felt something solid. It was soft and padded like a pillow but on something solid. He tried to move but found he was constrained on all sides. He couldn't shift his body more than a few inches in any direction. He reached his hand up and it struck something hard. Where was he?

"Hello," he said hesitantly. His voice sounded strange and unfamiliar.

"Hello?" he repeated, louder this time. The voice he heard startled him. It was not the voice he remembered, but he knew for certain it originated from him.

"Welcome back," another voice said. The voice was deep and strong, and even though it did not speak loudly, it shook him.

"Where am I?" he asked the voice. Again, his own voice seemed strange to his ears. Ethereal and wispy.

"You are in the mortal realm," the voice replied.

"The what?" he asked, shaking his head to try to relieve the confusion he felt.

"Do not worry, the disorientation will pass."

He tried to raise his hand again and it once again struck the hard surface. He tried his feet and found the same result. Was he in a box? He wished he had some light so he could see where he was. As if something had read his mind, a small light appeared above his head, illuminating his surroundings.

Strangely the sudden explosion of light did not hurt his eyes. Somewhere in his mind, he thought that it should have caused him pain, but it did not. He gazed at the small light and saw that it was a tiny locket. The locket hovered just above his face, shining with pure white light. Wait—he knew this locket.

"Is that better?" the voice asked.

"How did you know I wanted light?" he asked curiously. "I did not ask for it."

"I heard your desire for it in your mind."

"You read my mind?" He directed the question to the hovering locket, although he felt foolish talking to jewelry.

"Of course. I can also communicate directly to your mind. How do you think I am talking to you now? As a locket, I have no mouth."

"Do you have a brain?" he asked, smirking.

He examined his surroundings now that he had light to see with. He was lying down in a small room or possibly a cupboard of some kind. The entirety of the small space was covered in soft white pillowy material and had little room to move.

"Hey—am I in a coffin?"

"Yes."

"Yes, I am in a coffin or yes, you have a brain?"

"Both," the voice said blandly, apparently not picking up on the sarcasm. "I am sentient, though I do not exist and think as you do."

He shrugged off the voice's attempt at explaining itself. "Locket, why am I in a coffin?"

It was silent as if contemplating how best to respond to the question. "Because you are dead."

The revelation of his demise sent a shock wave of memories surging through his mind. He grabbed his head with his hands and attempted to curl up in a ball as the images thundered through his mind.

Pictures from his childhood as his family moved from church plant to church plant. His baby sister cooing. Pain washed over him at the sight. Pictures of school graduations and sporting events he had played flashed by next, bringing with them feelings of warmth and joy. He saw himself going through the academy and then finally graduating.

Eventually, the memories stopped at the face of a beautiful woman with long brown hair and luminous dark eyes. He knew her face, but her name... It was at the edge of his mind. Finally it hit him.

"Dana!"

He remembered everything now. Remembered how much he loved her and with the remembering came more pain. The pain turned to panic as a picture of his brother flashed before his eyes. He remembered the pain of the knife and not being able to breathe. He had died. Steve had killed him.

"I have to get to her. She is not safe—he will kill her!"

He flailed at the walls of the coffin, like a caged animal his pounding muffled by the pillowed sides.

"Calm yourself," the voice soothed. "She is safe for the time being."

"Calm myself?" he spat. "He will kill her. Do you understand? He will find her and torture her in ways I don't want to think about. I know he will. I may not know why my brother is doing what he is, but one thing I do know is that just like any other murderer, he will not want loose ends, and she is a loose end."

"Jared. She is safe. He has not harmed her."

His name washed over him like ice water, Jared froze. He blinked his eyes and grunted. It felt like he was waking from a dream, no, a nightmare. Or was this the nightmare? He could not be certain, but with the mentioning of his name came more memories.

He remembered the darkness. He shuddered at the thought of it and felt for the sides of the coffin in order to prove that he was no longer lost.

"You will not return to the darkness," the voice said in response to his thoughts. "You need not fear it. It was a place of transition and nothing more."

Jared went to blow out a long breath but found that he had none to expel. Curious, he reached for his neck and felt for a pulse. Nothing. How could that be?

"Locket, how... am I alive?"

The locket hovered and glowed but did not respond immediately.

"You are not alive, at least not in the biological sense. You exist still because I have chosen you and I will it to be."

"You what?" Jared asked incredulously.

"I will it."

Jared's thoughts raced again as he tried to grasp what this thing was saying to him. "Locket, what are you?"

"I am Tzedakah. I am Justice."

"Metaphorically speaking, or as in the actual spirit of?" Jared asked. This whole situation was so surreal, and he was having a hard time wrapping his head around it.

"Yes."

Jared frowned. This was all so impossible, and yet, he remembered dying and he remembered the darkness. He shifted uncomfortably. Not out of physical discomfort, but rather because he was beginning to get antsy. He glared at the locket still hovering above him. His fingers itched to reach out and grasp it. Before the thought had crossed his mind, he had done it. Had he done that on purpose or had something else compelled him?

"We will continue this conversation later. He is here."

"Who is here?" Jared asked.

"The one who converses."

Then the world went dark again.

Chapter Thirty

Jeremy Wagner sat on a small bench that resided near the walkway in a rather large cemetery, staring up at the night sky, his mouth slightly agape in awe and his legs swinging. This was his first time this far upstate, and he was awed by its beauty. Most people thought of New York as nothing more than a great sprawling metropolis, but to those who called the state home, they knew it to be so much more. Two mountain ranges, thousands of acres of undisturbed forests, lakes, rivers, gorges, and canyons made New York one of the most beautiful states in the union. It was a pity that when people thought of New York all they saw was the city.

This late at night, the cemetery was quiet and peaceful. Jeremy enjoyed the solace it brought. He wasn't a creep, mind you, and it was not his usual habit to spend his nights wandering around cemeteries, but of all the strange places God had led him to, this one was not so bad. The cemetery was well kept, and fresh flowers adorned many gravestones. Grieving families had erected crypts and set up memorial statues from the slight and unassuming, to the colossal and gaudy. All in all, it was a beautiful place—at least, if you were into that sort of thing.

He yawned and looked at his watch. It was getting late, and he really hoped that whatever had brought him here would happen soon. It was a clear chilly night, so he stood up and moved around a bit in order to warm himself. Jeremy stretched his average frame, and the bangs from his short, unkempt dark brown hair fell into his eyes. He blew at them, trying to get the wayward strands away from his usually laugh-lined bright brown eyes, but they stubbornly refused to comply. He puckered his lips, crossed his arms, and pouted like a toddler at his rebellious bangs.

Seriously, it was getting really late, and he just wanted to go back to his hotel room and crash. Of course, if he did, there was no way that God would let him sleep. No, He would keep him up all night, pestering him about duty and the importance of what he needed to do. What exactly it was he needed to do tonight, God had yet to reveal.

Jeremy exhaled and his hot breath condensed, making it look like he was breathing smoke. He breathed out again, only this time harder, growling like he imagined a dragon would. He'd have to ask a dragon if they really did make sounds like that if he ever met one.

Jeremy's eyes wandered up to the night sky. It was filled with stars. More stars than he had ever seen before. He could get used to this, he thought. It was nearly impossible to see even one star over the ambient light of the city, let alone the hundreds and thousands he was seeing tonight.

"It is time," a voice spoke.

"Really? Already? Gee, it only seemed like two seconds and not forever. I mean, I only got frostbite in one of my fingers, so that's good," Jeremy told the voice he knew so well.

It was God's. Of course, no one believed him when he told them that. When he was a kid, his own parents had tried to have him committed because they thought he was schizophrenic. To tell the truth, for a while he believed that, too. Then it had happened.

A little girl got lost in Central Park. Her parents called the police, and before long it seemed like the entire city of New York was out looking for the little girl. After a day of searching, the girl was still missing. He and his parents were helping look when the voice directed him to one of the bridges that dotted the park. Underneath it, he had found the girl.

She was unconscious and had a nasty gash in her forehead. She had fallen and struck her head and needed immediate medical attention. Thankfully, she recovered, and life returned to normal for everyone except him. Ever since that day, he realized that the voice that was speaking to him was real. He started listening instead of suppressing it.

"So, what is it this time?" he asked unenthusiastically. "A demon? No, I know, it's a restless spirit that needs me to help them find peace and move on. Maybe I should've brought a camera crew with me and we could film a ghost-hunting show."

God was silent, but Jeremy could sense His amusement. For some reason, God liked his sarcasm. Jeremy really did pity people who did not know this side of God's character. The Almighty had a wonderful sense of humor, as well as a highly developed appreciation of irony.

"With the jawbone of an ass," he muttered from the Bible, "I made asses out of..."

A strange sense of expectancy fell over him. Whatever was about to happen, it was important.

God led him farther into the cemetery and to a fresh grave where the grass had not yet had time to grow. Crouching down, he tried to read the name on the headstone. It was too dark, so he reached into his pocket and pulled out his cell phone. Blue light illuminated the etching.

"Jared Caddret," he read aloud. "He was only twenty-eight years old when he died. Now, that is sad. How did he die?"

Before God could answer him, the ground beneath his feet began to shift and he fell backward in fright. It took a lot to scare Jeremy. In all the years God had been talking to him, he had seen many things both amazing and horrific, but zombies clawing their way up out of the grave was a first.

A hand broke through the ground. Surprised, Jeremy jumped back up on his feet. Wide-eyed, he watched as the hand turned into an arm and then a man's head broke through the dirt. Strangely, he barely disturbed the dirt as he seemed to phase through the earth to stand atop the grave. To Jeremy, the being seemed to have floated up through the ground, more like a spirit than a zombie.

"Really?" Jeremy said out loud, staring wide-eyed at the man standing before him. "So, we really are ghost hunting? Seriously, I should've brought a camera."

The man Jeremy assumed was Jared Caddret seemed to be confused as he surveyed his surroundings. He held up his fist and a strange soft glow seeped through his fingers.

That's one big lightning bug clutched in his closed fist, Jeremy thought.

The man, like a basilisk, turned his eyes on Jeremy and paralyzed him with shock. To Jeremy's dismay, where the man's eyes should have been, there was nothing but writhing darkness.

Jeremy's eyes widened in recognition when he saw those nightmare black eyes. "Oh crap. This is not good."

He got up and casually brushed himself off while Jared scanned his surroundings as if seeing the world for the first time. Sighing deeply, Jeremy plopped himself down on a nearby headstone.

So, the Shogun was dead, Jeremy realized. He had to be dead if this—whatever he was—was standing here in front of him.

The man stopped looking around and fixed his eyes on him. Jeremy knew what those eyes saw when they fixed on people. At least, he had a vague understanding of what it was they saw. The Shogun had once told him about the dark gaze. Jeremy shuddered as the man continued to stare at him.

"See anything interesting?" he asked.

The man did not speak as his eyes continued to bore into him.

The intensity of his gaze never wavered as he spoke. "Honestly, I have no idea what I am seeing. It is like the world is the same, yet different. If that makes any sense?"

"Yes, actually it does," Jeremy replied, shifting uncomfortably. "So, I take it you haven't been dead long."

Jared's face fell at that, and the hand holding the locket dropped.

Jeremy smiled apologetically. "Too soon?"

The locket suddenly glowed brightly and shifted in Jared's hand, transforming. When the glowing finally died down and he opened his hand, the locket had transformed into a silver ring. Jared stared at the ring for a moment before compulsorily putting it on one of his fingers. He stared at the ring thoughtfully.

"I guess I haven't had much time to think about it," Jared replied, looking at the man again. "I am sorry."

Jeremy lifted an eyebrow. "Sorry for what?"

"For your life," he said matter-of-factly.

"Oh that. I guess you are seeing everything about me now. Hopefully, you won't want to kill me for that bad habit I couldn't shake during puberty."

"Just puberty?" Jared said, flashing a sarcastic smile.

Jeremy choked back a laugh. "Well, this is different—you have a sense of humor! From my experiences with the one I knew, people like you don't usually have one. Maybe the reanimation process is different for each individual. Reanimation is a good word for this, right?" He gestured to Jared with both his hands.

"My ring said reanimation is an accurate if simple explanation. At least, I guess it is my ring that is speaking," he said, examining the ring on his finger again.

"I have never seen it take on the form of a ring before," Jeremy said curiously. "Usually it is a sword. Of course, I have only known one of your kind and it was always in the shape of a Japanese katana when he had it. He liked to ask me questions about God and heaven. I guess he was curious."

"Are you a minister or a priest?" Jared asked. "My parents are pastors."

Jeremy slowly got to his feet and stretched. He shivered a bit from the cold and rubbed his arms with his hands. "No, at least not in the traditional sense, anyway. God talks to me, is all."

Jared nodded his head slightly.

"I know. It sounds crazy, right? But God really does talk to me. In fact, I usually can't get Him to shut up. I find it so ironic that the rest of the world complains about how silent He is. I just wish He would stop talking to me when I am in the shower."

"Interesting. Tzedakah says that you speak the truth."

"Well, he would know," Jeremy replied. "Anyway, can we continue this conversation back at my hotel room? It's freaking cold out here, and I am tired."

Jared suddenly lurched back as if avoiding some unseen assailant, and Jeremy bolted upright his eyes darting around searching for any signs of danger. The flap of bat wings reverberated through the air as a dark shadow darted past the two men. Jared's ring glowed, and with the speed of thought, it transformed into a large blazing sword. He crouched down and raised the weapon, searching for any sign of whatever it was that had just flown by them.

Even though Tzedakah did not speak to him directly, he could sense what it felt. Darkness. Danger. The connection the sword had made with him was so instant and complete, it was as if they were no longer separate beings but one singular entity. It felt strange at first; his instinct was to fight against the sword's intrusion into his consciousness. With this resistance, the connection wavered.

As if sensing the hesitation, the creature attacked again. This time the blow landed, sending Jared flying into his own headstone. It cracked under the force of the impact, the top part of it breaking off. Despite the power of the blow, he wasn't stunned. In fact, he felt no pain at all.

The creature hovered in the air, beating its enormous bat-like wings. It was humanoid in appearance but had large horns protruding from its head and bulbous red eyes. It wore dirty iron armor and brandished six-inch claws on each of its six fingers.

The creature bared its fang-filled maw and hissed, "What great fortune my dark master has given me tonight by delivering you into my hands. I, the great and powerful Baal Shaffar, shall have the privilege of slaying a fledgling Justice."

With a blur of motion, the demon threw itself at Jared again. Before he could react, the creature's nails were suddenly in his face, only inches from his eyes. Gripping Tzedakah with both hands, he managed to bring up the sword just in time to deflect the raking claws. Sparks flew and he could smell ozone as the nails scraped across the black metal. He pushed back against the demon and managed to fling its arm to the side, knocking it slightly off balance. Tzedakah screamed in his mind and he stumbled and shook his head violently as the sword attempted to invade his consciousness. The demon noticed the turmoil and grinned.

The demon lashed out with his tail, striking Jared hard on his legs, sweeping his feet out from under him. He knew he was falling and that he was in trouble, but his body felt heavy and slow like he was moving through water. The demon struck him as he fell, slashing his claws against his chest, ripping his shirt and tearing into his flesh. He felt the sudden pressure of the talons as they tore through his body and watched as gore and flesh sprayed into the air, but it was like he was watching it happen in a dream rather than real life. He barely registered the impact as he hit the ground.

Jeremy was unable to follow the movements of the battle, but he could sense that Jared was in trouble. He snapped into motion, drawing a small cross-shaped dagger from its hiding place in his coat, and launched himself at the demon. He landed on the creature's back just as it was lifting its arm for another blow, grabbed onto one of its wings for leverage, and drove the blade of his dagger into the back of the unsuspecting demon.

It howled in pain and thrashed wildly, trying to throw Jeremy off its back. He held on for dear life, riding the demon like a champion bull rider before it managed to grab one of his legs and pull itself free. It roared as it slammed Jeremy into the ground, leaving him stunned and gasping for air.

The demon glared down at the prostrate Jeremy, its red eyes burning with hatred. "Foolish human, I will rip you apart."

Jeremy groaned and tried to get up, but he was too dazed. "Sorry, but God says otherwise," he managed to croak.

The demon's eyes glinted menacingly as it stared down at Jeremy. It sneered, exposing enormous razor-sharp serrated teeth. "Your God will not save you—" The demon's words suddenly became indistinct gurgling and choking, and its eyes went wide in shock. It clawed at its chest frantically as the flesh there suddenly protruded outward as if something were trying to break free from inside its torso. Jeremy smirked as the blue glowing tip of a familiar black sword burst out of the demon's sternum.

The creature looked down at the protruding blade incredulously. Jared yanked it out and the gurgling demon fell to one knee, grasping at the gaping hole in its torso. Mortally wounded, the demon glared at Jeremy, who was still lying on his back, before dissipating into smoke as it passed from the mortal realm back to hell. The last thing to go was the creature's large red eyes which remained fixed on Jeremy until the very end.

Jeremy got to his feet, nursing his bruised left arm. He glared at Jared who was now shaking his head and seeming to be arguing with himself. "What the heck just happened?"

Jared frowned at him. "We were attacked by a demon. Tzedakah says it was the prince of Binghamton or something like that. It also says more are on the way."

Jeremy shook his head incredulously. "That's not what I am talking about. I'm not stupid, I know what a demon is. What I meant was, what the hell happened to you? You should've made quick work of a lightweight like that. God! The Shogun would have trashed that guy before I even knew it was here. I don't know what kind of cop you were in life, but you sure are a crappy... whatever you are."

"I don't know," Jared stammered looking down at the sword in his hands. "I don't know what happened. I think the sword tried to take me over, if that makes any sense, and I stopped it."

"Seriously?" Jeremy rolled his eyes. "We were in the middle of a fight for our lives, and you decided you didn't want the help of a supernaturally powerful talking sword? Wow, you really are a piece of work." He flung his hands up toward the sky. "God, what in the world were you thinking of bringing me here? Are you *trying* to get me killed?"

"Don't be so dramatic," Jared shot back. "What do you expect from me, anyway? Just ten minutes ago I woke up in a coffin and now, poof, I'm fighting demons and conversing with a talking sword."

The distant sound of flapping wings and howls snapped both men out of their pointless argument. Jeremy whipped his head back and forth as if unseen enemies hid in every shadow. Jared turned west and stared off into the night sky. "They are still a few leagues off, but they will be here soon. We should go."

"Okay, but they will most likely find us, no matter where we go in the city."

Jared's expression suddenly became glassy, and he seemed to be in some kind of trance. He turned to Jeremy and put his arm around him. His voice was the same but different somehow as if someone else was speaking through him. "Don't worry, I will protect us from them and take us somewhere where they will temporarily be unable to locate us."

Before he'd finished speaking, there was a brilliant flash of light and the two men were gone.

Chapter Thirty-One

Jeremy was hunched over a rather unremarkable bush, throwing up everything in his stomach and contemplating just how much he hated teleporting. He wiped his mouth on his sleeve and looked around. Just as he suspected, they were standing outside the door to his motel room.

"I guess there is no need to ask how you knew where I was staying, is there?" Jeremy said as he straightened up. "Who am I speaking with, by the way?"

Jared stared at Jeremy for a moment before he shook his head, attempting to dispel the disorientation he felt. "What happened? Are there more demons?"

"Well, that answers my question." Jeremy fished in his pocket for his room key. "Put down the sword; we are safe for now. Let's go inside and get out of the cold. I am exhausted, famished, and I have to pee."

Jared searched the night for any hidden enemies then, satisfied, he followed Jeremy into the motel room. Jeremy had already turned on the lights and tossed his coat over the nearest chair. The hotel room was nothing special, but it was clean, and Jared plopped into one of the desk chairs while Jeremy went to the bathroom.

Tzedakah still glowed but softer than it had when they were attacked. Jared studied the sword. The blade appeared to be made of some kind of steel, but a jet-black metal that was rough like iron. He ran his thumb across the edge, testing its sharpness. Even though the blade seemed weathered and aged, it was keen as the finest razor.

Jared was no scholar, but he did have a rudimentary knowledge of swords and ancient weaponry. When he was young, he had been fascinated by medieval history. This looked like a European long sword with a cruciform hilt.

Upon further inspection, he noticed that the hilt was in the shape of a scale held by a woman. The cross guard was the scale's beam, and the quillons were in the shape of pans. The grip was the shape of a woman's arm and had what appeared to be a white linen cloth wrapped around it. The entire weapon was wrought iron black, from the tip to the pommel, which was fashioned into the face of a beautiful woman wearing a blindfold.

Jeremy returned from the bathroom after a few minutes and opened the small refrigerator. He pulled out a half-eaten sandwich and a can of soda, popped it open, and drained half of the sweet liquid in a single gulp. Then he munched his sandwich. "So, any idea of what we are supposed to do next? I need to get back to the city tomorrow for work. I'd like to get at least a few hours of sleep before I have to head back. So, if we could speed this along, that would be great."

Jared looked up from inspecting the sword to gaze at Jeremy. Flashes of information raced through his mind in an instant, too fast for any human mind to comprehend. Somehow, he registered it all and not only understood what he was seeing but, remembered every bit of it as if he had a photographic memory.

"Why does your life flash before my eyes every time I look at you?" he asked. His voice still seemed strange to his ears as if someone else was speaking through him. "At least, all of the horrible things you have ever done or have ever been done to you."

Jeremy continued to chew on his sandwich as he contemplated the question. "Honestly, I don't know. I think it has something to do with the sword, it being the 'Spirit of Justice' and all."

"That makes sense, I guess. Why can't I see any of the happy moments of your life? You must have some that are not so... depressing."

Jeremy chuckled and drained the rest of his drink. "Well, once when I was two, my daddy gave me a candy bar before beating me. That was nice." He smiled. "Of course I have good memories, everyone does. But why do you only see the dark ones?" He shrugged. "I honestly don't know. Maybe you should ask the glowing ghost blade."

Jared scowled. "You really are no help at all."

"Sorry. I can tell you one thing, though. If you don't find a way to connect with that sword there, you won't be around for very long."

"Are there more demons out there?"

"Demons are the least of your worries, brother. They are lightweights compared to some of the other baddies I have crossed paths with over the years."

"Great." Jared sighed. "I hate the feeling of not being in control of my own actions. It's disconcerting."

Jeremy smiled. "I can see that. But, uncomfortable or not, you have to find a way to deal with it. On a different note, let me ask you something. Do you have the sudden urge to kill me?"

He shook his head. "That is the second time you mentioned me possibly wanting to kill you. Why?"

"Well, you are the new Spirit of Justice, after all."

"What does being Justice have to do with killing you?"

Jeremy grew serious. "When you looked at me, you not only saw what happened to me, but all the things I did. I am no saint. So, I've got to know, did you have a reaction to anything I did, or rather, did the sword?"

Jared's eyes seemed to bore into him as he contemplated the question. "Yes, kind of. I don't really understand what I saw or what I felt. I don't think it wanted to kill you. At least, not right now. Honestly, it is hard to distinguish between what are my feelings and what are the sword's. It's all so jumbled up in my head."

Jeremy crumpled his empty can and tossed it into the garbage next to the desk. "Well, I guess I can relax, now that I don't have to worry about you killing me in my sleep."

That settled, Jeremy yawned and decided he was going to call it a night. He had just made it into the bathroom to brush his teeth when he heard the door slam. Jared was gone.

"What the hell?" Jeremy swore as he grabbed his coat off the chair and ran out the door after him.

By the time he had made it outside and to the walkway, he could just make out Jared racing down the street toward the small gas station on the corner. He took off after him, moving as fast as he could. He watched as Jared reached the intersection and jumped across it in one supernatural leap. Jeremy was nowhere near catching up, and his breath was coming in short gasps.

Shots rang out, shattering the quiet.

No, God, no!

Jeremy redoubled his efforts and pushed himself harder. Just as he reached the intersection, he saw Jared standing stone faced in front of the convenience store. He watched, horrified, as a figure came running out and stumbled right into Jared who was waiting for him directly in front of the door.

The man, if that is what he could be called since he was no more than seventeen, stopped short before he ran directly into him. Jeremy could see that the boy had a gun in his hand and what appeared to be a bag full of cash in the other. Jeremy's pace had slowed from exhaustion and he gasped for air as he continued toward the inevitable confrontation.

The boy raised the gun and pointed it at Jared who stood staring at him, his sword ablaze. Getting closer, Jeremy could see that the kid in the black hoodie was tall and lanky, his wide-staring eyes wild.

"Don't do it, kid," Jeremy said to himself under his breath.

"What do you think you gonna do with that blade against my gun, man? I will cap your ass if you don't get out of my way," the kid said. He was trying to be intimidating but his voice cracked.

Jeremy had finally reached the other side of the intersection when Jared stirred. He twirled the glowing sword in one hand and pointed it at the young man. "Dejuan Johnson, you are guilty of the murder of Mary Salisbury," he said, his voice ethereal and frightening.

Jeremy reached the two combatants just in time to see Jared swing his sword at the boy with lightning-quick speed. Before the sword plunged through the young man, however, it stopped. Jeremy could see the terror on Dejuan's face as he stared at the glowing blade that was now touching his chest.

"Jared!" Jeremy shouted. "Stop—he's just a kid!"

Jared was grimacing and straining in a battle of wills. The boy, seeing his hesitation, raised his gun and fired. *Crack!* The shot echoed down the street.

The darkness in Jared's eyes seemed to grow in intensity and the atmosphere around him became palpably dangerous.

"No," Jeremy whispered as Jared plunged the glowing sword into the young man's chest.

The boy's eyes went wide, and his mouth opened but no sound came out. His gun clattered to the pavement at Jared's feet. Jeremy's nose was filled with the metallic smell of blood as the boy futilely grasped at the blade in his chest. He continued to watch in horror as the light in the boy's eyes finally faded and his struggling stopped. He slumped forward toward Jared, driving the sword deeper into his body.

The young man's head fell forward till it rested on Jared's shoulder. He carefully withdrew his sword from the boy and gently laid him down on the pavement. He placed a hand over the young man's lifeless eyes and closed them.

"I tried to stop myself," Jared said softly. "He shot the clerk during the robbery. I sensed it back in the room and Tzedakah took over."

All Jeremy could do was stare in dismay at the boy's lifeless body. He knew that Tzedakah's judgments were always just, but killing a boy like this, seemed wrong to him.

Jeremy's voice cracked as he said, "He was just a kid."

"I know. But he murdered the store clerk, and he was guilty."

"Guilty?" Jeremy retorted. "Jared, he was just a kid."

"I know," Jared shot back, the darkness in his eyes writhing angrily. "Don't you think I know that? I tried to stop but when he shot at me, I lost control."

Jeremy backed away in fright as Jared turned on him, the sword in his hand glowing brightly. "Whoa now, big guy. Just calm down."

Jared glowered at Jeremy, then turned his anger on the sword. "This is not me at all! I would never kill a kid, no matter what he had done." He looked up at Jeremy, who was bathed in the sword's soft blue light. "What kind of monster have I become?"

Jeremy had no answer for him. He just shook his head as he once again looked at the dead boy. He wished he had the right words to say to put Jared's mind at ease, but all he felt was sick.

The sword flared, and a pulse of blue energy surged out from it, hitting the convenience store. All the electronics sparked and went dark.

Ducking, Jeremy said, "What was that?"

Jared shrugged. "An electromagnetic pulse to knock out the cameras and destroy the recording of us. Come on, we need to go before the police get here."

With that said, he started walking back the way they had come. Jeremy took one last look at the boy before hurrying after Jared.

When Jeremy finally made it back to the motel, he found his door wide open and Jared sitting just inside the doorway on the floor. His head was back, his eyes closed. He appeared to be sleeping. The sword had returned to the shape of a ring. A faint dark blue band glowing softly on his hand.

Jeremy shut the door and eyed Jared as he moved to sit on the bed. Unsure of what to say, he decided that it was best to let Jared initiate any conversation. It did not take long before he spoke.

"What kind of monster have I become?" he said softly. Even though his eyes were closed, Jared's face was contorted into an expression of pain.

Jeremy sighed. "You are not a monster."

"Really?" Jared's nightmare black eyes flicked open. "Only a monster would murder a teenager."

Taken aback by the vehemence of Jared's words, Jeremy did not immediately respond. Only moments before, he had watched Jared kill the young robber, and he could not lie to himself that it hadn't bothered him. Even though the act had seemed to be cold-blooded, however, he knew that was not necessarily the case. The boy had murdered the store clerk, and even though what Jared had done still troubled him, from what Jeremy saw, the young man was unrepentant of his crimes.

Of course, the boy was most likely scared at having been caught and simply reacted to the obstacle in his way. In truth, however, what Jared had done, harsh as it was, could be construed as justice. Even though he knew this to be true in his head, Jeremy could not shake the sense of revulsion causing his stomach to churn.

Jared took Jeremy's silence as an affirmation of his conclusion. He grimaced bitterly. "Now I understand why you asked me earlier if I wanted to kill you. Perhaps you should be concerned."

Jeremy swallowed hard. "I figure if you were going to kill me, you would have done it already," he said with a confidence that he didn't feel. "Look, I can't imagine what you are going through, but I have known one other like you and he was not a monster. Dangerous, yes, but not a monster."

Jared leaned back against the wall. "The clerk had two kids," he said after a few minutes of silence. "She was a single mom working two jobs to support her family. Her husband had been killed in a drunk-driving accident a few years ago, leaving her alone to raise her two children. I don't know how I know that; I just do. It's like I can see everything.

"I cannot really put into words what I mean by that, though. It's something far more complex than just seeing with my eyes. When I look at you, I see this moment we are currently experiencing, but I also see every sinful act you ever committed in your past. I am right now watching you commit sins in the past, while you also talk with me here in the present. For me, you are both in your past and here in the present; there is no distinguishing between the two. They are both just as real to me as if they are happening right now."

Jeremy chewed that over. "I can see now why the others had no sense of humor."

Jared went on, brushing off his comment. "Even now the clerk—her name was Jane, by the way—her life is playing out before my eyes, giving weight and justification to the anger burning within me at the injustice of her death. All I felt when I took the young man's life was satisfaction. It was not hatred for the boy or a desire for vengeance, but rather a deep and overwhelming need to give her justice."

"Perhaps it was," Jeremy murmured.

Jared grimaced. "How could killing a kid be Justice?"

Jeremy shrugged. "He was a murderer, wasn't he?"

Jared contemplated that. "Yes, yes, he was."

"To us humans, justice is a fluid concept. We temper it with our own views of morality and what we feel is right and wrong, but Justice, in its essence, is not fluid but set in stone. It is black and white and absolute. For most of us, taking someone's life as a punishment for murder is unmerciful and harsh. Particularly that of someone so young. That's why most states have abolished the death penalty. But in truth, a life for a life could be seen as the very essence of Justice."

He stopped for a second, then rolled his eyes.

"Oh, and God wants me to remind you that His mercy far outweighs His wrath. Anything else You want to chime in about?" He aimed this question at the ceiling.

Jared chuckled and temporarily forgot his melancholy. The respite, however, was not long. "So, is this what my life is now? Am I simply the universe's executioner? An instrument of death?"

"Honestly, I don't know. I do know that God says you don't need to worry, you are not being punished." Jared started to say something, but Jeremy interrupted him. "Oh, and you're not going to go to hell, either."

He just stared at Jeremy, his mouth open in shock. "How..."

"How did I know you were going to ask me about hell? Like I've been telling you, God talks to me and He knew you were going to ask that. Look, man, I don't have any answers for you about what's happened, but what I do know is that you're not evil and you're not just some executioner. The sword may have a mind of its own, but there is a reason God pairs it with a human soul. What that reason is I don't know, but I have to believe that it is for good and not for evil."

Both men fell silent. Seeing that Jared was lost in thought, Jeremy decided to close his eyes for a few minutes. But sleep found him quickly and before long he was snoring. Jared sat in silence, not wanting to disturb his new friend.

Strangely he did not feel tired at all. Perhaps he did not need sleep. It was a strange concept for him, and he wondered if he would ever sleep again. One of the great things about sleeping was that it gave you a temporary reprieve from the problems that life brought. It kept a person sane. Would he stay sane?

"No, not in the mortal sense," came the voice in his head. The voice was somehow not as intrusive as before, so Jared didn't fight it. "You will, however, eventually decay."

"What do you mean?"

"No mortal can be Justice forever. Their soul cannot bear the burden."

Jared grimaced. "Great."

"You cannot truly sleep, as you are not truly alive, but I can help you rest, if you like."

Jared shifted to relieve the tightness from sitting in one place for too long. He was not really uncomfortable, but his mind felt like he should be. It was still responding to the echoes of his former life. "Tzedakah, how long will it take for me to... decay?"

The ring was quiet a moment. "The length of time is different for each bearer. So I cannot say."

"What happens when I do? Do I die? I mean, for real this time."

"He will come for you when it is time."

Jared screwed his face up in confusion. "Who will come?"

The ring was silent again. Jared was beginning to get impatient, but before he could lash out, the ring said, "We will talk of this another time. For now, you should rest."

"I don't want to rest. I want to know…"

Before Jared could finish his sentence, his consciousness simply shut down and he was thrust into a state of oblivion.

Chapter Thirty-Two

Dana lay on her bed staring at the ceiling. Her eyes were red and bloodshot from crying and she was completely disheveled. It had been a week since Jared died and the tears were still flowing. She wondered if she would ever stop crying. Everyone told her that in time the pain would lessen, and she would be able to move on with her life. The hole in her heart told her differently.

She covered her eyes with her arm and sighed heavily. Sleep had eluded her this past week. She had slept a total of five hours, maybe. Her brain screamed at her to sleep, but she ignored it. Thankfully, the captain had given her the week off to recover, but she did not care if she ever went back. In fact, she had been contemplating resigning from the force altogether. She could not imagine going back there without Jared. As soon as the thought of quitting hit her brain, she shut it down and scolded herself for even entertaining it. She was a good cop, and she loved her job and she was not going to let this tragedy define the rest of her life.

Her nose was running again so she reached for a tissue from her nightstand. She still had one arm over her eyes, so she had to use muscle memory to find the box. It was still where she left it, but it was empty. Groaning, she batted it to the floor and decided to wipe her nose on her pajama sleeve instead. It was crusty from all the previous times she had done so, but she did not care.

She had been wearing the same set of pajamas since she had returned from the funeral and they were very ripe. She was ripe as well, but she could not bring herself to take a shower. All she wanted to do was lay there and die. She realized she was being dramatic again, and mentally chastised herself. Her stomach grumbled at the hollow pit inside. Ignoring it, she hugged her pillow harder.

Her eyes fell on the alarm clock next to her bed. 11 p.m.

What day is it? she wondered.

Who cares?

She was not going to go anywhere anyway. As she lay there, a thought managed to make its way through the pain.

Is this what Jared would want?

Of course this was not what Jared would have wanted. No, he would want her to go on, to live her life.

But Jared was not there. He was dead.

He had left her, and she was furious at him for it. The vehemence of the thought startled her. Was she really angry? How could she be angry at him? After all, it was not his fault that he had been murdered. No, she was angry but not at Jared. She was angry at the whole goddamned world, but not him. She was angry at herself for being too late to stop it. She was angry at the NYC police who were obviously too inept to find out who did it, and she was angry at Steve.

Yes, but why?

Something in the back of her mind was screaming at her. Something was wrong, but she could not put her finger on it. What was it about Steve that made her skin crawl? She slammed her palm against her forehead to knock free whatever was hiding there. All she received for her efforts was a headache.

She gritted her teeth in frustration and screamed, "What are you trying to tell me?"

With a suddenness that took her breath away, the memory of her last moments with Jared flooded to the forefront of her mind. He had been trying to tell her something, but what was it? She had convinced herself that he was trying to tell her he loved her, but now she realized that she had missed something important.

The shock and grief of the moment had caused her mind to shut down, but somewhere deep in her subconscious the detective in her had been present and it had observed something. It was that ever-rational part of her that was trying to warn her, but about what?

Think! she told herself. *Get yourself together and think like the detective you are.*

She quieted her mind and went through all the details of that night. She recalled holding Jared and shouting for someone to call for help. She remembered him reaching up and pulling her close to tell her something, but his lung had been punctured by the killer's knife. He was unable to get enough breath to speak.

Frustrated, she closed her eyes and focused hard on that memory. No words had come out as his lips trembled, but something she had said... had struck a chord in him and made him frantic. What was it?

Retracing her movements from that night, the only thing she could remember saying to him was that he would be all right and that Steve had gone for help. It was then that it hit her. It was the mention of Steve's name that had gotten the reaction out of him. Why? Did he want her to tell him something? Perhaps he had been simply trying to tell her to tell his brother that he loved him.

No, that could not be it. Jared did love his brother, but she doubted his last thoughts would have been about Steve. Why then had he reacted so strongly at the mention of his name? Had he been trying to warn her about him? After all, he was already there on the scene when she had arrived. Why had he not been considered a suspect in both murders? She had been so filled with grief that she had simply taken his word about what had happened that night.

Come to think of it, even the NYC police had quickly dismissed him as a suspect. If this had been any other case, she would have instantly considered Steve as the prime suspect. Why had she simply dismissed the idea offhand? Sure, they had all grown up together and he was Jared's brother, but it would explain Jared's behavior at the mention of Steve's name.

Of course, no weapon had been found at the scene by the police, but had anyone searched Steve that night? She could not recall if they had. Of course, she was so overcome by grief and shock that she really would not have noticed. A peculiar haze seemed to be draped over her memories of that night, and up to this point, she had chalked it up to grief. Now she was not so sure.

It was more than unusual that absolutely no evidence had been found at the scene. No fibers or fingerprints. No shoe prints or any other evidence of any kind. Of course, Steve's fingerprints would have been all over the scene since he was the person who had discovered the bodies, but they would have been dismissed instantly. Still, there was the problem of the murder weapon. As far as she could remember, when she had arrived on the scene, he had not been holding a knife.

Of course, she had been so fixated on Jared that she most likely wouldn't have noticed if he had. He could have easily hidden it upon her arrival, but surely the police would have searched him at the scene. Every time she tried to recall anything about Steve from that night and what he had done or said, the memory was foggy and blurry. She remembered everything else in vivid detail, except Steve. It was as if someone had gone into her mind and had tampered with just the part of her memory that pertained to him.

Also, there was that eerie moment at the funeral when his eyes seemed to glow. Her rational mind would not accept that his eyes had indeed glowed red, but perhaps it was her subconscious' way of warning her about him. She had certainly not been thinking rationally at the funeral, and it was perfectly conceivable to believe that her mind could have conjured up such a thing to try to reach her through the grief.

Moreover, when Steve had passed her while carrying Jared's coffin, she was sure that he was smirking. At the time, she had convinced herself that her grief had been causing her to misinterpret things. Now she was not so sure.

Something was off about Steve, and she was going to find out what it was.

With a renewed purpose she got out of bed and went out into the kitchen. She ignored the food in her fridge and grabbed a diet soda instead. How long had it been since she'd had something to drink? God, had she been like this since the funeral? The thought of the funeral caused the pain to come surging back, but this time she suppressed it. If she allowed herself to feel the grief again, she would be crippled, and she had no time for that right now.

No, she scolded herself, why should she suppress her feelings? Her old martial arts instructor had taught her that emotions had the power to either cripple or propel you. She was done being crippled by grief. Now she would use that grief as fuel.

She thought of Jared, of how much she had loved him. How he'd been taken away from her before they had even had a chance to begin. The pain that had constricted her heart turned into fury. She had never been that helpless little girl type, not since her mother had left her and her father when she was ten. No, she was done wallowing. It was time for action. When she thought of Steve, a wave of anger swelled that was every bit as ferocious as her grief. If he'd had a hand in Jared's death, she was going to find out and bring him to justice.

No, she corrected herself. *No, I am going to kill him.*

The cop inside of her screamed in protest, but she shut the voice up. If she found out that Steve had killed Jared, there would be no arrest and no trial, only vengeance. She would have to be absolutely certain of course before she acted, but when the time came, she would act.

She was getting ahead of herself. First, she would need to investigate and find out what had really happened. Perhaps she was wrong about Steve and her grief was playing tricks on her, but deep down inside she doubted that. She finished off the soda and set the empty can down on her coffee table and looked around for her phone.

After a few minutes, she found it on the charger where she had left it and turned it on. She saw that it was Saturday and realized that she still had a few days left of personal time before she had to be back to work. She decided that she would go back to New York to where Jared had been killed and investigate the scene herself.

Of course, the NYC cops would probably not like her snooping around their territory and might take offense at her intrusion into their investigation. Even though she was a police officer, she couldn't expect them to allow her to look at any evidence they may have collected from the scene.

If she was going to do this, she needed to find a way around all the bureaucratic red tape. Since she had turned on her phone, it had blown up with missed calls and new messages and texts. Her most recent voicemail was from... Agent Johansson. What was he calling her about? Maybe he'd found out something about the family in the locket picture. She cued up the voice mail and put the phone on speaker.

"Hey, Dana. I just wanted to call and see how you are doing. I know we haven't known each other for very long, but I wanted to give my condolences and let you know that if you ever need anything, I am there. Anything, that is, except the truth about who really killed JFK. That I just can't tell you about.

"Anyway, I just wanted to let you know I was sorry. Jared was a good man. Well, take care of yourself, and hopefully, we will run into each other again. Oh, wait, before I go, we got nothing on that John Doe you guys got up there. It was a dead end. Looks like he was an immigrant or tourist or something who happened to be at the wrong place at the wrong time. Anyway, you take care of yourself, Dana."

Well, the John Doe was a dead end. That was not surprising with all of the people immigrating to the US of late. It was nearly impossible for the government to keep track of everyone coming in, and a lot of those people slipped through the cracks, with no electronic or paper trail. He most likely belonged to someone who was afraid to come forward and claim him due to their fear of being detained or deported.

Wait a minute, she thought. Johansson worked for the FBI. If anyone could get her around the proverbial red tape, it was him. He might even have information about the case the NYPD did not. The incident was, after all, remarkably similar to the killings by the Eastside Stalker. Maybe it had been red flagged by the FBI and he was already on it. If so, then he would have access to the crime scene and any evidence discovered. Of course, he'd not mentioned anything about the case in his message, so maybe she was just grasping at straws. But what did she have to lose by asking?

She ignored the countless text and messages from condolence givers and pulled up Johansson's contact information. Just as she was about to dial the number, her phone buzzed to life with an incoming call.

It was her captain.

Curses.

He knew she was still on leave, so why was he bothering her? She almost ignored it, but then thought he wouldn't have contacted her during leave unless it was important.

"Hello, Captain, what can I do for you?" she asked.

"Dana," the man said in his deep baritone voice. "Sorry to bother you during your time of grief, but I have a case that I thought you might want to look into."

She gritted her teeth. It took everything in her not to snap at the man. She did not need this right now. She needed to talk to Johansson and get to the city as soon as possible. The longer she waited, the colder the case would get. "I am sorry, Captain, but I am very busy. Perhaps you can give it to Handley and Winder instead."

"Dana," he said, "I am not *telling* you to come in. I wanted to give you the opportunity to come in."

Dana closed her eyes and rubbed her temples with her free hand. "What could possibly be so important about this case that would make me want to come in right now?"

"The body of a young woman was found in her apartment this evening by a maintenance worker. The apartment where she lived was the unit directly across from Jared's."

Dana was stunned into silence. What did he just say?

"They have not moved the body yet, but the officers on the scene said, by the look of the body she has probably been dead for quite some time. In fact, the only reason she was found at all was that the maintenance man was responding to a complaint about a bad smell. Of course, he cannot be ruled out as a suspect, but the management has backed him up on why he was in the apartment. I thought you might want to be in on this case since it hits so close to home. I don't think it is related to what happened to Jared, but with all of the homicides lately, you never know."

Dana was already halfway up the stairs. "I will be there as soon as I can. Who is on the scene right now?"

"Officer Small and Hernandez. The medical examiner is on route and should be there momentarily. Do you need the address?"

She threw her phone onto her bed and stripped off her pajamas. "No, I know where it is. Thanks for the heads-up, Captain."

"Of course. Let me know what you find, and Dana, let me know if you need anything else. We are all here for you."

"Thank you, I appreciate that."

"Any time. I'll let the officers on the scene know you are on the way and to wait for you before they do anything. Let me know what you find. Bye, now."

Dana pulled on her shirt and a pair of jeans. She looked at herself in the mirror and realized that she appeared a bit rough. But there was no time for a shower or makeup, so she just threw her hair up in a ponytail, grabbed her phone, and practically ran down the stairs.

What is the world is going on? she thought. Being a homicide detective, she dealt with death on a daily basis, it was her job after all, but now it seemed to her like her whole world was being swallowed up by it.

Chapter Thirty-Three

Jared's consciousness flooded back. Something was wrong. Tzedakah glowed fiercely in his hand and the radiance from the blade illuminated the small hotel room. His new eyes did not need the light to see, and he did not notice anything out of the ordinary. Jeremy was soundly asleep on the bed, his soft snoring reminding Jared of a cat's purr. All seemed well, but his sense of danger increased.

"The window," Tzedakah said urgently.

Panther-like, he moved to the large picture window and peered through the curtains.

Outside, a rather average-looking middle-aged Caucasian man with dirty blond hair was standing in the parking lot staring intently at the door to their room. At first glance, no one would consider this man a threat, but the same sense of danger that had jolted him out of his rest intensified.

Another man came walking up to stand next to the first. He was a tall African American man who looked to be about thirty. He was fit and muscular and wearing jeans and a tight sports T-shirt. Neither man acknowledged the other but simply continued to stare at the door as if they were waiting for something.

Like something out of a zombie apocalypse movie, people of all ages, ethnicities, and genders streamed into the hotel parking lot. Before long there were about thirty of them congregating in front of their door. Just like the first two who had arrived, none spoke or acknowledged each other, but simply stared at the door. They seemed docile, but he could not shake the now screaming feeling of dread.

"What the—?" he asked out loud.

Jeremy stirred and propped himself up and looked around groggily. He rubbed his eyes attempting to force the sleep away. "What's going on?"

"Be quiet," Jared hissed with more venom than he intended. "There are about thirty people milling around outside in the parking lot."

"Huh?" Jeremy shot out of bed instantly awake. "How long have they been there?"

He stumbled across the room, the fear that had been rising in his heart turning into full-on dread. As soon as he reached the window, he quickly drew back the curtain and his eyes went wide with terror. "Oh, crap."

"You know what's going on?"

"Yeah, I think." Jeremy pulled on his coat. "You see that aura emanating from them? Like a red stain in the air around 'em."

Aura was perhaps the wrong word to describe what he saw. Each person seemed to have tendrils of smoke flowing and moving about their bodies. The smoke writhed and contorted and was attached to each person like puppet strings attached to marionettes. The stain did not engulf the people but snaked its way into their souls.

"We need to move before they attack," Jeremy said, his eyes searching the scene.

Tzedakah drew Jared's gaze upward into the night sky. It was a clear night but in one area of the sky, the stars were blotted out by a large dark shadow. He did not need Tzedakah to know that the huge shadow blocking the stars was the tendrils' source. "I think I found the puppet master."

Jeremy looked up and grimaced.

"Can this night get any worse?" he growled. "I know. I know. You don't need to tell me who it is. I can sense his filth all the way in here."

Jared was about to tell him that he had no idea who it was that was out there when he realized that Jeremy was not talking to him. Tzedakah spoke the word "Dominion" into his mind. Confusion clouded his features as he tried to make sense of what it meant.

"Does Dominion mean anything to you?" he asked Jeremy.

"Yeah," Jeremy said as he frantically checked the locks on the door for the tenth time. "A nasty bugger of a demon who enjoys contorting and bending people to his will. Honestly, most demons don't bother with full-blown possession because it draws too much attention. Most prefer influence and manipulation. You know, intense thoughts or desires that you know you shouldn't have but can't seem to get out of your head? Suggestions. This guy likes to use straight-up possession. And trust me, unlike most demons, he is powerful enough to control more than one person at a time."

"How many people?"

"A lot. I've run into him a few times over the years, but I usually just steer clear and stay out of his way."

Jared frowned.

"What's up?" Jeremy asked.

"Tzedakah says that only a few of the people out there deserve death," Jared said, relaying the sword's message. "That means we're going to have to try to do this without hurting them too much."

Jeremy smiled ruefully. "Well, at least that answers the question of whether you are just an 'executioner for the universe.' Of course, I'm fairly sure that Dominion will not be so considerate of their wellbeing."

As soon as the words left Jeremy's mouth, he noticed movement in his peripheral vision and turned just in time to see ten people charging toward them. "Crap."

Jared was already on the move. He threw himself through the large window, shattering it, just before the first wave of drones reached their door. He took out the two closest to him with quick jabs, punching them so hard they flew spiraling away into parked cars. Jared winced, hoping that he hadn't done them permanent damage. Before he had time to dwell on it, he was engaged by the second wave.

The remaining eight from the first wave hammered on the hotel room door while the next ten advanced on Jared. Tzedakah glowed even brighter as they rushed to overwhelm him with the sheer force of their numbers. Jared punched and kicked, trying his best to pull his strikes.

An Asian woman struck him in the face with a force that was certainly not human; his head flew backward, knocking him into a man who was trying to drag him down from behind. His head hit the man's forehead with a sickening crack.

Hands clawed at his clothing, pulling him in every conceivable direction at once as the mob attempted to drag him to the ground. But he managed to stand his ground and he kicked another attacker's feet out from under him. The man fell backward and was consumed by the horde.

Jared heard a loud crash. Jeremy was shouting. Behind him, the motel door had given way.

Jeremy!

With a flurry of punches, Jared sent his attackers tumbling to the ground like dominoes.

Crashes and grunts came from the broken window of the hotel room as Jeremy fought for his life. Jared turned and ran in the direction of the fighting, but he did not get far before a drone reached out and caught his foot. He went sprawling to the pavement. He hit the ground and flipped himself over, but it was too late.

The drones piled on him grasping at him with hands far stronger than any human. He felt himself being pinned to the ground; his sword hand forced out to the side by three possessed people. They grasped at his fingers, pulling and tugging trying to remove the sword from his grip. As the horde covered him, he could hear Jeremy screaming. He would never get to him in time.

Chapter Thirty-Four

It took her about fifteen minutes to arrive at the apartment complex where Jared had lived. As she got out of her car and headed toward the officers at the edge of the crime scene, she wondered if anyone had removed his stuff yet. She'd been so out of it, she didn't know.

The officer at the edge of the tape saw her coming and he raised it for her as she approached. It was Officer Hernandez. She thanked him for the assist, and his eyes were soft when he looked at her, filled with pity and remorse. Oh, how she hated that look. She headed up to the crime scene as quick as her feet would go.

When she reached the third floor, she was greeted by yet another officer. This one was younger than Officer Hernandez and he did not recognize her at first. He leveled her a stern look. "Sorry, ma'am, but no one is allowed down this hallway unless they are police personnel."

Barely restraining an eye roll, she mustered up all her professionalism and flashed her badge. "I am

Detective Campbell, so I guess that qualifies me as police personnel."

The officer gazed down at the badge. "Sorry, Detective. You can go through."

"No problem. Has CSI arrived yet?"

"Yes, ma'am, they are in the apartment waiting for you."

"Thank you, Officer..." She paused to read the man's name tag. "Steveson."

Dana pushed past the man and made her way down the hallway to where the other officers were congregating. As she passed Jared's door, waves of emotion surged over her. She could imagine that this was all just a bad dream, that Jared could come barreling out of his door carrying a cup of coffee for her and asking about the crime scene. But that would never be.

The door to the crime scene was open. Inside, CSI technicians searched the room for evidence. The smell hit her before she even stepped into the room and she immediately knew why everyone was wearing masks. The stench of death permeated every nook and cranny of the small apartment. She grabbed her mouth to keep from gagging. The girl must have been dead quite some time for the place to smell so bad.

One of the men quickly came over to her and handed her a white dust mask. "Here, take this. It does not completely keep out the smell, but it does help a little."

She took the small mask and quickly put it over her face. The officer was right about it helping to lessen the strength of the stench of death. "Thanks."

"You're welcome," the man replied. He was a Caucasian man of about forty and of average height with short dark brown hair that had a bit of salt in it. She could not see his entire face, as it was hidden by the mask he wore, but his eyes were bright blue. Since his face was covered, it took her a minute to recognize that he was Dr. Hudson the coroner.

"Doctor Hudson, where is the body?" she asked. "Does it look like a homicide?"

"Yeah, third one tonight actually."

"Third one?" she asked curiously. "Where were the other two?"

"Across town. It's been a busy night. Hell, it's been a busy last few weeks. I feel like I haven't slept in a month. The other one appeared to be a robbery gone wrong. The clerk was shot and killed, and the young man we think was the robber was found dead outside the store."

"That's strange. Does it appear to be gang-related?" she asked as they made their way to the bedroom.

"Not sure. All of the money was still there, so whoever killed him was not interested in the money. He was stabbed by what appears to be a sword or edged weapon of some kind. Detectives Handley and Winder are there. Once the body gets to the morgue, I will examine it more fully. This one here was also stabbed to death."

"By a sword?" Dana asked incredulously.

"Looks like something smaller, a hunting knife possibly. Of course, I won't know until I get the body back to the morgue and examine it."

The stench of the decomposing corpse made it through her mask, and she gagged again.

"You okay?" Doctor Hudson asked.

She waved his question away. "Yeah, I'm fine. It's just really strong."

He nodded. "The body has been here for a while. From the rate of decomposition, I would say at least five days, possibly a week."

Dana approached the small bed. The entire area was covered in dried blood and she could make out quite a few nasty looking wounds on the girl's body. The young woman was naked and intertwined in the bedsheets as if in the middle of an amorous encounter that had all gone wrong. Her eyes were still open, and Dana couldn't help but feel that they were fixed on her. It unnerved her, but she refused to show it. She gazed into the woman's lifeless eyes and knew full well who had done this to her.

"I think I am going to have to call the FBI and let them know we have another Stalker body on our hands," she told the doctor.

"That's what I was thinking as well. Of course, I won't know for sure until I get her back and examine her more closely, but I would wager a week's pay that the wounds on her body will match those of the other two."

"Shit. If the press gets wind of this, we are going to have a panic on our hands. I am sure he has moved on since no more bodies have been found and this one looks to have been killed around the same time as the others, but that won't stop locals from panicking."

Her mind raced as she looked at the girl. Hadn't Steve stayed at Jared's house right before they had decided to go to the city? Come to think of it, the other bodies appeared right around the time he had mysteriously shown up, as well. Was it just a coincidence? Her detective mind did not believe in coincidences. Of course, she had no proof that Steve was involved, but too many coincidences pointed in his direction.

"You okay?" Doctor Hudson asked, knocking her out of her thoughts.

"Yeah, I'm fine," she said, unclenching her fists. "Let me know what you find after you have examined the body more closely."

She made her way out of the small bedroom past the bustling CSI technicians and out into the hallway where she was finally able to breathe again. They had been at it for hours, but she knew that they would not find anything. They never did with the Eastside Stalker.

God, if it's Steve killing these girls, how is he not leaving any evidence behind? she wondered. She knew that he was smarter than he let on, but she found it hard to believe that he could be some genius serial killer. *But isn't that what people say about every genius serial killer?* She pulled out her phone and dialed the captain. Either way, she would find out, and if he was involved, then she was going to kill him.

As she walked down the hallway, she didn't notice the eyes that watched her from Jared's apartment. Steve had been observing the unfolding scene since the police had arrived. What was happening to him? First, he had been so careless that he had almost allowed Jared to walk right up on him while he was dispatching his second victim in Binghamton. Then Jared had stumbled on to him after the show in the city.

Now the police were right across the hall, admiring more of his work. He really did need to control his impulses. Otherwise it was only a matter of time before one of the cops got lucky and he'd be caught.

He cracked the door a little wider just in time to see Dana pass by with her phone to her ear. She stopped only a few feet away from where he was watching. Damn, should he close the door and let the whole thing blow over, or go out and feign ignorance?

Steve cocked a smile. Of course he was going to go out and talk to her. It wasn't his style to sit back and skulk in the shadows, regardless of what the papers said about him. Sure, he liked to stalk his victims before he killed them, but not for the reasons the papers suggested. No, he liked the hunt; it was exciting. The more daring the kill, the more of a thrill he got out of it.

Happily meditating on his favorite subject, he moved his fingers as if flipping a knife, and was surprised to feel the cool weight of a one. He held a thin shiny ebony blade. It was sharp and beautiful as all such tools are. There was no handle attached to the blade, and to his amazement, it seemed to grow in his hand like a shadow growing in the fading light. He pointed it away from himself, and with breathtaking swiftness, it elongated until it struck the wall directly across from him. It hit the wall with such force that it cut through the drywall and did it without making a sound.

As quickly as the knife materialized, it was gone. Dissipated into the shadows.

Well, that's new, he marveled. It never seemed to amaze him just how powerful he was becoming. Nearly every day he discovered some new ability.

So many possibilities! If he could master this new gift, he would never again have to worry about the police tracing a murder weapon back to him. Impulse control be damned; he could kill people from a distance with such a knife. Of course, there was no fun in that. Now, tormenting them before going in for a close kill—that had potential.

He swung the door open and stepped out into the breezeway. Dana's back was to him, so he crossed his arms over his chest and leaned up against the door.

Surprisingly, he made no sound as he moved. In fact, even the noise from the door swinging open had been muted. It was as if some strange sound suppressing cloud surrounded him. Mere feet away, Dana still hadn't noticed he was there.

"Okay, Chief, I will keep you up to speed on the investigation. I guess my hiatus is over. You're going to need everyone on this if we are going to keep one step ahead of the press." She turned, and her eyes met Steve's. "Sorry, Chief, but I gotta go."

She hung up and lowered her hand to the duty weapon on her hip. Never taking her eyes from Steve's, she dropped the phone into her jacket pocket and turned to face him. Her dark brown eyes bored into his ice blue ones, giving away far more than she had intended to. He smiled at her warmly, but his eyes did not mirror that warmth.

"So what's going on?" Steve said, breaking the silence but not the tension. "Binghamton's finest have been here making a terrible racket ever since I woke up. I finally decided to crack the door and steal a peek when I saw you walking by on your phone."

His easy smile was disarming, and Dana's resolve cracked a bit. Maybe she was wrong about him. After all, they had grown up together and were practically family. Maybe she was just being paranoid and allowing the grief of Jared's loss to cause her to look for boogie men in every shadow. This was Steve, after all. *He may be a bit of a jerk*, she thought, *but he's not a killer*. Her hand dropped from her weapon.

"The maintenance man found another dead girl," she told him.

"Really? Any connection to the other two girls?"

Dana locked eyes with Steve, and suddenly the full weight of her emotional and physical exhaustion hit. Steve reached out to steady her, but as soon as his hand touched her shoulder, a jolt of anger surged through her, dispelling the weariness she was feeling. She batted away his hand.

"Don't touch me," she growled, her eyes flashing with fire.

Steve put his hands up and stepped back. "Whoa now, Dana, I was just trying to help. You looked like you were about to pass out. Jeeze, what's gotten into you, anyway? Your usual defensiveness seems to be turned up to eleven."

She glowered at him but did not relax. She watched him as he smiled warmly attempting to calm her. Her outburst had drawn the attention of some of the other officers and they looked ready to head over. She exhaled deliberately and calmed herself before waving them off.

"It's nothing. I'm just tired," she replied, attempting to mask the underlying suspicion she felt.

"I get it," he said, leaning back against the door frame. He reached into his pocket and pulled out a cigarette. Remembering that he had seen her smoking the other day, he held out the pack. She shook her head, so he shrugged and lit his cigarette.

Steve said, "I haven't seen you since the funeral. I would've come by to check on you, but I figured it was best to leave you alone for a while."

Dana's shoulders slumped. "Yeah."

Steve watched her as he exhaled, expecting her to say more, but she did not. After a few minutes of silence where she seemed lost in her own thoughts, Steve put out his cigarette. "Well, since the excitement is over for the night, I guess I'll head back inside. You take care of yourself and let me know if you need a friend."

"Steve," she called to him softly. Her head was bowed, her fists clenched at her sides.

A warm smile was painted onto Steve's face, but inwardly warning bells were going off in alarm.

She knows, he thought.

He reached back and allowed the inky darkness to coalesce into a blade. Dana was still not looking at him. His mind raced as he contemplated his next course of action.

The impulsive Steve wanted to damn the consequences and strike, but something inside warned him to pause. Maybe her sudden change in demeanor had nothing to do with him. Certainly if he attacked her now, a swarm of police officers would descend on him before he had time to escape. Plus, Dana was no slouch, and he knew she could handle herself. No, he would not strike just yet. He'd wait to see how this all played out before he acted.

Dana finally raised her head to look at him. Her large brown eyes bore into him with such fire that he felt uncomfortable under her gaze. When she spoke, her voice was calm and controlled but held the same intensity as her eyes. "I just wanted you to know that I will find out who killed Jared, and when I do, I will make sure that they never hurt anyone else again."

"I have no doubt you will," he replied. "And I am sure he will go away for a long—"

Dana cut him off with a raised hand. "No, Steve. Let me make this very clear. When I find them, and make no mistake I will, I am going to personally make sure that they never hurt anyone again. No trial, no judge, no passing go and collecting two hundred dollars. Just simple and unadulterated justice."

"Well now," Steve said, his lips curled in a smirk. "That is not very police-like of you. Besides, are you sure that when you do finally crack this case, you'll be able to handle what you find?"

As he spoke Dana noticed that he held one of his hands behind his back. He noticed the slight flick of her eyes and the suspicion that rose up in them and stiffened. They stood glaring at each other before Dana finally relaxed.

She sighed and turned away from Steve and walked back toward the waiting crime scene. He watched her go. He still could not be sure of what she knew, but he could definitely sense hostility and suspicion. Perhaps it was time for him to learn just how much she knew.

"Oh and by the way," Dana said. "Were you staying here with Jared before we left to go to the city?"

"Yeah. I crashed on the couch. Why do you ask? Does it have something to do with the dead girl in the apartment across the hall?"

She smiled a disarming smile, but it was obviously forced. "Well, the estimated time of death is right about that time. You didn't happen to see anything, did you?"

He cocked his head as if in thought. "No. Not that I can recall. Of course, I crashed pretty hard that night."

"Anybody who can verify that?" The predatory look in her eyes belied her friendly smile.

Steve's smile widened into a harsh grin. "Just Jared, I'm afraid."

She shook her head and walked away. He watched her go, his thoughts racing.

Then she yelled over her shoulder, "Hey, don't leave town. We may have a few more questions for you."

"Am I a suspect or something?" he asked nonchalantly.

She didn't even bother replying. It was obvious Dana was toying with him to see if he would give anything away. He smiled wickedly. Yes, it was definitely time to find out what she knew.

Chapter Thirty-Five

The horde of attackers got heavier as people piled on him. Strangely he still felt neither pain nor the pressure of being crushed. Despite the grasping fingers trying to hold his head down, Jared turned toward the hotel door. He could not see Jeremy but heard a fight coming from the room. At least Jeremy was still alive. Someone had got Jared's hand and was attempting to pry open his fist and remove the sword, but his grip held firm.

"Don't worry. As long as our connection is strong, nothing can separate us," Tzedakah spoke into his mind.

"That's good to know," he said through grunts. "I guess me throwing you into a lake like Excalibur is out of the question, then?"

He managed to get one arm free of the bodies and grabbed a middle-aged blonde woman by her hair. Too hard. Her head whipped back, and her neck snapped from the force. She flipped end over end, skipping off the ground like a pebble on water. Her body flopped over, her head bent and facing him, her eyes fixed and lifeless.

Jared gritted his teeth in frustration and anger. His dark eyes saw everything about the woman who now lay dead. She was a schoolteacher with two children, a good person who had tried her best to live her life helping others. He had not intended to kill her, and his heart ached at the thought of her children growing up without their mother. As he continued to look at her, he saw that the red stain melted and faded away.

So, killing them removed the influence of the stain, but it would be murder. No, killing them was not an option. Even Tzedakah agreed they needed to find another way. Jeremy was running out of time, and he had to get these people off him quickly so they could regroup and figure out their next move. He gritted his teeth in frustration and reached inside himself, allowing his connection to Tzedakah to get stronger. Doing so was hard for him, because the more he allowed the sword in, the more he felt like he was losing himself.

As soon as he opened his consciousness to Tzedakah, its power surged through him. The blade in his grip burned with a bright blue fire. He growled through his teeth and let out a guttural roar, as he slowly muscled his way to his feet.

Bright blue surges of energy swept out from him, tossing off the people clinging to him. One man stubbornly hung onto his neck, refusing to let go, somehow managing to ignore the energy that jolted through his body. Jared reached up with his free hand, grabbed the man by his shirt, and hurled him to the side. He struck a parked car, denting the door, and went limp.

Jared ran to the motel room where he knew Jeremy was still fighting. Just before he reached the doorway, he heard Jeremy yell something unintelligible and a brilliant blast of intense light exploded from the opening. Instinctively Jared put his arm up to shield his eyes from the bright light. As soon as the light subsided, three men and two women came stumbling out of the door. They seemed to be dazed and staggered confusedly blinking and rubbing their eyes from the shock.

A disheveled Jeremy casually walked out of the door as the disoriented people stumbled away. He plucked at one of the sleeves of his coat. "I know. I know!" he said out loud. "I know I should have done that sooner, but I was distracted by the demon zombies trying to rip my face off. Anyway, not to tell You how to do Your job, but if You had intervened sooner, my favorite coat would not have gotten ripped. Oh haha, very funny."

He walked over to where a surprised Jared stood. "That'll only stop them temporarily, so we really should get out of here before they recover, or their boss shows up."

Jared cocked his head and looked at Jeremy. His spirit appeared to be merged with God Himself, and it was so bright that it actually hurt his eyes to look at him. As he watched, the energy slowly faded until it was nothing more than an aura of residual power shrouding him.

"What was that?"

Jeremy stuck a finger through the large tear in his coat and wiggled it. "My favorite coat, with a hole in it! It's not like I have the money to just go around buying coats all the time."

"Jeremy," he snapped. "Stop worrying about the coat and answer my question."

Sighing, Jeremy left his torn jacket alone for the moment. "A light burst. It's what usually happens when God or an angel shows up. Too bad their boss was not in that room; he most likely would've been fried and this whole mess would be over. Of course, that would just be too easy, wouldn't it?" This last statement was directed at the sky. "Well, one good thing came of it. The ones that were touched by the light will not be able to be taken over again. So that's something, anyway."

A loud roar bellowed from directly above them and reverberated through them like a shock wave. About thirty feet up, a large shadow darker than the night sky hovered in the air. Jared could see that the tendrils of spiritual power were coming from it. Some of the tendrils had been severed, but enough remained connected to be a concern. He had already seriously hurt and even killed a few of the possessed people. He needed to end this quickly before more innocent people were injured.

"You ready for round two?" Jeremy put his back to Jared's.

The people that Jared had stunned were now stalking toward them. Tendrils leached out from the dark silhouette above him, weaving and twisting into a massive network of threads that connected to each one of the possessed people. His vision dimmed and his thoughts became sluggish and disconnected as Tzedakah invaded his mind. He pushed back vehemently at the intrusion and the blade backed off at his resistance and tried a different tactic. The image of him severing the cords that bound the people appeared in his mind.

"I understand," he said out loud.

Jeremy glanced back at him. "You understand what?"

Before Jared could respond, the nearest person charged him. It was a freckle-faced teenager with his long brown hair tied up in a ponytail. Red tendrils snaked around the boy's body; Jared swung Tzedakah at them. They dissolved as soon as the blade made contact, releasing the boy from the possession.

The kid stopped in his tracks, blinking in confusion. "What's going on?" he asked. "Where am—"

New blood red tendrils of spiritual energy snaked toward him and wrapped themselves around his mind. He convulsed in pain and screamed as he fought the influence of the demonic puppet master. His eyes clouded over, and his body went limp as he lost the battle of wills and was reconnected to the horde.

The young man charged at him again and Jared once again went to cut the spiritual threads, but before his blade could slice them, the boy swung his arm up to block the strike. The sword bit deep into the boy's arm, severing the hand but missing the tendrils. Jared looked on in horror as blood spurted from the place where the boy's arm had been. Incredulously the boy did not react to the injury but swung his other arm hard at Jared's face. He evaded the blow easily and swung Tzedakah, once again attempting to sever the demonic connection.

The boy jinked sideways and backhanded the blade with the same arm he'd just attacked with, once again deflecting the blow away from the connecting threads. This time the blade severed his arm at the bicep, and the momentum from the boy's swing sent the severed arm spinning through the air, spattering blood across his face and torso.

Laughter echoed from the hovering shadow, and it infuriated Jared. The demon was using the boy's body as a shield, and at the rate the boy was losing blood, he wouldn't live much longer. As if on cue, the boy's eyes flickered and rolled up into his head and he passed out.

Jeremy was hard pressed at his back, using every trick he had to keep the attackers on his side at bay. It would not be long before he was overwhelmed. The boy that Jared had injured hung limp in front of him in the air. His body listed backward and to one side like a discarded marionette as his lifeblood poured from the stumps where his arm and hand had been.

As he watched, the boy's face twitched and contorted with pain and his eyes flared to life with recognition. The young man looked at him with such fear and panic that Jared's heart broke. His eyes pleaded with Jared, and he mouthed, *Help*.

"Hold on!" Jared shouted as tears streamed down the young man's face.

Then the life in the boy's eyes faded and went out. His head slumped and his wispy spirit slipped out of his body.

"Joe," Tzedakah whispered into his mind. "His name was Joe."

Laughter bellowed from above and the horde halted and froze at the sound. He could hear Jeremy panting behind him, but everything else had faded away, replaced by a blinding and all-consuming rage.

"Injustice!" The word roared through his very soul, giving definition and purpose to the seething fury. Everything that Joe could and would have been flared before his eyes and was aborted.

"Injustice!" he heard himself shout. The words exploded from his lips with the force of a thunderclap, emitting a shock wave that sent people, cars, and anything else that was not bolted down hurtling away.

Tzedakah glowed angrily and Jared thrust his arm upward and the people who had been thrown in all directions suddenly froze in place. The cars and debris kept careening outward until it all crashed violently into anything and everything in its way.

Jared stood, his arm raised above his head, in an empty crater encircled by crushed cars and debris. The remaining people who had attacked him hung suspended, motionless, and stunned, in the air around him like a twisted mobile. Jeremy, who had not been affected by the shock wave, stood dumbfounded, his mouth agape, staring at the carnage.

Tzedakah flared and torrents of blue-black energy arced from the sentient sword, surging into the suspended individuals. As they trembled and shook, the energy found its way to each connecting strand and used the tendrils as conduits to flow up and into the unseen puppet master. The demon howled in pain as power surged into him from a thousand different directions. Jared swung Tzedakah downward and the tendrils that connected the evil spirit to his pawns evaporated.

Jeremy watched in awe as the people who had been possessed slowly and gently descended back to Earth. Every one of them was unconscious, oblivious to the nightmare going on around them. Up in the sky where the surges of energy had converged, there hovered the monster Dominion.

"He looks angry," Jeremy commented. "Definitely hurt from your, whatever-that-was. But the real battle is only just beginning."

Jared's dark eyes writhed angrily as he glared up at the massive demon lord. "No," he replied in a voice that did not seem like his own. "The battle is already over."

Dominion roared furiously down at the two men and bared his long dagger-like teeth. His bat wings beat furiously as he fought to keep himself aloft. He clapped his fists together, then drew his hands apart. A long glowing curved sword of energy materialized in his hand.

"I will tear you to pieces, fledgling," he spat.

Jared was suddenly behind the demon lord. All Jeremy registered from the movement was a slight gust of wind as Jared seemed to materialize from thin air. Before the demon had time to perceive what was happening, Jared had struck him so forcefully in the back, he hurtled to the ground like a meteor.

"Oh, crap!" Jeremy muttered as the demon meteor streaked directly at him. He threw up his arms and shouted a quick prayer to the Lord. "Okay, God, now would be a good time to make Yourself known."

Jeremy squeezed his eyes shut and braced himself for the impact, but nothing happened. After a few seconds, he tentatively opened one eye to survey the scene. Since he had not felt himself being ripped apart by a cataclysmic explosion, he was sure that he would see the pearly gates of heaven with Saint Peter beckoning to him.

"You okay?" an angelic voice asked.

Jeremy looked up and squinted at the person who had spoken to him. Upon seeing who it was that had saved him, he stood and heaved an exasperated sigh. Sanctuary stood over him, his two flaming swords glowing fiercely as the remains of Dominion dissipated into blood-red smoke.

"If it had been any other angelic being standing here, I would have said yes, but since it's you, that would be a definite *no*."

"Your gratitude for saving your life is duly noted," Sanctuary dryly replied as he replaced his twin swords in their scabbards on his back.

Jared's feet touched the earth. He collapsed and fell to one knee. He braced himself on his sword.

"What happened?" he asked through gritted teeth.

"You nearly killed me, that's what happened," Jeremy fumed.

Sanctuary reached down to help Jared up. Jared took his hand and allowed the big man to lift him to a standing position.

"Tzedakah took control of you during the battle," Sanctuary replied. "I assume that the bond you two share is still tenuous at best, so he felt the need to intervene."

It was only then that Jared became aware of the surrounding destruction. His black eyes went wide as he surveyed the scene. "Oh God, did I do this?"

Sanctuary nodded, his golden eyes examining the small man standing before him. He could still see Tzedakah's power surging around him. "You will need to learn to control the link between you and the sword so it will not feel the need to supersede your will in the future."

Jared's eyes went from disbelief to anger in a flash. He lifted the sword up and glared at the still glowing blade. He gritted his teeth and growled audibly at the weapon. To Jeremy and Sanctuary, it looked like he was only staring at it. Both men knew that Jared was having it out with Tzedakah through the mental bond they shared.

Somewhere in the cold night, sirens wailed.

"I hate to break up this touching moment," Jeremy said, "but we really need to go."

More sirens could be heard now closer and coming from many directions, and the people who had been controlled by Dominion were beginning to stir.

"Now would be preferable."

Sanctuary turned and put his hand on Jared's shoulder. "We need to go. Your issue with each other can be addressed somewhere more private."

Jared blinked his eyes and looked up at Sanctuary as Tzedakah's glow faded. "We agree. Who are you, anyway?"

"Introductions and pleasantries can wait till we are far from here." He turned his gaze from Jared to the sword. "If you would be so kind, please teleport us away from here before we are discovered by the humans."

Tzedakah's radiance flared until the energy exploded in a bright blue flash. A cop car followed by an ambulance pulled into the parking lot just as the flash blinked out. The police officers shielded their eyes from the light burst and slammed on their breaks, the ambulance screeching to a halt behind them. When they were finally able to see again, the three men had vanished.

Chapter Thirty-Six

Still agitated from her confrontation with Steve, Dana headed for her car. While she had a hard time fathoming that he was involved with Jared's murder, but she couldn't ignore the very loud warning screams of her instincts every time he came around. She made it halfway to her car before she heard an explosion thunder in the distance.

She scanned the horizon, searching for the source of the noise. Car alarms blared somewhere in the distance, and she heard the faint sounds of sirens. The other officers stopped packing up their gear and they looked slightly confused as they discussed what they had just heard. She cautiously made her way to where they were congregating.

"Did anyone see what happened?" she asked.

Officer Lee shook his head. "Sounded to me like an explosion and possible impact tremor."

Lee's alert but composed demeanor told Dana that he was a combat veteran. Most of the remaining officers seemed unsure of what to do and meandered around talking quietly amongst themselves.

Suddenly Lee pointed to the sky at about two o'clock. "There. It's a bit of a ways off, but I think I saw residual flashes that could have come from an explosion."

Dana turned to look in the direction Lee was pointing and what she saw was so absurd, that at first, she did not believe her eyes. Forks of blue-black lightning streaked up from the ground, striking an object hovering in the air. The light show was brilliant and fantastic and easily visible for miles around.

Just as quickly as the dazzling display of radiance had begun, it ended.

"Did everyone else just see that?" a female officer asked.

A few officers murmured replies. Then everyone's radios and cell phones went off at once.

"All available officers, 10-33 at the Red Roof Inn on 590 Fairview Street. Officers and emergency services already on route," said a calm female voice.

Dana glanced down at her phone and saw a text from dispatch and knew at once it was about whatever they had just witnessed. "Okay, everyone," she said, "head to your vehicles and let dispatch know you are on route. Lee, do you have a cruiser with you?"

He shook his head and pointed to the female officer who had spoken earlier. "I'm with Dawes, ma'am."

"Dawes, can I borrow your partner for a few?" Dana asked her.

The woman nodded. "He's all yours, Detective."

"Thanks," she said. "Come on, Lee, I am over here."

Lee fell in line with her, confirming her guess that he was former military. Before they had even gotten halfway to where Dana had parked her sedan, they heard a faint noise that sounded like a roar followed by another loud clap. Both officers stopped dead in their tracks and turned back to face the direction they had originally seen the lightning.

"I don't see anything," Lee said quietly after a few seconds of scanning the horizon. "Whatever made that noise must be below our field of view."

"Agreed." Dana turned and quickened her pace. "We better get moving."

As the two officers headed away, neither of them noticed the dark figure that watched them from the shadows. Steve had also heard the explosion and had come out to investigate.

It was obvious the cops were riled up about something. Every single one was running around like a chicken with its head cut off. As Dana and her new friend got in her car, a wonderful thought popped into his mind. He could solve the Dana problem right here and now.

Binghamton was obviously in chaos at the moment. What better time was there to strike? After all, if the explosion he'd heard was some kind of terrorist attack, then the deaths of two random police officers would most likely be attributed to that and not investigated any deeper. He would have to kill both her and the officer with her, and that was impulsive. He had promised himself he was going to be less impulsive. But... he could always work on that tomorrow.

Pointing in the direction of the two officers, he imagined a blade made of dark energy shooting from his fingertips. Nothing happened. He turned his hand over and stared at it, confused. He was certain he had imagined the same knife he'd conjured before, so why had it not manifested?

The first time had been effortless, so he doubted it was from a lack of effort. He tried again, concentrating harder this time just for good measure, and was met with the same result. Frustrated since his prey was about to get away, he grimaced and examined his hand again. Perhaps if he thought back on what he had been doing and thinking when it had first manifested, he could discover what he was doing wrong.

Steve tapped his lips. "Well, all I remember thinking was how much fun it would be to kill Dana."

As soon as the feelings of anticipation entered his consciousness, dark energy tingled in his hands. Smirking, he again raised his hand and pointed it at the unsuspecting officers. This time a thin dark blade coalesced from the shadows.

Dana and the other officer were in the car now with the engine started, so he changed his aim to one of the back tires. His plan was to blow out a tire, forcing them to exit the car directly in his kill zone. At least, so he thought. He really had no idea what the range was to his new weapon, but today was as good a day as any to test its limits.

He made his hand into the shape of a gun. Just as he suspected, the blade warped to his imagination and extended out past his index finger, allowing him to better aim the shadow blade. He closed one eye and aimed for the back tire facing him.

"Boom," he said as he lowered his thumb.

The shadow blade exploded silently from his fingertip and raced toward the car. Before the darkness had gone two yards, it was intercepted and deflected by a glowing thin purple and black sword. As soon as Steve's eyes registered the newcomer, he felt a slight breeze pass by his body that ruffled his hair.

Unfazed, Steve lowered his arm and cocked his head to one side. The man was absolutely absurd. He was clad in black with a large-brimmed hat with a red feather sticking out of it and dressed as if he belonged at the Renaissance Faire. He replaced his rapier in the scabbard on his hip and smiled at him maliciously. Steve was instantly struck by the man's nightmare black eyes.

Steve was in awe of the man's obvious strength. He could sense it emanating from him in waves of power. The man watched the two officers speed off down the road. As soon as they were safely out of view, he scrutinized Steve with his dark eyes.

"Well now, what do we have here?" he said. "I see you have grown since last I saw you, infant."

Steve squinted suspiciously and allowed the dark energy to form in his fingertips again. "You're like that damn China man who was following me, aren't you?"

The Musketeer laughed out loud. "China man? Monsieur, how absolutely delightful. I have not laughed so hard in a *siècle*. Well, in your tongue, I think it is a century. In a fashion, I suppose that I am. I am, how you say, more..." He snapped his fingers. "Malevolent. Yes, that is a good word for it."

Steve tried to process what was happening to him. He had supernatural powers and he was pretty sure he knew where they came from, but this... this was just bizarre. He really had to wonder if he'd finally lost it.

"Are you real?" he asked.

The Musketeer smiled at Steve the way a cat would a mouse. "Am I real? Monsieur, you have the ability to conjure shadow weapons and you ask if I am real?"

"Well, can you blame me? Your manner of dress is a bit... out of date. Besides, I was raised Christian.

Demons and angels I get, but you, now that is something new entirely."

The Musketeer waved away Steve's confusion. "My boy, there is much about the universe you do not know, but now is not the time for teaching. Let me ask you, what were you planning on doing to those two *policiers*?"

"I was going to kill them."

When Steve declined further elaboration, the Musketeer said, "Oh, mon ami, you really are such a blunt instrument."

Not sure if he was being insulted, Steve shrugged. "Why did you stop me?"

"Because, my boy, now is not the time for killing dear Dana. You need only be patient a little while longer."

Steve was not sure who or what this man was or what his intentions were. That made him nervous. He casually put a hand behind his back and allowed the dark energy to build up in his fingertips just in case.

As if the man could read his thoughts, he turned around so his back was facing Steve and raised both hands up. "If you think you can hit me, then go ahead and strike."

Steve's eyes went wide as the man suddenly vanished. Before he even had time to wonder where the man had gone, he felt a sharp object pressing against the small of his back. It was at that very moment that Steve realized just how outmatched he truly was. A fear like he had never experienced before petrified him.

The tip of the Musketeer's rapier bit into his skin as the man leaned closer to speak in Steve's ear. "As fun as this little distraction is, mon ami, time is ticking away, and our window of opportunity is short. Now listen to me very carefully since I will not be repeating myself. Find a woman you fancy and go be a blunt instrument. When you do, he will sense it and he will come; and when he does, you will understand why I stopped you tonight."

Steve managed to stutter, "Who will come?"

But there was no reply.

It took him some time to dare turn around to see if the man was truly gone. His heart was still racing from the confrontation. Whoever the Musketeer was, one thing was certain: he was no ordinary human being. Steve could still feel the spiritual echoes left by his immense power.

The words the Musketeer had said right before he vanished resounded in his mind. "Find a woman you fancy and go be a blunt instrument."

That was simple enough. It was time to go hunting. The night was waning fast, and he was dying to try out his newly discovered powers.

So with a smile, he stalked off into the shadows.

Chapter Thirty-Seven

Jeremy threw up again. He hated teleporting, and twice in one night was definitely a record for him. Since he was from the city, he had no idea where they were. He did recognize that they were on the roof of a rather tall building. Of course, "tall" was relative. Compared to the lofty skyscrapers of downtown Manhattan, even the tallest buildings here looked small.

"We are still in town," observed Sanctuary. "I had hoped for a destination that was farther away, but this will do for now."

"At least Dominion is gone. For the moment." Jeremy sat in the corner with his eyes closed, holding his stomach and feeling miserable. "That's something anyway."

Jared stared out at the night sky. It was late or early, depending on your perspective. Soon the sun would be cresting the eastern horizon and the day would begin for the ordinary people of New York's Southern Tier. He still could not get Joe's terrified expression out of his mind. No matter what argument anyone made, he knew it was his fault the young man was dead.

Sanctuary placed his large hand on his shoulder. "Jared, I am sorry it took me so long to find you. I was detained. What has Tzedakah told you so far?"

Jared continued to stare off into space lost in his own thoughts. It took him a minute to realize that someone had spoken to him. "I'm sorry. What did you say?"

Sanctuary scrutinized him for a few seconds before he spoke again. "It was nothing important. How are you adjusting?"

"To being a murdering monster? Not well." He spat.

"Jared, it is not as it seems. You are not a murderer; in fact, you are the farthest thing from it."

"Tell that to the young man whose arms I cut off," he retorted. "Oh, that's right. You can't; he's dead."

"That was not your fault," Jeremy interjected.

Jared turned on him. "Oh really? How about the teenager back at the convenience store? Was he my fault?"

Jeremy had no idea what to say to comfort him, so he went back to nursing his nauseated stomach.

"What is it Tzedakah has told you?" Sanctuary asked.

Jared glared at his sword. "Not much. It keeps trying to invade my mind and I don't like that. I never liked alcohol—never even tried drugs—because I don't like the feeling like I'm out of control. These mental intrusions are a thousand times worse."

"I see. Now I understand why it took control of your actions earlier. Unfortunately, there was probably no other way for it to protect you. You were in more danger than you realized, and even though Jeremy is a fine fellow, I am sure he was very much out of his depth."

"I'm sitting right here, you know," Jeremy said. "Yeah, he is a bit full of himself, isn't he?" This last statement was directed to the sky.

"Tzedakah's actions may seem harsh," Sanctuary continued, "but I can assure you, they are absolutely just. In fact, Tzedakah is the living embodiment of justice, and every action it takes is for that purpose and that purpose alone. To mortal perceptions, justice can at times seem harsh and unfair, but justice is the one force in the entire universe that is absolutely and always impartial."

"So, it was *just* for that young man to die?" Jared asked incredulously. "He was being controlled by a demon and had no idea what he was doing. How could his death be justice? I don't buy it."

Sanctuary grimaced. "Jared, not all things are as they seem. To a normal mortal, possession is frightening and incomprehensible. It is the stuff of nightmares and legends, but in reality, it is not so mysterious. To be frank, no one can be possessed if they do not want to be. Yes, it is a process of influences and persuasion that steers a person toward an eventual destination, but in the end, the person must follow willingly."

Jared fell silent. The situation still seemed wrong to him, but he had to concede that there was much about the universe he did not understand. The fact that he was alive and walking around was confirmation of that. Even so, killing people like this did not sit well with him.

He turned his head slightly and looked at Sanctuary out of the corner of his eye. "And what about what Tzedakah does to me?"

The big man pursed his lips. "That is a different matter entirely and will require a bit more explanation."

Jared shook his head. "I thought you'd say something like that. Who or what are you, anyway?"

"I have many names, but you may call me Sanctuary."

"Yeah, of all of God's minions, he is the one who is the most meddlesome," Jeremy said. "And you don't have to take my word for it. You will see for yourself before long. Ask him what happened to the last person he 'helped.'"

"That is enough, Jeremy," Sanctuary chastised. "Your problems with me have no bearing on the current situation. You and I both know the severity of what it is he is facing."

Jared could feel Tzedakah in his head. He had not completely forgiven the sword for its earlier intrusion, but he was beginning to see that it was important that they find a way to work together. Whether he liked it or not, this was his new reality, and he had to find a way to cope.

"I apologize for taking control of your body," Tzedakah said, sensing how Jared's mood. "I hope you understand that I had no choice. I know this is difficult for you, but you need to start trusting me."

Trust you? Jared thought. *How can I trust you? It's not like we are partners or something. It's funny, really. In the normal world, weapons are instruments to be used by men, but I have the feeling that the roles are reversed when it comes to us. I am the instrument being used by you. You ask me to trust you, but how can I when you keep using me as some kind of tool?*

"If you would trust me, then I would not need to 'use you,' as you say. But the longer you fight me, the more unpleasant our time together will be."

"Jared?" Sanctuary inquired, concerned after a few minutes of prolonged silence.

Jared turned his gaze from the sentient sword and looked up at Sanctuary. "Sorry. We were talking."

Sanctuary nodded. "I know you feel trapped, but what is happening to you is of the utmost importance to the world as a whole. Sometimes what is required of us for the greater good must take priority over our own desires."

"And there it is, the 'you need to sacrifice for the greater good' speech," said Jeremy getting to his feet. "Well, that didn't take long. I think this is a new record for you, Sanctuary."

Jeremy and Sanctuary continued to square off, but Jared was no longer listening. His black eyes were fixed on the horizon.

"You can sense him as well, can't you?" Tzedakah asked.

Jared nodded and clenched his teeth in rage. His grip tightened on the sword and for the first time since he had been reborn, he allowed Tzedakah in unhindered. At first, he wanted to struggle against the sudden rush of emotions he felt from the sword, but he calmed himself and let the sensations flood over his mind.

The compulsion to move and act was so intense that it threatened to overwhelm all his human reasoning. He could feel himself being lost to the driving hunger. It was like nothing else in the world existed but one thing: justice. For the first time since this had all started, he felt he understood the sword and what it was they were meant to do.

The change in the atmosphere was tangible. Jeremy and Sanctuary turned to look at Jared. Even

Jeremy's human eyes could see the power radiating off him like tongues of blue-black fire. Sanctuary took a step toward him, alarmed by the sudden surge of spiritual power.

"Jared, what's wrong?" he asked concerned.

Jared glanced back at his two friends, and the darkness that had replaced his eyes danced. Before either man could react, Jared leaped off the rooftop and vanished in a burst of crackling energy.

Chapter Thirty-Eight

The woman was beautiful. Her long flaxen hair was pulled up into a ponytail and it bounced provocatively as she ran. Her eyes were an amazing bright blue and her milky white skin glistened with sweat. She was full-figured and curvy but had the tight stomach of a fitness instructor. She was dressed in yoga pants and a hoodie and looked to be in her mid-forties. Doubtless, she could have been a model or actress, and Steve smiled as she jogged up to the intersection where he was waiting and stopped next to him.

Panting, the woman put her hands on her hips as she cooled down. She was oblivious to everything around her, including Steve standing next to her. But he noticed her and drank in every detail.

When she finally became aware of him standing there, the woman acknowledged him politely yet dismissively. She checked her smartwatch and sighed. She was out for her morning run but had awakened a little later than usual. Now she needed to cut it short to get back in time for work. Smiling politely at Steve, she headed back the way she'd come.

Before the woman had even made it a meter, Steve struck like a viper. His shadow blade lashed out and sliced the back of her hamstring. Unsure of what had happened, the woman stumbled forward and dropped to one knee. The cut had been so precise that it had sliced cleanly through her skintight pants, leaving only the slightest incision.

The woman gritted her teeth from the sudden intense pain, tears welling in her eyes. She groped at the back of her leg and cradled it to her body protectively. She was in shock as the blood dripped down her leg and pooled at her feet.

When she noticed the dark red stain on the ground next to her, her face went paper-white. She tried to stand but stumbled and fell backward, hitting her tailbone hard on the pavement. She was still in shock and could only whimper as she looked around for help.

Her eyes met Steve's. He smiled warmly and ambled toward her, and she exhaled thankfully through gritted teeth when she realized she'd managed to get his attention. But the searing pain in her leg made it impossible for her to explain the seriousness of her injury. The woman was in so much pain that all she managed to say to him as he kneeled down next to her was a barely intelligible, "Please call 911."

"Just calm down, getting all worked up only makes it worse," he said, pretending to assess the situation. "Now, tell me what happened."

"I—I—" she started.

The world swam, and the woman blinked to regain focus. She wanted to stand, but the searing pain told her the leg would not work. All she could do was grasp it as her blood leaked out.

Steve pulled her hand away and probed the wound. "Okay, I can feel where it's bleeding from. Looks like you got a nasty cut here. Any idea how that happened?"

The woman shook her head, tears streaming down her cheeks.

"I've got it," Steve said, clamping his hand on the wound.

The jogger closed her eyes and exhaled releasing some of the built-up tension. Her face was tear stained and she was deathly pale, but thanks to her unknown rescuer, she felt a little better.

"Thank you," she started to say before her words were strangled by a rush of excruciating pain.

She thrashed and screamed out in agony as Steve cruelly dug his fingers into her open wound. Even though it was early morning, this was upstate New York. No one was around to hear her cries.

He was in ecstasy right up to the point where the woman passed out from pain and went limp. Furious that his fun was interrupted, he kicked the prostrate woman. Seriously, he had seen more fight in a puppy. He had just decided to put the poor girl out of her misery when he felt a surge of immense power materialize behind him.

Remembering the Musketeer's words, he allowed the dark energy that resided in him to build up in his fingertips. Now the demonic force flowed out of him instinctively as if it had always been a part of him. Energy coursed through his entire body, electrifying him with unimaginable power.

Steve's newfound demonic senses bristled at the spiritual pressure of the man who slowly walked toward him. The authority emanating from him was similar to the Musketeer's, yet decidedly different. It was as if both men were different sides of the same coin. He was dressed all in black like the Musketeer and brandishing a glowing sword, though he was wearing a long-tattered trench coat instead of the Musketeer's traditional tabard.

Even with his dark powers, Steve knew he should be afraid of the man, but the intoxicating effect he felt from the demonic energy he'd unleashed flooded him with confidence. It was not until the man had moved close enough for Steve to see his face that his nerve faltered. The face he beheld was the face of his dead brother.

"No," he hissed in disbelief. "This is not possible."

Jared advanced toward his younger brother. His nightmare black eyes churned angrily and Tzedakah's glow increased with every step. In truth, Jared did not see his brother when he looked at Steve. All he saw was the monstrous atrocities he had committed. All he saw was murder.

Jared pointed Tzedakah at his petrified younger brother. Power swelled in the blade of the sentient sword, arcing and convulsing in anticipation. Jared's face was hard; Steve knew that the person who stood before him now was no longer his older brother.

The thought came too late to him, however, as Jared unleashed the pent-up energy. The power exploded from the blade with the sound of a thunderclap and surged toward him like a lightning bolt. He knew that he would not be quick enough to evade the blast. He had resigned himself to his fate when a voice inside said, "Let me take control."

Chapter Thirty-Nine

Jeremy ran to the edge of the roof and searched in vain for any trace of Jared. He knew it was futile, but he had to make sure, anyway. The Holy Spirit was screaming in his mind that danger was nearby, but he ignored the warnings.

"This is not good," he said frantically. "I know that this kind of thing is not my usual forte, but he's kind of grown on me and I don't want to see him dead. Well, at least re-dead or whatever it is that happens to him."

Sanctuary paced behind him, scanning the horizon as if he was searching for something. "His link with the sword is tenuous at best and that puts him in real danger. Tzedakah will do his utmost to protect him, but sword bearers are at their most vulnerable shortly after they are first called."

"Called, that's a very diplomatic way to put zombified," Jeremy retorted. "Where do you think he went? Honestly, he could theoretically be anywhere in the known universe, right?"

The thunder of an explosion echoed in the distance; blue-black lightning flashed.

"I'm pretty sure I know where he went," Jeremy said.

"Agreed," Sanctuary replied. "He most assuredly needs our help. Are you up to the task?"

Jeremy sighed heavily. "Well, since you asked so nicely, yeah. Besides, God has been screaming at me for the last couple minutes about it, so I don't have much of a choice either way. Trust me, if I tried to leave, He'd find a way to get me there, anyway. He's good at that."

Sanctuary smirked at Jeremy. "I am aware."

Jeremy huffed, "Yeah yeah yeah."

Sanctuary put his hand on Jeremy's shoulder. "I truly am glad to have you with me, my friend, and I am very thankful you were able to be here when I was not."

"Alright, enough with the mushy stuff already. You gonna fly me there or am I going to take the bus?"

"The bus, of course," chuckled Sanctuary. "I may have the strength of ten men, but I am not that strong."

"And there is the son of a gun we all know and dislike," said Jeremy. "Wow, I didn't think you had a sense of humor. I thought being serious was a prerequisite for your line of work."

"Perhaps you are rubbing off on me," he said, turning to take him by the arm. "We really do need to go."

As soon as Sanctuary touched Jeremy's arm, his eyes went wide in surprise. He jerked suddenly to the right, away from the angel's touch and away from the edge of the roof where they were standing. His momentum sent him as far from the angel as was humanly possible just as a ball of violet energy erupted between them. The force of the explosion pushed Jeremy towards the center of the roof and sent Sanctuary reeling through the air.

Jeremy's last-minute maneuver had saved his life, placing him in just the right position for the blast wave to throw him away from the edge of the roof instead of off it. He did, however, strike an industrial air-conditioning vent with enough force to crack a few ribs and knock the wind out of his lungs.

He lay still on his side, gasping for air. He could taste blood in his mouth but was unsure if it were coming from internal or external injuries. Thankfully, Jeremy had been listening, and he had heard God's warning just in time. He had been distracted but responded quickly enough to prevent himself from being splattered all over the pavement below. He knew that they were still in danger, so he tried to stand, but nearly passed out from the pain. Something was definitely broken. All he was able to do before the pain became unbearable was roll onto his back and turn his head toward whoever it was that had attacked them.

Sanctuary had already recovered from the unexpected ambush and had both his flaming blades out and at the ready. The fire from his aura had deflected most of the energy from the blast, but a few tendrils of crackling power arced around him before dissipating into the atmosphere. When unveiled, the angel was imposing, but the aura of the person nonchalantly leaning on the guardrail was just as impressive.

"God forgive me," Jeremy whispered, "but oh shit."

The Musketeer smirked as he tapped his lips with his free hand. His rapier was in his other hand still surging with power and he casually flicked it in the air.

"Now, now," he mocked. "We mustn't interfere with the children's fun."

Chapter Forty

The police radio in Dana's car squawked as she barreled down an empty street. Apparently, two more explosions had been reported in different areas of the city and officers were being rerouted from the initial location to those neighborhoods. The radio chatter was predominantly from the officers who had been rerouted and they were all talking at the same time, trying to discover what was going on in their normally calm municipality.

Lee was buckled in and holding on to the handle over the window casually. Of course, his face was as stoic as ever. Dana took a hard left turn and he leaned into it gracefully like a pro, not showing any signs that the movement had disturbed him.

I bet all this action reminds him of wherever he was deployed, she thought.

Dana's cell phone suddenly came to life as she made another sharp turn. Lee picked it up. "Officer Lee. Yes, sir, she is currently driving. Absolutely, sir."

Lee pushed an icon on the dashboard's touch screen and the captain's baritone voice came through on the car speakers.

"Dana, you there?"

"Yeah, Captain, go ahead," she replied.

"You headed to Fairview, or have you rerouted to one of the other locations?"

"We are headed to Prospect, sir," she answered. "It's the farthest out and most of the other officers are headed downtown or to the initial incident, so I figured we'd go there."

"Good. I was going to send you that way. People are waking up and the reports coming in are... strange."

Dana and Lee both glanced at each other. The captain was a veteran police officer and he had experienced pretty much everything that a person could during his many years on the job. So for him to be unnerved...

"What do you mean, sir?" Dana asked, trying not to allow the anxiety she felt to show in her voice.

"Now take this with a grain of salt, but witnesses are claiming that there are two men fighting in the street."

"Okay. So, are they the suspected bombers?" Lee asked. "Perhaps an internal dispute or something like that."

The captain said, "Honestly, I am a little hesitant to repeat what was reported. The reports are that one of them is carrying a glowing sword and that he is shooting lasers out of it like some kind of science fiction movie."

Both Dana and Lee said, "What?"

"Are you serious?" Dana added.

"Dead," replied the captain. "That is why I wanted you to head that way. I need a level head on this, and you are the best officer I currently have in the field. Handley and Winder are still finishing up their earlier homicide investigation, and I notified Agent Johansson about our new possible Stalker victim. I am waiting for him to call me back."

"Is Agent Johansson on his way?" Dana asked.

"As far as I know, he left about two hours ago. Said he would call when he got into town. You call me as soon as you get to the location and let me know what the hell is going on."

"Will do, Captain."

Neither officer spoke as they continued to drive down the now awakening streets. All that could be heard was the wail of their siren and the occasional screeching of Dana's tires as the city flew by. Both of them found it hard to believe that a sword-wielding warrior was roving around the city blowing things up with lasers.

Dana had a thought and she reached for the icons on the dashboard. A phone rang through the car speakers. It only rang twice before a male voice answered. "Dana? What the hell is going on up there?"

"Tom. I am not really sure," she managed as they took a particularly hard turn. "That's why I'm calling. All hell seems to have broken loose. We have multiple explosions and possible—and I hesitate to say this—sword-wielding aliens or something like that."

"Okay... is there more than one of them? Be specific. What exactly are the reports saying?"

Dana was surprised by Johansson's tone, which seemed apprehensive. "Well, all I know is that the reports stated that two men were fighting. We are heading in that direction now and I thought I'd call you to see if there was any rumored terrorist activity that you knew of."

Johansson sighed heavily on the other end of the call. Dana could tell he was losing his patience. "All I can say is that this is not a terrorist attack. At least, not as far as I can tell. But what I need to know from you, is how many of the reported assailants have swords?"

Dana was stunned into silence. She had just told him about multiple explosions and medieval weapon-wielding combatants in the streets and he was concerned with how many of them had swords.

"Dana. How many of them have swords? This is important."

"I don't know for sure, but the captain only mentioned one."

"Okay, I want you to do me a favor," he said, sounding relieved. "Do not under any circumstances go near them. Do you hear me? Do not go near them."

Dana and Lee shared a look of incredulity at Johansson's warning. They were police officers and unknown assailants were endangering the people of their city. Getting involved was their job.

"What exactly do you know, Tom?" she asked him. "Because from where we sit, it sounds like you know more about what's happening here than you are willing to divulge."

"Dana, I'll be there in about an hour. Please don't do anything until I get there. You have to trust me on this, okay? I honestly don't know what's going on, but I do know things that you don't, and I am asking you as a friend not to engage any of the suspects until I get there, okay?"

"Well, we can't do that, Agent Johansson," she said and pushed a button to cut him off before he had a chance to protest.

Chapter Forty-One

Steve had no idea how it had happened, but he had somehow managed to evade the blast from Jared's sword. He found himself about ten feet away from where the power had traveled, crouching in front of a split and burning pine tree. A sinister shroud of shadowy energy flowed all around him, protecting him like a shield.

The voice inside spoke again, instructing him to permit the dark energy to flow into his hands. Just like when he had conjured the daggers, the shadows coalesced into something of form and substance. This time, however, instead of a thin dagger, two large scythes manifested around his hands.

"My power is yours," an eerie voice rasped in his mind. "Take it."

Steve shook violently as wave after wave of demonic power coursed through his body. Before his body had stopped trembling, some sort of sixth sense warned him that danger was upon him. Faster than human eyes could track, Jared dashed at him with his sword poised for a killing blow.

Steve grinned as he easily maneuvered out of the way and swung a shadow scythe to parry the strike. He punched out with the other scythe, slamming Jared in the gut, throwing him backward.

Jared spun through the air like an acrobat and landed on his feet. Without even a second's hesitation, he regained his footing and attacked Steve again. This time, however, Steve was ready for the assault and he met him blow for blow. To mortal eyes, the two brothers appeared as nothing more than indistinguishable blurs of movement as they clashed.

After a few minutes of intense action that ended in a stalemate, the two brothers separated. Jared waited with his free hand in front of his body and his sword arm extended out to his side. Tzedakah burned blue flame, mirroring the fierce expression on his face. Steve's expression was one of absolute bliss. He tightened his grip on his weapons and flexed his muscles, reveling in the boundless strength he felt.

"This is absolutely unreal!" he shouted gleefully like a child opening a Christmas present. "Such unlimited power! Such might! Oh, how I wish I had known of this power sooner. I'd wondered if I had allowed something in all those years ago. I'd always suspected that it had been working for my benefit. But this—this is beyond anything I ever could have possibly imagined."

His words were lost on Jared who only saw all the foul things his brother had done. Murder after gruesome murder flashed before his eyes in a cruel montage. Sadly, evil had entered Steve when he was very young, giving Jared a lifetime of wickedness to witness.

Jared would have been horrified and even saddened at the revelation of just how far his brother's darkness went if he had not been overtaken by Tzedakah's endless need to bring evil to justice. Still, despite Tzedakah's overwhelming compulsion, Jared maintained a glimmer of will that belonged to him and him alone. This was the reason why, when he attacked again, he chose to defy Tzedakah by attempting to incapacitate his brother rather than kill him.

Steve saw Jared move, but this time he was too fast. He tried in vain to react, but it was futile. Jared's movements were so quick that he was upon him and past his guard before he even had time to raise his shadow weapons. He struck Steve with Tzedakah's pommel ten times before his body even registered the damage.

When his body finally felt the pain, he doubled over, and Jared followed up with an uppercut so strong, it launched him backward like a missile. He reeled end over end before crashing into a parked car.

Steve lay partly embedded in the side of the car. The door had wrapped around his body, covering his left side completely while leaving his right partially exposed. The black shroud that had encased his body dissipated. Jared feared he had killed his brother, but he approached him cautiously just in case.

The streets were unusually empty considering all that had just transpired. Sirens could be heard blaring in the distance as local authorities were finally responding to the chaos that had erupted around the city. Likewise, the inhabitants of Binghamton were all waking up from their night's rest, ready to start their busy days. He was mentally and emotionally exhausted, and the commotion of the world around him faded away as he focused on the moment at hand.

When he reached Steve's prone body, Jared bent down to see if he was dead. He touched his neck, feeling for a pulse. Steve's heartbeat was slow but still there. He stepped back and looked at his brother. He looked peaceful. Jared tried to remember what his brother had been like when they were kids, but all his new eyes saw were the terrible things the killer had done.

One moment had changed his little brother forever. Just one fateful day. Jared remembered that day like it was yesterday. He had forgiven his parents and God for baby Hope's death, but Steve never had. Bitterness and anger had consumed him. It twisted him inside and broke him.

Jared's new eyes allowed him to see how the evil entity that now inhabited his brother had used Steve's pain as a conduit to latch onto him. Once the demon had won his trust, he transformed him into a monster. Slowly it had encouraged his murderous impulses until his every thought was consumed by them. Upon seeing his brother's life unfold before his eyes, Jared realized just how true Sanctuary's words had been about the workings of devils.

With a suddenness that incapacitated Jared, Tzedakah invaded his mind. He felt every painful and raw sensation that each of Steve's victims had experienced. Their pleas for mercy broke his heart and their despair forced tears to his eyes. Biting pain erupted over his body from a thousand wounds that were meant to torture, and he dropped to his knees overwhelmed. He wept bitterly and prayed for death as Steve's victims had before he finally ended their lives.

"Execute him," Tzedakah demanded. "Justice requires that he die for his transgressions."

"No!" shouted Jared. "I will not."

"Yes. You will."

Chapter Forty-Two

All Jeremy could do was watch helplessly as Sanctuary squared off against the Musketeer. He was thankful to God that he was alive, but he wished there was something he could do to help his friend. Using every bit of his remaining strength, he once again tried to get to his feet. But just like before, the pain was too much, and he collapsed.

"Darn it," he hissed through gritted teeth. "You're lucky I am all beat up, you French jackass, or I would come over there and beat that stupid grin right off your face."

The words slid right off the Musketeer who stretched casually if he were getting ready for an exercise class. When he finished, he pulled at his gloves, swished his blade through the air a few times, and settled into a defensive fighting stance.

He gestured broadly at the angel. "Well then, mon ami, I guess it is finally time for us to see who is the strongest."

Sanctuary crossed his flaming swords. "Renault, I can assure you this will not take long."

"Of that, I agree."

Both combatants warily watched each other from across the roof in an old-fashioned standoff. Sanctuary was the first to move. He darted to the side, trying to flank his opponent. The Musketeer instantly read the move and twisted away from the angel's double swing while simultaneously blocking his blades and shoving them away from his body. The parry left Sanctuary's back exposed and the Musketeer in the perfect position to take advantage of the opening.

But when he swung, all he struck was air as Sanctuary backflipped away from his attack. The angel somersaulted twice then hovered high above the rooftop, out of his adversary's reach. His beautiful golden wings extended like that of a gigantic bird of prey.

The Musketeer huffed. "Don't you think that is cheating, just a little bit?"

Sanctuary smiled down at the slender Frenchman but said nothing.

The Musketeer disappeared in a violet lightning bolt of motion, zigzagging through the air toward the hovering Sanctuary.

He slammed into the angel, who crossed his blades and took the full force of the blow. Sanctuary was shoved back but managed to maintain his balance.

The Musketeer grinned gleefully as he began to drop. "I shall enjoy clipping those beautiful wings of yours, Sanctuary."

This time it was Sanctuary's turn to attack. He streaked like a rocket toward the descending Musketeer. Terrified, the Musketeer twisted his body just enough to avoid the full force of the blow but went spinning violently into the building below. With the agility of a cat, the Musketeer managed to right himself just before he slammed into the rooftop. His boots struck the concrete hard, but he redirected his momentum into a forward roll.

Then he planted his feet and launched himself upward, back into the night sky. Sanctuary was ready for the maneuver and plummeted toward the Musketeer. They collided in midair like two freight trains, sending a shock wave in all directions.

Metal clashed against metal as the two combatants fought. Jeremy still couldn't help. He could barely follow their movements. But he could pray. And as soon as he reached out to the Lord, he could feel God's healing power pour into his broken body. It was not enough to repair his broken bones, but it restored a measure of his strength.

He was still unable to stand, but he could sit up and lean against the industrial air-conditioning unit he'd hit earlier. As he did, he turned his head just in time to see one of the combatants slam violently into the rooftop. The reinforced concrete cracked and bowed from the impact, releasing a cloud of debris that obscured Jeremy's vision.

When the haze finally cleared enough for him to see, his heart sank. Sanctuary lay prone and motionless in a small crater of fractured concrete and steel. Both of his blades were missing and the ethereal fire that usually surrounded him was extinguished.

The Musketeer's cruel laughter pierced the silence as he emerged unscathed from the shadows. He sneered down at the angel who struggled to rise. "I guess I win!"

Sanctuary growled angrily, but the Musketeer kicked him in the face. His head snapped backward, bouncing off a dislodged slab of concrete with enough force to shatter it.

"Tsk, tsk," said the Musketeer as he ambled over to Sanctuary's limp body. He readjusted his gloves, gripped his rapier with both hands, and raised it up over his head with the point facing downward.

"I had hoped that you would be more of a challenge." He sighed. "But sadly, you never really stood a chance. I know I can't truly destroy you, angel. But know this: as soon as I am done with you, I will take my time with the prophet."

Jeremy's rage rose as the Musketeer taunted his friend.

"God," he pleaded, "I know You are listening, so please give me the strength to wipe that infuriating smile off the face of this humongous piece of crap."

To Jeremy's great delight, heavenly power built up in his right hand.

"This one's for the Shogun!" he whispered.

The Musketeer was too busy with Sanctuary to notice the sudden change in spiritual pressure, so the blast of divine power that shot from Jeremy's outstretched hand took him completely by surprise.

To Jeremy's immense satisfaction, there was no smile on the Musketeer's face as he went soaring off the edge of the building. He fell straight down, just as two police cruisers arrived. Thanks to the paralyzing effects of the divine energy that had struck him, the Musketeer was unable to move or teleport. He struck the ground hard and bounced twice before coming to a stop a few feet from two startled police officers.

"Who's going to take his time now, jackass?" Jeremy shouted triumphantly at the roof's edge.

Jeremy's shout roused the stunned Sanctuary. His eyes flicked open, and he sat up gingerly. The heavenly radiance that usually encompassed him returned as he rubbed his neck. He turned to look at Jeremy who had slumped sideways a bit from the kick of releasing so much spiritual power. Besmudged and bruised, he was so exhausted that he couldn't even right himself. It took everything Sanctuary had not to laugh.

"You good now?" Jeremy asked sarcastically when he realized the angel was amused. "I can come over there and help you up if you like. It's not like I just saved your hide or anything like that."

Sanctuary forced the grin off his face and got to his feet. "I'm sorry, are you going to be alright?" he asked, concerned.

"Oh yeah. I mean, I'm sure the massive internal injuries I probably sustained will heal on their own, so I'm good. Didn't need my spleen, anyway. What the heck does a spleen even do?"

Sanctuary gingerly walked over to him, reached down, and picked him up. Jeremy nearly passed out from the pain. His head lolled and his eyes lost focus as Sanctuary walked to the edge of the building.

They peered down, hoping against hope that they had finally managed to incapacitate the Musketeer. All they saw were two dead police officers and a handful of people milling around, looking confused.

Jeremy blinked to clear away the fog in his head. "I think I am going to need a hospital," he slurred. "Or a walk-in clinic at least. Maybe a veterinarian. God has assured me that I am not going to die, at least not yet. Right now, dying might be preferable."

Sanctuary made a decision as he looked out at the horizon. Whatever it was Jared was currently encountering, he was going to have to face it alone with Tzedakah. That would have to be enough. Sanctuary prayed that their bond was strong enough to overcome whatever challenges they were facing. But Jeremy needed immediate medical attention, and for now, there was nothing more either of them could do to help him.

"Hang in there, brother," Sanctuary said as he extended his enormous wings, gently rose, and headed for the nearest hospital.

Chapter Forty-Three

Steve's eyes were closed, but he was not unconscious. Whatever the entity was that had been helping him, it had minimized the damage from the impact to next to nothing. He cracked open one of his eyes and saw his brother crouched in front of him, holding his head as if he were in pain. Unsure of what exactly was happening to Jared, he decided it best to play possum and figure out his next move.

Jared's eyes were squeezed shut. His face was contorted in an expression of intense anguish. Steve had no idea how it was possible that his brother was alive. It all felt surreal, like he was trapped in some sort of low-budget horror film or something. In fact, this whole day had been one long walk into the paranormal and the bizarre. Perhaps he was having some sort of psychotic break, but he decided to go with it either way.

"I will not!" his brother suddenly shouted.

"He is going to kill you," the voice in his mind rasped. "You must destroy him first."

Kill me? Steve thought. *I suppose it does make sense.*

Why else would his brother come back from the dead?

Well, maybe to see Dana, he surmised. Only a fool like his brother would rise from the grave just to save a girl. The girl he could never see as anything more than a friend until it was too late. Maybe instead of a revenge movie, he was in some ridiculous paranormal romance story instead.

It was time to put an end to Jared, this time for good. He reached inside to his unseen benefactor and it once again provided him with demonic power. The shadows coalesced around him and this time his muscles expanded and swelled from the unrestrained power.

With a roar of defiance, he ripped his trapped arm free and sprung at his brother. Steve's shout brought Jared back to his senses just in time to see both of his fists bearing down on his face. Before he could react to the sudden attack, Steve struck him square in the jaw with a double-fisted uppercut that sent him careening through the air.

Steve threw his arm forward and a line of shadow energy surged from his fingertips and rocketed toward Jared. The shadow took on the form of a large tentacle with thousands of two-inch-long barbs protruding from it. The tentacle wrapped around Jared's leg and bit deep into his calf. Steve pulled his arm down, redirecting his brother's momentum and sending him hurtling toward the ground.

Jared struck the road so hard that he put a man-sized divot in the asphalt. He could feel Tzedakah screaming mentally at him, but his voice was distant and distorted as if it were trying to reach him through water. Before he was able to sort out why his connection to Tzedakah was strained, he felt himself being flung up into the air once again.

Steve repeatedly slammed his brother into the ground like a rag doll, cracking the road in several places. Jared was not taking any real damage from the continuous beating, but his broken connection to Tzedakah made it impossible for him to counter it. Over and over again he smashed into the ground before Steve finally let go of him and sent him hurtling through the air.

Dana and Lee came barreling around the bend in the road just in time to see him being launched in their direction. Dana slammed on the breaks and the car swerved and stuttered, halting just before an airborne Jared flew past their windshield. He hit the ground a few feet from the stopped car and tumbled toward the river.

Before either of them could process what happened, Steve lunged past them using the hood of Dana's car as a springboard. The car rocked as he launched off it with so much force that he caused the frame to bend and the windows to shatter.

Steam poured from the car's hood and both airbags went off. Dana's heart was beating out of her chest. The front of her car was flattened, and both front tires had exploded.

"What the hell was that?" she asked.

"It looked like a man and then possibly another man," Lee said with his usual calm demeanor. Other than a few small cuts and bruises, he seemed none the worse for wear.

"I know it was a man," Dana snapped. "Gosh Lee, what exactly did you do in the military? Nothing, and I mean nothing, seems to rattle you."

He just looked at her and shrugged. "The usual things."

Lee, who had completely recovered from the shock of the accident, pointed to a woman who was sitting on the sidewalk only a few meters from them. "I think we may have a civilian hurt over there, ma'am."

Dana peered through the broken glass in the direction where Lee was pointing. Just as he had said, there was a woman sitting on the sidewalk, clutching her leg and crying for help. She might have heard the lady's cries if it wasn't for the loud ringing in her ears.

Lee popped out of the car and rushed to where the woman sat. Dana, on the other hand, gingerly extricated herself from the crushed car, and made her way over.

Lee had his hand pressed firmly on one of her upper thighs and with his other hand, he was fumbling through one of his pants pockets. Before long, he retrieved a rolled-up bandage and gently started wrapping it around her injured leg. The woman was pale from loss of blood and shock, but otherwise not in any immediate danger.

Dana looked for the two men who had disappeared by the river. What in the world was going on? If Lee had not confirmed that he had also seen them, she would not have believed her own eyes. It just wasn't possible, was it?

"Promise me you won't engage them," Johansson had said.

That son of a bitch knew what was going on and he had refused to tell her. Had he known that something was off even back during the Stalker investigation? Come to think of it, she didn't remember anyone calling in the FBI in the first place. Johansson just showed up out of the blue. That was not how interagency relations worked. No one had questioned it because he was FBI.

Moreover, he had brushed them off when they had gone to the city to check into the investigation. At the time she had not thought anything of it, but now it all made sense. He had even minimized the importance of a body disappearing from the morgue as if dead bodies got up and walked away all the time. To his defense, he had warned her not to get involved, but it was too late for that now.

She drew her weapon and turned to Lee. "You got this?"

People were starting to congregate around them, but otherwise, they were keeping their distance. He looked around at the bystanders and then nodded. "Yeah, I can handle this. I will call for EMS and back up. Are you sure you're going to be okay going off by yourself?"

She had to find out just what was going on and did not have time to wait for help to arrive.

"Yeah," she said setting her jaw. "I hope anyway."

She turned and quickly started off in the direction the two perpetrators had fled. Before she had gone far, however, Lee called out to her. "Detective!"

"Yeah?" she responded, impatiently turning around.

"Get that son of a bitch," he said with a smile.

She smiled back at him and gave him a quick salute before she continued her pursuit.

Chapter Forty-Four

Jared finally came to a halt when he crashed into a huge oak tree just on the edge of the river's waterline. Luckily, his body had come to a stop in a sitting position against the tree trunk. Leaves flitted down around him. Jared did not have time to enjoy them, as his brother came crashing through the tree line.

"Jared," Tzedakah whispered. "Trust me."

He gritted his teeth and shook his head. "No. Not if it means killing my brother," he said.

"You must," he pleaded. "We are almost out of time."

Steve reached his brother and bent down so they were face-to-face. He leered at him, revealing a mouth full of teeth elongated into the shape of tiny daggers. His eyes were wild, demonic, and glowing blood-red. His fingernails had extended into vicious claws, which he raked against Jared's chest.

"I must admit," he said in a voice more guttural than before. "I was somewhat sad when I was forced to kill you back in New York. Sure, I hate Mom and Dad, but I never held any ill will toward you."

Jared met his brother's gaze and glared at him angrily. He wanted to kill him. He wanted Justice, not only for himself, but for all of Steve's victims. Suddenly, as if he had turned on some kind of switch, he could hear the sentient sword's voice clearly once again. He realized at that moment, that the more he desired justice for his brother's victims, the stronger his connection with Tzedakah grew. Tzedakah hated injustice and his brother had become an avatar for everything he despised. By allowing himself to want justice, which required his brother's death, he was bringing his desires in line with the longings of the sentient sword.

Even so, he could not bring himself to kill his younger brother, no matter how much he deserved it. Strangely, Tzedakah was silent. He could still feel the raw emotion of the sword through their mental link, but he was no longer demanding Steve's death.

"Why?" Jared asked his brother.

His voice was hollow and ethereal and no longer resembled his former one. It didn't seem to originate from Jared's body either, but rose as if from some distant, invisible realm. Steve was confused when he heard it and backed away.

"I have to say, big brother," he said warily, "this new you is quite frightening. I mean, I am literally becoming a demon from hell, but you—you are a whole new level of terrifying."

Even though Jared could now hear Tzedakah clearly, he still did not trust him. He did not want to hurt his brother, despite the fact that he was a monster. Deep down in his heart, however, he knew that Tzedakah was right and that his brother had to die.

"You asked me why," Steve said, lowering his guard and taking a step backward. "Well, I killed you because I was afraid you saw me murder the girl at the show. I knew that even if you wanted to, there was no way you could overlook that. I mean, when we were kids, you couldn't handle having anything bad on your conscience. There was no way you'd be able to keep quiet about something like that."

He shrugged and scratched his head with his long nails. "If you were hoping for something more profound, I am sorry. Sure, I was a bit jealous that you were able to move on from Hope's death and I was not, but that wasn't why I killed you. Really, it was simply wrong place, wrong time.

"Now, if you are asking me why I kill people, well, that is a different matter entirely. Long story short, I hate God for not saving Hope while you all get to live. By killing people, I hurt Him and that makes me happy. Sure, hearing myself say that out loud now makes me realize that I have some pretty deep issues, but at this point, I really don't care."

It was at that moment that Dana emerged from the small tree line next to the river. It was nautical twilight so there was just enough light for her to make out that there were two people in front of her, but not enough to see any distinguishing features. She raised her duty weapon and pointed it in the direction of the two men.

"Binghamton police!" she shouted. "Put your hands on your heads and get down on the ground."

Jared's eyes went wide, and Steve grinned mischievously, as they both recognized her voice. The two brothers stared at each other, neither moving as Dana shouted more commands.

Jared's connection to Tzedakah was not yet whole, so he was not fast enough to stop his brother when he turned toward Dana. With frightening speed, Steve launched a thin shadow dagger at her while slamming his fist into Jared's face.

The stream of shadow shot through Dana so quickly that it took her a moment to register that she had been impaled. Her eyes went wide with shock when she saw the long shadow blade sticking out of her stomach. She tried to scream but all that came out was a wet gurgle as her legs lost their strength and she toppled to the ground.

Steve clapped his hands and laughed maniacally at his good fortune. "Well now, big brother, look who has come to the rescue! I knew it was only a matter of time before I would have to kill dear Dana, but who would've thought I'd get to kill her in front of you the way I killed you in front of her. I've gotta say, the man downstairs is far more helpful than the one upstairs. You chose the wrong side, brother."

Jared tried to rise, but he felt sluggish and slow like he was moving through liquid. He had to get to Dana, but his body would not respond fast enough. He could feel Tzedakah just at the edge of his consciousness, but he could not connect with it. Even now when Dana was in mortal danger, he still could not bring himself to kill his brother. He did not trust Tzedakah because it wanted him to kill his brother; hence, the disconnect between him and the sentient sword.

Steve slugged him again, sending him back to the ground. He then reached down and grabbed him by the hair, jerked him up, and making him face Dana's prone body.

He breathed in his brother's ear. "Do you think she is still alive? If she is, how long do you think she has? An hour? Ten minutes? It really is a crapshoot, isn't it? I mean, I'm not exactly precise with my aim, so I may have hit her kidney or some other vital organ. Or I may have missed everything entirely. You never know, really."

He let go of his brother's hair and his head dropped back to the ground. Jared lay on his stomach. Dana's moans had stopped, and she wasn't moving. All he could do was watch her helplessly as his brother stood over him.

"I think I'll do this the old-fashioned way," Steve said as he reached into his pocket and pulled out a medium-sized hunting knife. "There's no need to rush, so I might as well take my time and enjoy myself."

A soon as he turned toward Dana, a shot rang out. Steve looked down at his chest in surprise as a large red stain formed in the center of his shirt. He looked up to see Dana on her knees with her pistol trained directly on him, holding her stomach with her other hand. Their eyes met and he saw not only recognition in them, but death. He smirked, and she unloaded her clip in his torso.

Steve stumbled back, jerking violently as the bullets ripped through his body. *Click, click, click—* Dana's clip was empty. She was still dry firing when her strength finally failed, and she slumped in the grass.

The sun crested the horizon, bathing the scene in light just as Steve's legs gave out and he toppled face-first into the river. The last thought he had before his consciousness faded away was that he hoped he'd have the chance to tell God off before he went to Hell.

Dana turned painfully onto her back. Her vision was hazy, and she knew that it was only a matter of time before she passed out. The man Steve had been assaulting gingerly rose to his feet and stumbled toward her. The lightness she felt in her head increased and she fought to stay awake as the figure approached.

She knew she should be frightened as the man reached down and lifted her head into his lap, but she didn't have the strength. He stroked her hair and spoke something to her that she couldn't make out. His voice not only sounded odd to her ears but a thousand miles away. Strangely, it was soothing to her. She felt that she should know it somehow.

Dana could feel herself slipping away, but she needed to know who this person was. So, with all her remaining strength, she willed herself back to consciousness. For just a moment, her vision cleared. The face that appeared before her eyes made her heart skip a beat.

As the darkness overtook her, she smiled and breathed, "I love you, Jared."

Chapter Forty-Five

Jared watched anxiously from the tree line as Officer Lee worked to save Dana's life. Thankfully, the officer who had found her had the hands of a surgeon and the skills of an emergency room doctor, so it did not take him long to stop the bleeding and stabilize her. Nevertheless, if she did not get to a hospital soon, she wouldn't make it.

Tzedakah glowed brilliantly and a faint blue aura appeared around Dana's body. She relaxed and her breathing grew steady.

"I have done what I can for her," he said tentatively. "Now her fate is in God's hands."

Jared nodded. It took everything in him not to rush to her side. He desperately wanted to be with her, to be the first thing she saw when she woke up. If she woke up. The thought of her dying both infuriated him and broke his heart at the same time. Oh, how he wished he had been strong enough to kill his brother when he had had the chance. It was a regret he knew he would carry for the rest of his life, however long that would be. He silently prayed that it would not be long since the thought of living without her for even a moment was unbearable.

Both of them watched, hidden from view, as a helicopter appeared overhead. Lee leaned over Dana, shielding her from the debris kicked up by the helicopter's rotors.

As soon as the helicopter landed, a big man wearing a brown suit and a Boston Red Sox cap jumped out and headed over to Dana and Lee. He crouched down and shared a few words with the officer before signaling to the chopper. Two more men wearing EMS uniforms and carrying a stretcher exited the side door and ran to retrieve Dana.

Jared watched helplessly as the men returned to the aircraft with Dana in tow and lifted her up into the open door. The big man and the medic followed suit closing the door just as the aircraft lifted off the ground. The helicopter rose into the air hovering for a few seconds before moving forward and passing over the horizon and out of sight.

As soon as the aircraft was gone, a squad of police officers arrived. They moved slowly and methodically, canvassing the area for any signs of the two perpetrators who had been reported to still be in the area. Not wanting to be discovered, Jared disappeared in a flash of blue light.

He reappeared down by the river where his brother had fallen. There was no sign of Steve's body, but the current was moving swiftly, so it most likely had been swept downstream. Even after all he had done, Jared found it impossible to hate him. Steve was his younger brother, and he would always love him unconditionally in spite of what he had chosen to become. He hoped that in death his brother had found some measure of peace. Sadly, however, the blood of the people he had murdered still cried out for justice. Even in death, he could not escape judgment.

He felt the presence of someone watching him from behind but did not turn around. "Late again, I see."

The angel walked up and stood next to him and stared down at the river, as well. "So it seems."

"Where is Jeremy?"

The angel looked up into the heavens. "At the hospital, but don't worry, he will live. We were attacked shortly after you left, and he was injured severely. Thankfully, he will recover with no lasting complications. I have known him for a long time, and he has seen worse."

Jared nodded but said nothing. Neither of them spoke as the river carried on its never-ending course. Was life like this river, Jared wondered, a continuously flowing stream always rushing toward a predetermined end? Did his brother truly choose his path, or, like Jared, was his path chosen for him?

He raised Tzedakah up and examined the softly glowing blade. He wanted to hate the sentient sword but found that he could not. In truth, it was only doing what it was designed to do. To hate it was the same as hating a lion for hunting or a storm for blowing. Still, he could not help but feel that he had been trapped by it somehow.

"I did not choose this," he said softly.

"I know," Sanctuary replied. "The ways of God are mysterious. Even we angels do not always understand them. Sometimes the road He asks us to walk is a hard one."

Jared nodded and glanced over at the rushing water. "And sometimes," he said, finishing Sanctuary's thoughts, "someone has to be the one who sacrifices so others can live."

Sanctuary looked at Jared with sad eyes. "It is the way of things," he said. "But I am sorry that this burden has fallen on you."

"It didn't," Jared said. "It fell on her."

Neither of them spoke again as they stood on the riverbank and continued to watch the water flow by.

Epilogue

The Musketeer materialized somewhere in the woods at the top of a steep ravine. He hated the forest and much preferred the hustle and bustle of the big city to the dull quiet of nature. Cities were filled with people and people brought chaos; he loved chaos. What he was seeking, however, had come to rest somewhere deep at the bottom of this ravine.

With a sigh, he leapt from the edge into thin air. Wind rushed past as he dropped, nearly snatching away his precious hat. He grabbed it just before a particularly strong gust stole it from him.

The rapier on his hip flashed violet, and his momentum slowed to a crawl. He landed on his feet, as soft as a feather, patted his trusty weapon, and scanned the area. It did not take him long to spot what he was looking for. About two meters away, next to two large rocks, lay the broken body of a man.

With a slight skip in his step, he sauntered over to the mossy boulders. He had to watch his footing because the stones were covered in algae and extremely slippery. He hated getting his boots wet.

He grabbed a large stick to shove the body onto its back, so he could examine it better. Steve's battered and bloodied face looked up at the Musketeer who tsked thoughtfully. Was the boy dead? Alas, no; there was the subtle rise and fall of his chest.

Steve's eyes flicked open.

"Well done," the Musketeer said. "You are still alive. That is a truly fortunate thing, mon ami, because there is still much that needs doing. I am not finished with you just yet."

JW Kiefer 316

Coming early 2025

Please enjoy a sneak peek of the eagerly anticipated
second installment of the bestselling Justice Cycle
Series.

For more information go to:
JWKIEFER.com

Chapter One

The branches slapped at her pale skin, leaving red welts and deep, painful scratches. She ignored the pain and continued to blindly run through the thick foliage. She squinted her dark green eyes, trying to see in the dying light as the sun slowly slipped below the horizon, plunging the world around her into darkness.

No! It was too soon. Please, God. I am not far enough away yet.

Her eyes darted back and forth, searching the growing blackness. Every tree looked like a pursuer and every shadow a threat. The musty smell of moss and damp leaves filled her nostrils with every ragged breath she took. She stumbled blindly onward, ignoring her fatigue.

Crack. Her breath caught in her chest. Was that a branch breaking? Had they found her already? She strained to hear, but the constant thumping of her heart in her ears made it impossible.

She ignored the burning in her muscles and ran, renewed terror driving her forward. She had to escape. Had to reach freedom. They wouldn't be far behind. She had pretended to be unconscious, and when she was sure they were asleep she had made her escape. At least, she thought they were asleep. They never came when the sun was out. She shivered, remembering those horrible nights. She had learned quickly to fear the sunset.

Her dirty t-shirt snagged on a jutting tree limb, twisting her painfully and nearly causing her to lose her footing. She grimaced at the tearing sound it made and the smoldering agony that erupted in her left bicep. Tears filled her eyes, causing them to burn from the sudden wetness, and she blinked rapidly, trying to clear her vision. She ignored the pain and blindly stumbled onward, waving her hands back and forth in front of her body, attempting to feel for obstacles.

Pain erupted in one of her bare feet as she snagged it on a raised tree root, and she lost her balance. She fell forward, landing hard on her knees, scraping them and widening the rip in her shirt, exposing one of her breasts.

They had kept her barley clothed and shoeless, allowing her only a long t-shirt and underwear. It wasn't sexual but rather done to keep the captives disoriented and feeling exposed and powerless. A vulnerable captive was less likely to attempt an escape.

Well, they had sorely underestimated her. She may be barely clothed and fatigued, but she would be damned if she were going to simply lie there and wait to die.

She was too exhausted and injured to care about her exposed chest, so she rolled over into a sitting position. Her back heaved as she gulped in the clean night air, sending her into a fit of coughing. She curled up into a fetal position as pain shot through her torso. Each desperate breath felt like knives being rammed into her chest. Her lungs felt like they were made of iron and each breath seemed to barely be taking in any oxygen. She felt like she was drowning.

Calm down, Sophie. You are hyperventilating and you need to slow your breathing down before you pass out.

Her heart still raced, and her lungs still felt like cement, but with each deliberate breath she took she could feel herself calming and her breathing slowly returning to normal. She sat back on her hands and continued to deliberately exhale until she felt sufficiently recovered enough to scan her surroundings.

All she saw were trees and shadows, so she closed her eyes and listened. The sounds of the forest came alive. Crickets chirped loudly and something moved just to her left, disturbing the dead leaves and branches, causing her to jump. She focused on the noise for a few seconds until she was sure it was nothing. An owl hooted in the distance, and she could hear the soft gurgling of a stream.

Her eyes popped open. *What was that sound?* She closed her eyes again and listened. Faintly, somewhere in the distance, she thought she heard a dog barking. Where there was a dog there had to be people, and where there were people, she could find help. Using all of the strength she had left, she slowly rose to her feet and started shuffling off in the direction of the faint barking.

As the sound of the animal grew louder, her heart began to beat faster. Waves of relief washed over her, and she began to sob softly as she hurried towards the noise. She was going to make it. She was going to find help. Thank God for upstate people who leave their dogs outside. Never again would she make fun of rednecks and good old country folk.

It was becoming harder for her to see as the faint traces of sunlight slowly lost their fight to the encroaching darkness. She squinted in the dying light and moved her hands from tree to tree, feeling her way as she inched forward. Up ahead she saw, like a lighthouse beaming faintly in a storm, a dim ray of white. It was a light. She quickened her pace, stumbling blindly through the trees towards her salvation.

Crack. Her head snapped up and her eyes went wide in terror. Something was there, just beyond her sight. *Crack. Crack. Rustle.* She bolted as fast as her emaciated body would allow in the direction of the light. Whatever had been watching her from the darkness gave up all pretense of stealth and charged after her, tearing through the foliage.

Her breath was ragged and coming out of her in wheezing gasps as she stumbled forward, heedless of any obstacles in her way. The dog became increasingly agitated as she drew closer, and its barking was intermingled with yelps—as if it were trying to break free of a restraint. Just a little farther.

Suddenly leaves and small branches began to rain down upon her, causing her to have to slow her pace. She heard the cracking and rustling of foliage and saw the branches bow and sway as something big tore through the trees above her.

She thought her heart was going to beat right out of her chest as the adrenalin and fear kicked in, full force. She watched in horror as the branches broke and bowed until whatever it was reached the clearing where the light and dog were. The dog let out a feral growl before yelping in pain and going silent.

She gathered her courage and gritted her teeth in frustration. "No!"

A growl of rage and impotent frustration burst out of her, scaring her with its intensity, and she ran as fast as she could in the direction of the light.

"No! No! No!"

As she drew close enough to finally see the large white farmhouse, her survival instincts to fight kicked in. She expected to see whatever had killed the dog appear at the edge of the clearing, but it didn't. Then something far worse happened.

Her teeth began to chatter uncontrollably, and her breath condensed in the air in front of her like tiny clouds as a wave of intense cold washed over her. Her muscles twitched and contracted in response to the cold, and she stumbled and fell to the ground, unable to move.

She lay there in the fetal position, shaking violently as her body attempted to ward off the invading cold. Her jaw muscles tightened and she bared her teeth, gritting them to stop the shivering. As she lay shaking, a pale, delicate, woman's foot appeared near her face. It was bare, and so white it was almost translucent. The nails were perfectly manicured and polished a light ice blue.

She knew those feet. Using what little strength she had left, she turned her head so she could see the thing that stood looking down at her. The eyes that looked back at her were almond-shaped and the color of the sky on a cloudless day. As beautiful as they were, they held an edge of cruelty to them like the eyes of a predator.

The woman shook her head and her long, straight, black hair fell into her face, slightly covering her delicate, angular features. She brushed it away and clicked her tongue against the roof of her mouth disapprovingly.

"Dear Sophia. You have been an awfully bad girl."

Sophia met the woman's gaze with defiance. She wanted to say something witty, but she was too tired and still shivering too much to speak.

The woman closed her lovely eyes, and her face was serene as she breathed in deeply through her nose and then exhaled. Her hair seemed to constantly sway in some unseen wind as it fell gracefully down to her waist. Her white dress, which was so low-cut that it barely covered her breasts, also swayed in the unseen breeze, making her look more like a wraith than a solid being. Her skin was so pale that it seemed to glow, making the effect more pronounced.

"I so love the smell of defiance. It makes everything taste so much more...delicious."

The pungent smell of decay and death drifted in on the wind, causing the woman to scrunch up her nose. She pulled her lips into a sneer, revealing a mouth full of sharp, elongated canine-like teeth. Sophia had to fight her gag reflex as the stench almost made her vomit.

"Is the animal dead?"

A dark silhouette stepped out of the darkness and into the light. The creature was humanoid in appearance but with limbs that were too long for its frame and clothing that was torn and filthy. Its dirty, stringy hair grew out of the bulbous scalp like patches of dry grass, and its mottled grey skin clung to its frame, making it look like the starving children they show in commercials. Its beady, black eyes looked down at Sophia, showing an unabashed malice.

"Yes, my lady."

It moved closer to them, and the smell of decay was intermingled with the distinctly sickly-sweet metallic scent of blood. It did not take its eyes off the prone girl as it spoke. It smiled, showing a mouth full of razor-sharp teeth that still had flecks of gore hanging from them. It lifted its hand, pointing one elongated clawed finger at Sophia.

"Can I eat her, Mistress?" it croaked in a dry, grating voice. "I am so hungry. Always so hungry."

The woman's face twisted into a mask of savage rage, and she turned on the creature. Before Sophia could register what was happening, the woman had the thing by the throat and was lifting it off the ground with one arm.

The woman was beautiful and terrible, and exuded the power and grace of an apex predator. The creature struggled in her grip, its feet flailing as it tried to free itself. The woman bared her teeth and hissed.

"Now, Nayati, do I need to repeat the lesson we went over the other night?"

Nayati stopped struggling and went limp. "No, Mistress," he replied softly. "No lesson is needed."

She dropped him unceremoniously and he sat on the ground, coughing and gasping for air. She dismissed him and turned to Sophia, who was still shivering uncontrollably.

"Now, where were we? Ah, yes. We were discussing your disobedience. What shall we do about that, my dear? I should just let Nayati have you and be done with you. Use you as an example for the others, but there is something in your smell that appeals to me. Any thoughts? What would you do if you were in my place?"

Before Sophia could reply, a man's shocked cry startled them. It came from the farmhouse. Apparently, the owner of the dog had discovered its mutilated corpse. Sophia's heart jumped with hope and she mustered her strength and shouted.

All she managed was one word before a kick from the woman knocked the breath out of her lungs. She gasped and choked as tears filled her eyes.

"Be silent!" she snarled. "Or I will tear you apart myself."

Muffled angry voices and more commotion could be heard as others came out to see what the man had been shouting about. Sophia whimpered and tried to drag herself in the direction of the people.

"Help me," she wheezed softly through gritted teeth. "Please."

Another wave of intense cold struck her, and she curled up into a ball, shaking and groaning.

"I said be quiet."

The woman turned in the direction of the people, her face intense. She then looked down at Sophia and grinned, her eyes wild with malice.

"Nayati, dear. Are you still hungry?" She never took her eyes off the prostrate girl as she spoke.

Sophia's eyes went wide in horror. "No. S...s...stop. I will ga...go with you, just stop. Please."

Sophia heard the wendigo tearing through the trees before she even had time to finish her sentence. The white lady continued to look at Sophia, her face stern like that of a disapproving parent as the screaming started.

"This is what happens when you do not obey, little one. Innocent people die. And make no mistake, this tragedy is your fault. If you had simply done what you were told, these people would still be alive."

Sophia curled up into a ball and wept. It was her fault after all. She had tried to save herself and, in the process, had got an entire family brutally murdered.

The shouts turned to pleas of mercy, and then she heard a child's scream that turned into croaks of pain. She covered her ears, trying to block out the shrieks. It didn't work. She could still hear them. They would be burned in her mind forever.

Acknowledgement

So, now that you have read this book of mine, I would like to take the time to acknowledge a few people. Well, a few people is most likely a gross understatement, as the folks who know me will attest.

First off, I want to thank you the readers for deciding to pick up my book. I know you have a gazillion other options to choose from, and from the bottom of my heart, I thank you for taking a chance on my little novel. I sincerely hope you enjoyed it.

No good author worth his salt could write his first acknowledgment page without mentioning the two people who brought them into the world. Unless of course you were born in a test tube, cloned from someone else's DNA or are an AI. If this is the case, then you will either despise me for having wonderful and supporting parents, or simply be confused.

Since I am none of those things and have saints for parents, (they actually are saints by the way. They have the halos to prove it.) I want to thank them for always believing in me even when I didn't believe in myself. Without your love and encouragement I never would have finished the race. Well, without you I would not have been here to start the race, so…thanks for that as well.

Next, I would like to thank my kids Emma and Connor. From the moment you first opened your wee lil eyes, my heart was yours. My greatest delight in this life is being your dad. It has been, and will continue to be, my greatest responsibility, honor, and joy. You are my happiness.

The next people on my hit list are all of the wonderful friends I have made along the writer's way.

I couldn't have asked for a more supportive and inspiring community. You are all mad and you talk to imaginary people, but hey, all the best ones do. From all of the people who have created, hosted or guest starred on "The Dead Robots Society" podcast, to JR Handley, Tim C Taylor and Walt Robillard who have been my valued companions on this journey, I thank you. In truth, thanking you seems like too small a sentiment for how much of an impact you have had on me, but it will have to do.

Of course, I could not forget my lovely editor, Lauren Moore. You took my overly extensive ramblings and helped me turn them into something marvelous. I learned so much from working with you and my story is certainly better for it. Your patience and kind criticism are the backbone of this book.

Lastly, I would like to thank my God and my King Jesus Christ. You always have and always will be the center of my life. I owe everything to you.

Jay (2021)

Authors Note

I hope you enjoyed reading Death: Book 1 in the Justice Cycle. If you did, or even if you didn't, I would appreciate it if you would leave a review. Every little bit helps.

If you would like to be kept up to date with upcoming books, sign up for my newsletter, or check out my Blog, you can find me at JWKIEFER.COM.

Thanks again.

Jay

About the Author

J W Kiefer is a father, minister, novelist, script writer and blogger who hails from the Southern Tier of Western New York State. He has a degree in Theology and Church management as well as a degree in liberal arts. He is also a reserve Green Lantern; and when duty calls, can be found assisting the rest of the core in interstellar matters. An avid vocalist and worship leader, he loves to belt out Disney tunes, especially when it is most awkward and embarrassing for his children. His other pursuits include knitting, canning, watching paint peel, and observing the occasional pot hoping to see it boil.

If you are interested in more information about J W Kiefer he can be found at: JWKIEFER.COM

Other Works from the Author

Dark Mater: a short story in the Anthology: Storming Area 51 (A Bayonet Books Anthology Book 2)

USAF Colonel Christian Racene is a husband and father who works long hours as one of the Presidents science advisors. When he is inexplicably called away to the mysterious complex known as Area 51, he discovers that project Wonderland, a program that has been based on his research on dark matter, has been relocated to the facility. Colonel Aliya Johnson head of Project Wonderland has asked for his help specifically because she has encountered an enigma that only he can solve. What Christian finds there will challenge his views of the universe and possibly all of reality itself.

Dark Mater is a short science fiction story that can be found in volume 2 of the Bayonet Books anthology *Storming Area 51*.

www.ingramcontent.com/pod-product-compliance
Lightning Source LLC
Chambersburg PA
CBHW031438240626
47154CB00001B/311